He wanted more than just to hold her. Far more.

What he didn't want was to move from her.

He eased his arms from her, anyway. Reaching between them, he circled her wrists with his forefingers and thumbs. He brushed his lips to her temple. "Do you have any coffee?"

Amy blinked. Confusion masked the banked yearning in her tone. "Sure." Her brow furrowed as she looked up at him. "You want coffee?"

"No," he admitted, his breath warm on her face as he brushed his lips over hers. "It's just that we need to do something before I kiss you."

Her heart jerked in her chest. "You just did."

"That wasn't a kiss."

The longing she'd veiled threatened to surface as his smoky gray gaze moved over her face, lingered on her mouth.

"It wasn't?"

"Not even close," he murmured.

"Maybe you should show me how it's done."

Dear Reader,

I believe in the fairy tale.

Really.

That said, I'm not naive enough to believe every prince will be wealthy or ride in on a white horse. I've also never heard of a man who has remained consistently charming. I know too many Cinderellas who have to wipe runny noses, work weekends and do laundry. Happily-ever-after isn't a guarantee. It takes work. I *know* all that. So why do I believe in something that started out as a myth and became a children's story? It's because of what, for me, is at the core of the modern Cinderella tale: that love is often found where a person least expects to find it, and that good things happen to good, ordinary people.

I hope you believe in the fairy tale, too.

Love,

Christine

THE MILLIONAIRE AND
THE GLASS SLIPPER

CHRISTINE FLYNN

SPECIAL EDITION®

Published by Silhouette Books

America's Publisher of Contemporary Romance

SILHOUETTE BOOKS

ISBN-13: 978-0-373-24870-4
ISBN-10:   0-373-24870-9

THE MILLIONAIRE AND THE GLASS SLIPPER

Visit Silhouette Books at www.eHarlequin.com

Printed in U.S.A.

Books by Christine Flynn

Silhouette Special Edition

Silhouette Books

CHRISTINE FLYNN

admits to being interested in just about everything, which is why she considers herself fortunate to have turned her interest in writing into a career. She feels that a writer gets to explore it all and, to her, exploring relationships—especially the intense, bittersweet or even lighthearted relationships between men and women—is fascinating.

With thanks to Lois Faye Dyer for the premise and the invitation, to Allison Leigh and Pat Kay for being such inspirations and to all three of you for making The Hunt for Cinderella come to life.

Prologue

J.T. Hunt sat sprawled in a deep, wing-backed armchair in his father's spacious library, his head resting against the smooth leather. With a highball glass of hundred-year-old bourbon balanced on one thigh, he was trying hard to stay awake.

Beneath the long Tiffany lamp hanging over the pool table, his half brothers Justin, four years younger than his own thirty-eight, and Gray, older by six, killed time playing a game of eight ball. It was obvious from the muttering that Gray hadn't played in a while. Their other half brother, thirty-six-year-old Alex, watched from a matching armchair a few feet away.

The last time they'd all been together at the Shack, as they'd long ago christened the multimillion-dollar estate on the shores of Seattle's Lake Washington, had been a month ago. That had been when their father, Harrison Hunt, the billionaire founder of HuntCom, had suffered a heart attack. J.T. couldn't remember how long it had been for him personally before that. He tended to be the black sheep. The prodigal. Though he was more circumspect than he'd been in his youth, he felt an outsider nonetheless. He only came to the home he'd been raised in when he absolutely had to.

He supposed that was mostly because he felt he had little in common with his tech-genius father and his half brothers, other than his passion for his portion of the business. As director of real estate development and the company's lead architect, he lived, ate and breathed his work designing the structures that held everything from HuntCom's thousands of employees, to the products they manufactured and shipped worldwide. The only thing that mattered as much to him as his work was the isolated island in the San Juans his father had bought when J.T. was a teenager. Hurricane Island was the only place on the planet where he felt anything remotely resembling a sense of peace. It was too bad he couldn't stay long enough to sail out to it for a while.

"Does anybody know why the Old Man called this meeting?" Justin asked as he tapped one of the balls with his cue stick.

At six foot three, as long and lanky as the rest of them, Gray gave a shrug. "My secretary said he wouldn't tell her the reason."

Alex sat forward at that. "Harry called you himself? Me, too." He waved his bottle of Black Sheep Ale toward J.T. "What about you, J.T? Did you get the message from his secretary, or from Harry personally?"

"From Harry." Rubbing his eyes with his thumb and forefinger, he yawned and leaned forward himself. With his elbows on his thighs, he dangled his glass of bourbon between them. "I told him I'd have to cancel meetings in New Delhi and spend half a day on the corporate jet to get home in time, but he insisted I be here."

The trip made no sense to him, either. Since Harry's health

didn't seem to be the issue, given the vigor in his father's voice when he'd called, J.T. couldn't imagine anything the man wanted that couldn't have been handled by phone, fax or e-mail. Harry had practically perfected the technologies. The least he could have done was use one of them.

Running his hand through his dark hair, he looked at his Rolex. With the thirteen-hour time difference between Seattle and New Delhi, at the moment he had no idea what time his body clock was on.

He'd just decided it wasn't worth figuring out when the hall door burst open. Six feet six inches tall, his black hair nearly devoid of gray, Harrison Hunt strode into the expansive room with its rich cherry wood paneling and handbound collections of books. Black, horn-rimmed bifocals framed blue eyes sharp with the intelligence that had invented the software and technology that had made HuntCom a household word.

"Ah, you're all here. Excellent." His energy totally belying the heart attack he'd suffered only a month ago, he headed for his massive mahogany desk. Four chairs faced it. "Join me, boys."

As Harry settled himself into his executive chair, J.T. watched Justin lean against the wall. Gray moved behind one of the chairs, remaining there while Alex leaned against the wall not far from where Gray stood.

Rising, J.T. stayed the farthest back, separated from them all by a long credenza defining the seating areas.

Harry frowned first at Justin. "Why don't you sit down?"

"Thanks, but I'll stand."

That frown swept them all.

With an impatient shrug, Harry muttered, "Very well. Stand or sit. It makes no difference to the outcome of this meeting." He paused, clearing his throat. "Since my heart attack last month," he began, "I've been doing a lot of thinking about this family. I've never thought a lot about my legacy, nor about having grandchildren to carry on the Hunt name. However, the heart attack made me face some hard truths I'd ignored. I could have died," he said flatly. "I could die tomorrow."

He rose from his chair, leaned forward with his knuckles resting on the desktop. "I finally realized that, left to your own devices, you four never will get married…which means I'll never have grandchildren. I don't intend to leave the future of this family to chance any longer. You have a year. By the end of that year, each of you will not only be married, you will either already have a child or your wife will be expecting one."

Absolute silence met his emphatic proclamation.

That silence stretched, lengthened.

"Right," J.T. finally muttered. Like that's going to happen, he thought.

Still leaning against the wall, Justin stifled a grin and looked over at Gray. Gray looked amused. Alex lifted his bottle and tilted it to his mouth.

Harry didn't seem at all dissuaded by their collective lack of interest.

"If any one of you refuses to do so," he calmly insisted, "you'll all lose your position in HuntCom and the perks you love so much."

Justin stiffened.

Alex lowered his bottle.

Gray's amusement died. "You can't be serious."

"I'm deadly serious."

J.T. didn't bother getting upset. He didn't believe a word of the threat. "With all due respect, Harry," he said, fairly leaking patience he didn't feel. "How will you run the company if we refuse to do this?" Ice clinking, he lifted his glass toward his half brothers. "I don't know what Gray, Alex or Justin have going on right now, but I'm in the middle of expansions here in Seattle, in Jansen and at our New Delhi facility. If another architect has to take over my position, it'll be months before he's up to speed. Construction delays alone would cost HuntCom a fortune."

Harry appeared unfazed. "It wouldn't matter, because if the four of you refuse to agree, I'll sell off HuntCom in pieces. The New Delhi facility will be history and I'll sell Hurricane Island."

Having just made it clear he knew full well how important that island was to J.T., his unflinching gaze settled on Justin.

"I'll sell HuntCom's interest in the Idaho ranch." His glance shifted to Alex. "I'll shut down the Foundation if you refuse to cooperate." His hard stare finally met Gray's. "And HuntCom won't need a president because there will no longer be a company for you to run."

Alex took a step forward. "But that's insane. What do you hope to accomplish by doing this, Harry?"

"I mean to see you all settled with a family started before I die. With a decent woman who'll make a good wife and mother," he insisted. "The women you marry have to win Cornelia's approval."

"Does Aunt Cornelia know about this?"

Justin posed the question before J.T. could ask it himself. Personally, he hadn't had much to do with the widow of Harry's business partner. At least, not as an adult. As a kid and a teenager, the woman had seemed to be around only when he was in trouble. Where the others regarded her as something of a honorary aunt, he thought of her mostly as the woman who'd insisted to Harry that J.T. needed restrictions. She was good at calling a person on their behavior. From what he'd heard from Gray, since he was the brother he dealt with most, she was also the only person Harry ever really listened to.

"Not yet."

"So," Justin said, looking somewhat relieved by that. "Let me see if I've got this straight. Each of us has to agree to marry and produce a kid within a year—"

"All of you have to agree," Harry cut in. "All four of you. If one refuses, everyone loses, and life as you've know it—your jobs, the HuntCom holdings you each love—will be gone."

"—and the brides have to each be approved by Aunt Cornelia."

"She's a shrewd woman. She'll know if any of the women aren't good wife material. Which reminds me," he added abruptly. "You can't tell the women you're rich. Or that you're my sons. I don't want any fortune-hunters in the family. God knows I married enough of those myself. I don't want any of my sons making the mistakes I made."

Considering the history the man had with each of their mothers, J.T. had the feeling he wasn't the only one biting his tongue at that glaring understatement. He lifted his glass, waited to see who would be first to tell Harry to take a hike.

Harry drew a deep breath. "I'll give you some time to think about this. You have until 8:00 p.m., Pacific Time, three days from now. If I don't hear from you to the contrary before then, I'll tell my lawyer to start looking for a buyer for HuntCom."

With that, he moved from his desk and walked out the door.

The moment he closed it behind him, every one of them swore.

"It's not going to happen," J.T. insisted. "He'll never sell HuntCom. As for the rest of it…"

"He can't possibly be serious," Justin concluded.

Alex's scowl deepened. "Maybe he *is* serious."

From where he remained back from the others, J.T. listened to his half brothers debate whether or not Harry meant what he said. The uneasy possibility existed that he did, and none of them wanted to lose what mattered to them. Yet not one of them said he was ready to cater to the man's demands.

J.T. knew he was beyond tired when he didn't bother to mention what an insult those demands were.

Sleep, he thought. He needed sleep. "So we're all agreed?" he asked. "None of us are caving in to his crazy ultimatum?"

Justin nodded. "No question. Even if I wanted to get married, which I don't, I wouldn't do it because Harry decided it was time to settle down."

"Settling down." J.T. shook his head, shoved his fingers through his hair. "That's not happening. I'm never home long enough to have a dog. What would I do with a wife?" He set his now-empty glass on the credenza with an audible thud. "No offense, but I haven't slept since yesterday." He hadn't even caught a nap on the flight. He'd spent the entire trip trying to resolve the design problem he'd been working on when he'd been summoned. "I'm heading home to crash."

"I'll see you at the office tomorrow," Gray told him as they all moved toward the door. "We need to go over the figures for that possible plant in Singapore."

"Singapore," he muttered. "My head's still in India. Let's do it when I get back next week."

"Not a problem."

"Give me a ride downtown, will you? I took a limo here from the airport."

Gray told him he'd be glad to, then pulled his cell phone from his pocket when it rang yet again.

"It's my secretary, Loretta," Gray said. "She's at the office working on the white paper for the buyout. If you don't mind, I'll talk to her on the way."

Accustomed to being available at all hours himself, J.T.

told him he didn't mind at all and took advantage of the twenty-five-minute drive into the sprawling city to check his own messages, text back responses to most of them and decide what to do for a meal.

He was hungry for pancakes, which meant it must be morning, body time. Since it was night in Seattle, he phoned for takeout from Rico's. The Italian restaurant was on the ground floor of the building where he owned a penthouse with black granite and cherry wood in the kitchen and a million-dollar view of Puget Sound from nearly every room. Rather than go through his matronly, enormously efficient assistant, Kate Cavanaugh, who was probably feeding her husband at this hour, he then called HuntCom's chief pilot himself to let him know he'd need the plane ready for a trip back to New Delhi in the morning.

For now, he wasn't wasting another second's thought on Harry's insane ultimatum.

A day later—the middle of the night where he was, midday where his half brothers were—a conference call from his brothers demanded that he rethink his position. They all agreed that had their father's threat involved only money, they'd have collectively ignored the man's demand. It wasn't just money, though. It was about the things and places Harry knew mattered most to them.

Because of that, and because J.T. didn't want to give up the island or be responsible for his brothers losing what was important to them, he agreed with what Justin proposed. Even though there were serious doubts about finding marriageable women who didn't know who they were, and about how each man could get that woman to stay married after the deception was revealed, they would meet Harry's terms. But only if he signed an agreement preventing him from ever blackmailing them again.

Gray wanted the agreement to be ironclad, signed, witnessed and notarized so Harry couldn't throw out any new conditions.

What J.T. wanted as he hung up the phone and headed into his bathroom in search of an antacid tablet was to know how Harry thought something that had never worked for him should work any better for any of his sons. As far as he was concerned, no matter what happened, he'd just kissed his life as he knew it goodbye.

Chapter One

J.T. rubbed the back of his neck as he watched the numbers of the downtown office building's elevator ascend. A run was definitely in order. Or a workout in the hotel's gym. There was nothing like working up a sweat to lessen tension—with the possible exception of sex. Since he didn't know any women in Portland, Oregon, and since he wasn't into one-night stands, a workout seemed his best option for loosening the knots and easing the restiveness he could never quite shake.

His broad shoulders lowered with a long expulsion of breath.

He didn't want to think about women just then. Aside from making him aware of a different sort of frustration, since it had been a while since he'd had the pleasure of intimate female company, thinking about women reminded him that he was supposed to be looking for one.

He still couldn't believe the ultimatum his father had delivered two months ago. Two and a half, he mentally grumbled, reminding himself that the clock continued to tick.

His jaw worked in a slow grind as the numbers continued to climb. Justin had discovered he was a father not long after that meeting, but no one knew if he was making any progress with his little girl's mom. As far as J.T. knew, the guy still didn't want a wife. He knew for a fact he didn't want one himself.

He wanted nothing to do with the whole home-and-family thing. He knew firsthand that commitment on that level simply didn't work. He couldn't even remember his own mother, his father's second wife. She had bailed when J.T. was two, leaving him to a series of nannies, au pairs and the two succeeding stepmothers who'd pretty much ignored him before they'd abandoned him and their sons, too. They'd literally taken the money and run, which had pretty much proved to him long before he graduated from high school that women could be bought.

He'd learned a couple more valuable lessons back then, too. He'd learned that women pretended to care only when they wanted something in return. And that the best way to get any attention from anyone was to get into trouble. A visit from a truant officer was usually good for at least a ten-minute audience with his father. That was often the most time the man spent with him all week.

The elevator slowed. Over the quiet drone of the Muzak, a refined ding announced his floor.

He didn't cause problems now. At least, not the kind that involved threats of expulsion or fines for speeding tickets. He'd refined his talent for trouble into a tendency to merely break or bend any rule that didn't suit his purpose. His opinion of women, however, hadn't changed much. His father's rules for the Bride Hunt were that the women not know who they were or anything about the family wealth. When he got around to looking for a woman, which he was still in no rush to do, his personal requirements would be more specific.

The woman would have to have good genes. Preferably, in a tall, leggy blonde sort of way. She couldn't come with any emotional or familial baggage. And she needed to have a career she wanted to keep so she'd have interests of her own. His father had said that the woman had to fall in love with him—not that he had to fall in love with her. Not that he believed for an instant that his father's demands could be met—which was why he was about to implement Plan B.

The elevator doors slid open. Stepping into a wide hall, vaguely aware of the sounds of construction coming from a floor below, he noted the plaque on the wall indicating the direction of the suite he was looking for.

Plan B was to have everything in place to open his own architectural firm so he'd have something to fall back on when his father sold out. He figured that would happen in nine and a half months, when the time for the hunt expired. The logistics of that new venture became the sole thoughts on his mind as he opened the door marked Kelton & Associates.

A spacious reception area of white walls, gray industrial carpet and a wide mobile of what looked like stainless steel boomerangs greeted him. Beneath the slowly moving mobile sat a large amoeba-shaped Lucite secretarial desk. A state-of-the-art computer monitor and telephone system, lines ringing, occupied the short side of the curved L.

He'd chosen to interview this particular marketing firm because of its reputation for being cutting edge, and its relatively small size. Small meant fewer people who might recognize him. It was also half an hour away by air and two and a half to three hours by car from Seattle, which meant that it operated outside the sphere of core support businesses

HuntCom used in the Seattle area. To avoid the publicity that would come if news of his endeavor got out, he wanted to keep everything under wraps until implementing it became absolutely necessary.

His first impression of the ultramodern decor was that it echoed the firm's cutting-edge hype. His second was that there was no one manning the reception desk. There wasn't a soul in sight.

Or so he was thinking when a totally preoccupied young woman in a gray sweater and skirt barreled around the corner from a hallway. Her dark head was down, her arms loaded with files. Judging from her direction and her speed, her destination was the ringing telephone on the desk. Before he could do anything more than think about stepping from her path, she walked right into him.

Her startled gasp met the rustle of papers and the soft plop of files hitting the carpet. Of the dozen thick folders she carried, half of them hit the floor. The other half she clutched to her chest as she dropped to her knees.

"Ohmygosh. I'm so sorry." Flushing to the roots of her barely chin-length, chopped brown hair, she grabbed a file. "Our receptionist isn't in today, so I thought I'd work out here so I could get the phone…" She shook her head, flushed. "Never mind. Please," she murmured, clearly embarrassed as he crouched beside her and picked up a file. "I'll get these. You don't have to help."

Ignoring her insistence, he reached past her for another file. Closer to her now, her scent drifted toward him. Something fresh, faintly herbal and unexpectedly, inexplicably erotic. Caught off guard by the quick tightening low in his gut, he jerked his focus to the delicate lines of her profile. As he did, she looked up—and went still the instant her dark eyes met his. A quick, deep breath, a quicker blink, and her glance fell away.

Young, he thought. That was how she looked to him as he scanned the fine lines of her profile once more. Pretty. A little self-conscious. And impossibly…innocent. As edgy as he'd felt lately, he figured her to be about a lifetime shy of his own admittedly jaded thirty-eight years. The thought made him feel older, and edgier still.

Her focus remained on her task. "Please tell me you're not Jared Taylor."

The name caught him momentarily off guard. To protect his plans, he'd made the appointment using his full first name and his mother's maiden name. He needed to remember that. "Sorry," he replied, "but that's me." He handed her another file as his eyes narrowed. "You wouldn't be Candace Chapman, would you?"

Still looking a little flustered, she took the file, reached for another. She had a beautiful mouth. Full. Unadorned. Kissable.

With a frown, he reminded himself that she also didn't look a day over twenty-two. Not exactly jailbait, but not fair game for a man who preferred women who held as few illusions as he did when it came to the opposite sex.

"No. I'm…no," she repeated. " I know you have a one-o'clock with her, though. I can get these. Really," she insisted, her focus on the transparencies and computer disks she quickly pushed back into a folder. She reached past him for another disk. Bumping his knee with her forearm, she pulled back, apparently deciding that disk could wait. "If you'll have a seat, I'll let her know you're here."

He handed her the disk and another file, then watched her snatch up the rest and start to rise. Snagging her upper arm, rising, too, he helped her to her feet.

"Thank you," she murmured, and aimed an apologetic smile at his chin before she reached across the desk to punch a button on the ringing phone.

Her tone totally professional, she answered with a brisk, "Good afternoon, Kelton & Associates," as she dumped the files on the desk.

His glance ran over the curve of her narrow hips, down to where her slim skirt ended modestly at the back of her knees. Her slender legs were covered with dark gray tights. The black ballet flats she wore spoke of comfort and practicality. Nothing about the way she dressed could be remotely construed as provocative. Yet he found himself thinking her body looked as taut as the muscles in her arm had felt, when a tall, leggy blond in killer heels and a lipstick-red suit rounded the corner into the reception area.

"I'll need ten copies of this report, too, Amy. And when you get a chance—" she continued, only to cut herself off when her head snapped up and she saw him standing there.

The young woman at the desk immediately transferred the call she'd answered and put another on hold. "This is Mr. Taylor," she informed the blonde with a nod in his direction. "He just arrived. Ten copies," she repeated, and slipped into the secretarial chair to straighten the files she'd dropped while telling whoever was on the line that the person he wanted to speak with wasn't in but that she'd be happy to transfer him to her voice mail if he wanted to leave a message.

The thirty-something ad executive in the red power suit gave him an easy smile as she extended her perfectly manicured hand. In that same moment, she managed a blink-of-an-eye once-over that somehow managed to take in everything from his Italian leather shoes to the quality of his open-collared dress shirt and hand-tailored sport coat and the neat cut of his dark, slightly graying hair.

"Jared Taylor. I'm Candace Chapman." Eyes the pure blue of a summer sky held his. Expertly applied makeup turned her strikingly attractive features flawless. "I've looked forward to meeting you. It's always exciting to be in on the birth of a new company." She tipped her head to one side, the motion causing her shining, shoulder-length hair to shimmer in the overhead lights. She snagged it back with her left, noticeably ringless, hand.

"Hold my calls, will you please?" she asked the young woman now heading into another hallway with the report she'd been handed. "Would you like coffee?" Candace asked him.

His attention diverted as much by the woman speaking to him as his reason for being there, he replied, "Please. Black."

"And two coffees?" she called after her infinitely more nondescript subordinate.

"So, tell me, Jared," she continued, only to quickly pause. "May I call you Jared?"

Since he'd been J.T. all his life, "Jared" would definitely take getting used to. "If I can call you Candace."

"Of course." The charming smile was back. "Anyway," she continued, leading him past offices with employees at drafting tables, "you mentioned on the phone that you're new to the Portland market. Are you planning to offer your architectural services only in Oregon, or all of the Northwest?"

She and the agency knew exactly how to make an impression. The first thing he noticed when she led him into her corner office at the end of the hall was an expansive view of the city, its river dividing east side from west and several of the dozen bridges linking them together. Then there were the industry and civic awards on and above a black-lacquered credenza behind the matching executive desk. Photos in sleek frames of Candace and an older woman who looked much like her shaking the hands of presumably important personages graced the opposite wall.

Rather than sit in the executive chair behind the desk, she

headed for the end of the room and one of four barrel chairs spaced around a low cube-shaped coffee table.

"I'm not limiting myself," he replied, as they settled themselves. "I'll go wherever the client wants."

She crossed her long legs, carefully adjusted her skirt and balanced a yellow legal pad in her lap. "And your market will be business developers?"

"And companies looking to build new facilities. I can handle anything from a single-level building to multilevel campuses with subterranean access and egress."

"So we'll need saturation in trade and financial magazines," she concluded. "Do you mind if I ask what sort of advertising you do now?"

He told her he did none himself, then danced around the nature of his present situation by explaining that he was with a company that designed industrial complexes in Europe and Asia. He didn't say a word that wasn't true, he just omitted a lot as he went on to tell her that his partners didn't yet know he was leaving. No one in the company did. Because of that, because he was striking out on his own, confidentiality was imperative.

It was as he was speaking of the need for discretion that he realized the associate she'd addressed as "Amy" had entered the room. With his back to the door, he didn't see her until he noticed Candace give her a nod and she moved to his side.

Holding the small tray she carried low so he could take his cup, she accepted his "Thanks," with a quiet "You're welcome," then set the tray with the other mug soundlessly on the cube.

The gaminelike woman was the antithesis of the chic advertising executive with the obvious business savvy and not-so-subtle sexuality. Even as the girl in gray slipped back out, her motions quiet, efficient, the woman across from him shifted to cross her legs the other way.

The motion immediately drew his glance to the length of her shapely calves. A man would have to be drawing his last breath not to notice legs like hers.

"No one outside the offices of Kelton & Associates will know of your plans until the time comes to unveil them," Candace assured him. "Everyone from our assistant," she said with a nod toward the now empty doorway, "to our graphic artists knows it would hardly be to our advantage to ruin the impact of an advertising campaign or alienate a client."

"Just so we understand each other."

She touched her pen to the corner of her glossy red mouth. "I'm certain we do. So," she said, "talk to me about your vision. Do you have a mission statement?"

She asked intelligent questions, took notes, and spent the next ten minutes having him do the talking to get as much information as possible. He spent the next ten letting her impress him with previous work they'd done for their clients and confirming what he'd learned about the agency in his research. By the time Candace gave him a tour of the place and started introducing him to the various people on the agency's creative team, she was well on her way to convincing him that Kelton & Associates was the firm he needed to launch his new venture.

It also became enormously apparent that Candace Chapman hadn't a clue that he was Harrison Hunt's son—and, unless he was totally misinterpreting her subtle cues, that she might be interested in something more than designing him a company logo and getting that logo recognized in the right circles.

The last thing he'd expected to find when he'd walked in the door was a possible candidate for the Bride Hunt. But he couldn't deny the possibility staring him in the face. While she reminded him of any number of other beautiful, sophisticated women he'd known over the years, as ambitious and career driven as she seemed, she might well meet his criteria for a wife.

Because of that, and because of his father's rules, he surreptitiously pocketed his Rolex on his way out of the graphics department. On his way into Film Media where he met Sid Crenshaw, their techno and art wizard, he made a point of claiming that every penny he had was going into his new business, so he really needed whatever campaign they designed to work. He wanted Ms. Chapman and the entire K.A. team, as she called them, to think him an average, modestly successful architect who lived part-time in Seattle, presently worked mostly overseas and wanted to open his own firm in the Northwest so he could return to living in the States.

He handled the logistics of paying the retainer without writing a check or otherwise exposing his identity by claiming to be in the process of setting up a separate account for his new firm. Candace didn't bat a single lush eyelash when he said he'd return the contract she would send him with a cashier's check for five thousand dollars to cover their preliminary work. She'd simply said that would be fine, and offered him her hand to seal the deal after they'd entered the reception area, where he found himself glancing around for the young woman who'd run into him when he'd first arrived.

"So we're agreed," Candace said, as he absently withdrew his hand. "We'll have a preliminary presentation for you next week." She tipped her head, her blue eyes steady on his. "If you have any questions or ideas in the meantime, call me. If you're in town, I'd be happy to meet and discuss them."

A faint smile tugged at his mouth. Not "we'll talk on the phone." Rather, "we'll meet." He had to give her points for being direct. He liked that in a woman. It took the guesswork out of the whole dating thing.

Thinking he'd give her a call to meet for a drink after he

looked at his schedule, he reached for the door. "I'm sure I'll be in touch," he assured her, and found himself taking one last glance toward the empty Lucite desk.

He was looking for her assistant. Not sure why, even less certain why he felt a twinge of disappointment at not seeing her, he moved into the hall, headed for the elevator and punched the down button.

He was in the process of dismissing that disappointment as being totally irrelevant when the elevator dinged, the door slid open and he heard a feminine voice down the hall call "Hold that, please?"

The missing assistant hurried toward him with an armload of manila envelopes, stacks of letter-size white ones and a half-dozen Express Mail packs.

He stepped inside the empty elevator, blocked the closing sensor with his arm.

"Oh, thank you," she murmured, and stepped inside herself.

Moving to a back corner, she aimed a smile toward his chest. She said nothing else, though, as the doors closed and he glanced from his corner to where she stood hugging the mail. The overhead light caught faint hints of gold in her baby-fine brown hair as the elevator began its descent. A few of the wisps that fell beneath her eyebrows had caught at the corner of her long, dark eyelashes.

With her arms full, she pulled her focus from the descending floor numbers, ducked her head and lifted her shoulder to dislodge the strands. She'd yet to meet his eyes. Wondering if that was because she still felt flustered from their first encounter or if she was just preoccupied, he started to ask if she always moved at a run.

The lights flickered just as he opened his mouth.

An instant later, the lights went out as the elevator jerked to a stop.

Chapter Two

Amy couldn't see a thing. In the darkness of the stalled elevator, she couldn't hear anything, either. No Muzak. No mechanical grind and whir that might indicate a frozen pulley motor. The construction noise from the tenth floor that had tormented the building's tenants all week was gone. Except for a terse, "What the...?" seconds ago, even the big man next to her remained silent.

As far as she could tell, Jared Taylor—all six-foot-two, beautifully masculine inches of him—didn't move from his corner. Neither did she as she waited a handful of seconds to see if anything else would happen.

Nothing did.

"Are you claustrophobic?" she heard him ask into the dark.

"I haven't been before." She drew a cautious breath. The way her day was going, however, discovering a new phobia was entirely possible. So far, she'd overslept, which meant she'd missed her bus so she'd had to take her car to work. She'd dented her fender pulling into the parking garage because she'd been in such a hurry, then arrived late to find that the receptionist had quit. She'd then nearly knocked over the firm's newest client because she'd been worrying about a call she received last night from her grandmother and hadn't been paying attention to where she was going. Now, the Fates had pulled the plug on the power. "But there's a first time for everything," she conceded. "How about you?"

"The only thing that bothers me right now is not knowing why we're stalled." He paused, listening. "I don't hear a fire alarm. If someone had tripped one, the elevator should have gone straight to the first floor and opened. It must be something else."

The mail she'd hugged landed on the floor. "There's a phone by the doors."

She had absolutely no desire to stand there conjuring scenarios. Apparently, neither did he. Even as she reached out to find the brass panel to the right of the elevator doors, she felt him moving beside her.

She reached the panel first. Groping over it in the dark, she felt his arm bump her shoulder as he reached past her.

His palm landed on the back of her hand. Since her hand wasn't covering what they were both looking for, she pulled her fingers from beneath his and patted farther to her right. As she did, his sleeve brushed her cheek. Or maybe her cheek brushed his sleeve. Whichever it was, she could feel his big body at her back. His heat permeated her sweater as his hand, or maybe it was his elbow since he seemed to be reaching over her, bumped a spot above her temple.

He must have heard her quick intake of breath.

"Sorry," he muttered, his deep voice above her. "What did I hit?"

"The side of my head."

She thought she heard him swear. She knew for a fact that she felt his hands curved over her shoulders and ease along the sides of her neck. As if feeling for the point of impact, his palms slid up and cupped above her ears.

"Where?"

She barely breathed. "My temple."

"Which side."

"Right."

His left hand fell to her shoulder, the fingers of his right eased into her hair as if feeling for a knot.

"Are you okay?" he asked.

Her heart was already doing double-time. The feel of his big hands should have put it into overdrive. Yet, his touch, the concern in it, the gentleness, seemed almost…calming. Or would have had she let herself truly consider it.

"I'm…fine. Really," she murmured. "You didn't hit that hard."

The disquiet in her tone had changed quality. J.T. heard it as certainly as he'd felt her go still the moment he'd touched her. Realizing he was the reason for both, aware that he'd reached for her without thinking, he eased his hands away.

"There's an emergency button by the phone." Urgency returned to her voice. "Below it, I think. Here. I've got it."

She must have pushed the button. Or someone trapped in one of the other two elevators had just as anxiously sent the emergency signal. Somewhere in the shaft below them, an alarm began ringing.

Conscious of that distant sound, more conscious of the lingering feel of her soft hair against his fingers, he took a step back to give her room when she said she'd found the phone.

"Joe, is that you?" she asked after half a minute went by.

"This is Amy from the twelfth floor. I'm stuck in the elevator with a client. I'm not sure," she said after a moment. "Somewhere around the ninth or tenth floor, I think.

"We're okay," she continued. "We'd just like to know what's going on.

"Will do," she finally murmured. "Thanks."

J.T. heard a patting sound as she searched for the receiver's cradle. It was followed by the click of plastic against metal when she found it and hung up.

"The power's out in the whole building. Something tripped the main breaker."

The construction, he thought. He remembered hearing the distant sound of a power saw when he'd first come in. "Did he say anything else?"

"Just that we're not supposed to panic. If the power doesn't come back on soon, they'll call the fire department to come get us."

"Are you okay with that?" A heavy hint of masculine caution laced the deep tones of his voice. "The not panicking part?"

"I'm not sure yet. I've never been stuck in a dark elevator before."

Thinking she sounded okay for now, hoping she'd stay that way, J.T. leaned against the elevator's back wall. "Who's Joe?"

"The building's maintenance supervisor. He's been here forever."

A moment ticked by. Another. From a few feet away, he heard her draw in a long, deep breath.

"These things don't just fall down the shaft," he told her, "if that's what you're worried about. There are redundant systems in place to keep that from happening."

"How many?"

"Aside from the static brake, there's at least one safety and a governor. Since we're nowhere near being over weight capacity, that system should keep us right here until the power comes back on."

"You know that for certain?"

"I do."

"How?"

"Because I've read the specs when I've designed these things into buildings. Different companies have different features, but they all have the basic safety elements."

A considering silence preceded her quiet "Oh."

Silence intruded once more. Within seconds Amy could practically feel it echoing off the walls. Or maybe, she thought, crossing her arms tightly around herself, what she felt was the disturbing combination of nerves and the memory of the heat that had shot through her when she'd first met his eyes. They were the color of old pewter, the deep silver gray of a cloudy sky. But that was all she'd noticed before that odd heat had caused her to look away.

She'd never really felt that disturbing, intriguing sensation before. That…electricity, she supposed. She'd heard about it. Read about it. Tried to imagine it. But not once in her twenty-five years had she actually experienced the jolt that had made her heart feel as if it had tightened in her chest and darted warmth straight to her belly.

She'd felt the sensation again when he'd curved his hand over her shoulder and slipped his fingers through her hair. Only, then she felt something else, too. Something she hadn't even realized she'd craved until she'd felt his compelling touch. Simply to be cared for, to be cared *about*.

"So," she said, too uneasy with the elevator situation to refute the wholly unwanted admission. Not that what she'd felt with him mattered, anyway. Men like Jared Taylor, tall, dark and gorgeous men with ambition, sophistication and drive paid no real attention to her. Certainly, not the sort her beautiful, equally sophisticated stepsister received. She'd seen the way he'd straightened when Candace had walked in, caught the way his eyebrows arched ever so slightly as his glance moved along the length of her body. She'd seen the quick, reciprocating interest, too, as Candace had checked out his left hand. He hadn't been wearing a ring. Amy had noticed that herself when he'd helped her pick up the files that had scattered at their feet. If the guy was single, odds were that Candace would have him asking her out by the end of their next meeting.

Silence had intruded again, heavy, uncomfortable. Later, she could wonder if she'd ever find a man who would look at her with that unmistakable, purely male interest. Right now, she just needed for him to talk to her. Or to talk herself. That silence did nothing but let her too active imagination head in directions she really didn't want it to go.

"So, Mr. Taylor," she began again.

"It's Jared," he corrected. "And you're…Amy…?"

An introduction seemed totally reasonable under the circumstances.

"Amy Kelton," she replied, and would have offered her hand had she any idea where to find his.

"Kelton? Are you any relation to the Kelton in Kelton & Associates?"

"Mike Kelton was my father. He owned the agency before he passed away."

"He did?" He seemed to hesitate on a number of levels. "I mean, I'm sorry. About your father."

"Thanks. Me, too." It had been nearly five years, but the shock of her dad's sudden death and its unsettling aftermath still caught her off guard at times. Mike Kelton had been a man in his prime. Or so everyone had thought when he'd gone out one morning for his usual run, and promptly suffered a massive coronary.

"The firm went to his wife," she explained, her tone matter-of-fact. This man was a client, after all. As long as the firm bore her father's name and she was part of the team, she would protect its members—no matter how ambivalent she personally felt about some of them, or how invisible she usually was herself. "She was his business partner. Jill Chapman Kelton. She's Candace's mom. You would have met her, but she's touring a client's plant today."

J.T. frowned into the sea of black that prevented him from seeing features he remembered mostly as being delicate. Her eyes were dark, long-lashed and shot with flecks of gold, though why he remembered that from the few seconds she'd actually made eye contact with him, he had no idea.

From the nearness of her voice, the young woman who apparently held more interest in the firm than he would have ever suspected, remained by the wall a couple of feet away.

He knew the agency was a mother-daughter enterprise from his own quick research into the firm and Candace's recitation of the firm's hierarchy a while ago. She'd even pointed out the classy, silver-haired version of herself in the photos on her trophy wall. What Candace hadn't mentioned was that her assistant was her stepsister, and that her mother had inherited the firm from Amy's dad. Not that she'd had any reason to mention it, he admitted to himself. He hadn't asked anything about the company that would have given her reason to bring it up.

"So you're interning," he concluded, thinking it the only way to explain the younger stepsister's subordinate position. "You're in college and learning all the jobs on the way to becoming a partner yourself."

"Actually…no. I'm Jill and Candace's assistant, the bookkeeper and gofer for just about everyone else."

"You're not going to be part of the agency?"

"Not in any way other than I already am. The company belongs to Jill." Candace would become a partner in a few months, though. Her mother had promised her a quarter interest when she turned thirty. If Candace wanted to tell him that, she could. It wasn't her place. "My only financial interest in it is in what she pays me."

"Are you okay with that?"

A shrug entered her voice. "I have to be."

He hadn't expected the acceptance in her response. Or maybe it was the resignation. Baffled by whatever it was, his basic sense of fair play insisted that she should have shared the ownership of what appeared to be a very successful operation, not merely been there to support the women now running it.

"Why do you have to be?"

"Because I need the job to help support my grandmother," she admitted, too concerned about being trapped to care that he was so blunt. They were talking. That was all she cared about just then. "Jill pays me too much to go anywhere else."

"Do you live with your grandmother?"

"No, I... No," Amy repeated, and promptly told herself she really should shut up. At the very least, she should change the subject. She couldn't begin to deny the unease she felt knowing she was ten stories up, trapped in a box with nothing but whatever mechanical wizardry he understood but she didn't to keep it from dropping to the basement. She just wasn't in the habit of sharing her problems with people she knew, much less with a stranger she'd be faced with again when he returned for his next appointment.

"Then, she lives with you," he concluded.

"She's in an assistant living facility."

"What about your stepmom?" he asked, before she could move on. "Why isn't she supporting her?"

"Because Grandma Edna is my responsibility. She's my mom's mom and the only real relative I have left," she allowed, though she might not have added the latter had she not been where she was. If the elevator fell, there wouldn't be anyone to see that the increasingly eccentric older woman was properly cared for. Edna could be a handful. Jill couldn't stand her.

"Can we talk about something else, please? Tell me about your company," she suggested, desperately wanting not to think about falling down the shaft. "You must be excited about pulling it all together. Is having your own firm something you've always wanted?"

J.T. didn't know which caught him more off guard just then; her obvious resignation to her position in the company, the abrupt change of subject, or her assumption that he felt any excitement at all about his possible venture.

She'd also just confronted him with the sudden need for an acceptable explanation for his own circumstances.

He could hardly tell her that the idea of starting his own company had nothing to do with realizing a dream. It had simply been the logical thing to do, given what his father had thrown at him. He couldn't tell her, either, that once he'd decided what he had to do, that he'd approached the task with the same methodical, get-it-done attitude he intended to tackle in his pursuit of Candace—the potential bride. There had been nothing resembling excitement involved.

The thought gave him pause. Standing there with the dark masking his disquiet, he couldn't honestly say he felt energized, eager or enthusiastic about much of anything he did anymore. Even his last climbing trip in the Swiss Alps had left him oddly dissatisfied and restless. It almost had been as if pushing himself to conquer yet another mountain was no longer enough.

He didn't care at all for that unexpected thought, or the

strange, empty sensation that came with it. Certain both were there only because he was being pushed to do things he didn't want to do, he dismissed the matter as inconsequential—and simply told her what he could of the truth.

"I didn't start thinking about my own firm until a couple of months ago. It just seemed like it was time."

"To break out on your own?"

"Something like that."

"Then, this isn't a goal you've worked toward for a while."

He hadn't been prepared for the conclusion in her voice. Or, maybe what he hadn't expected was her insight.

A hush fell between them, long seconds passing before her soft voice finally drifted toward him.

"I'm sorry."

"For what?"

"Overstepping myself. I didn't mean to pry." Sympathy joined the apology in her tone. "I just assumed that starting your own firm was something you'd wanted to do."

She clearly recognized that it was not.

For a moment J.T. couldn't think of a thing to say that wouldn't sound like confirmation—or like too much of a protest. He handled his life the same way he played poker. Straight-faced and close to the vest. He wasn't given to showing his hand. Yet, in a matter of seconds, this quietly unassuming woman had recognized his ambivalence and pretty much called him on it.

Feeling exposed, not caring for the sensation at all, he dismissed her perception as a fluke. At least, he did until he considered what he'd learned about her job and realized she might well be wrestling with her circumstances, too. The inherent unfairness in her situation did strike a vaguely familiar chord.

"What would you do if you didn't have to work for the agency?"

Amy shifted against the wall, uncomfortable with having trespassed onto sensitive ground. She wasn't usually so straightforward with a client. Not that Jill had her deal with any of them directly very often. Most of her contact was over the phone or by mail. It was just that this man's vague responses had left her with the feeling that his new venture had been precipitated by something unexpected. A divorce, perhaps. Or a problem within the firm he now worked with. Personality problems within the partnership. Cutbacks.

Whatever the reason, he didn't seem to her to be at all enthused about striking out on his own. She'd simply responded to that. Much as she'd responded to his touch moments ago, and the tension she sensed in him now.

That faint tension seemed to reach toward her, wrap itself around her, increase her own.

Not at all sure what to make of her reactions to him, she tried to ignore them all. "If I could do anything…"

A faint thud sent her heart into her throat.

Her voice dropped to a whisper. "Did you hear that?"

"Hear what?"

"It sounded like something hitting metal."

"Might have been a door. Is the stairwell near the elevators?"

"It's just around the corner."

"They're probably evacuating the building. Go on," he coaxed, sounding far less concerned than she felt. "You'd… what?"

The elevator doors were too thick to hear much of anything else going on beyond them. It was also possible that they were stuck between floors, which meant they were further insulated by the six or so feet of crawl space and whatever else existed between the building's various levels from anyone who might pull the doors open from the outside.

Thinking of how big he was, how quietly powerful and

confident he seemed, she inched closer to his voice. "Get a degree in marine biology," she said, "find a research position, then tackle the rest of my life list."

More concerned with being stuck while everyone else was leaving than with the list she'd barely begun to complete, she strained to see if she could hear anything else.

All she heard was the curiosity in Jared's voice. "Life list?"

"It's a list of things I want to do before I..." *die* wasn't a word she wanted to use just then. "Before I'm too old to get around," she concluded.

"Getting your degree is at the top of it?"

"At the top was to buy my own home." Having her own home had been at the top of her list ever since her father had married Jill and sold the one she'd grown up in. She'd promised herself then that she'd someday have a home no one could take from her. "I did that a few years ago," she told him, ever grateful for the down payment allowed by the modest insurance policy her father had kept for her.

Trying to stay focused, she thought about the next item on the old piece of blue notepaper she kept tucked in her nightstand drawer, and skipped right over it. Admitting her hope—her need—to have a family of her own felt far too personal, especially since he was undoubtedly only trying to distract her from thoughts of where they were.

"Next is to dive off the coast of Australia," she added, thinking her odds of accomplishing any of that roughly equal to acquiring a fairy godmother. She had neither the prospects, the time nor the money her dreams required. Given her present obligations, she wouldn't for a very long time. "And in the Bahamas and Hawaii." It was also a wish list, after all.

The curiosity in his voice remained as he asked how long she'd been diving. She told him her dad taught her when she was eleven, but that she hadn't done much in the past couple of years. "No time," she explained, thinking she'd love to be on any of those islands just then. Anywhere to be away from where she was.

Maybe she was a little claustrophobic after all. Or maybe the unease she felt was fear of falling.

She didn't realize she'd spoken her last thoughts aloud. At least, not until she felt him move closer and his hand touched her arm.

The moment it fell away, she realized what he'd done.

He'd let her know he was right there, close enough to reach, if she needed him.

"You're doing fine," he assured her.

"Do you think we should try to get out?"

"Doing anything other than staying where we are for a while would probably just get us into bigger trouble. They know we're here," he reminded her.

"In the movies, they show people going through the little door up there."

"What they don't show in those movies is that the hatch is usually bolted from the outside. Even if this one isn't, I'd rather not crawl around on top of this thing trying to find a way out in the dark." J.T. didn't mind an adrenaline rush. He'd hang off a cliff face suspended by ropes and gladly spend the time working out his next move and enjoying the view. But that kind of risk was different from hanging onto greased cables while standing on a box that would start moving the instant the power came back on. He'd have little control in that situation. Being in control was what his life had been about for as long as he could remember.

"I wouldn't have a clue where I was in relation to anything else," he admitted, willing to bet the best Bordeaux in his cellar that she didn't really want to crawl around up there, either. "I have a thing about wanting to know my next move."

"So we forget the hatch," she murmured. "What about prying open the doors?"

"The problem there is if we're between floors and one of us is crawling out when the power comes back on." Had he been alone, he probably would have already tried that. He'd risk his own neck. He didn't care to risk anyone else's. "The car will move. The floor remains stationary. It's too easy to get crushed."

He thought she shuddered.

"And you know these things because you've worked with elevator companies," she concluded flatly.

"Call it a perk."

Amy swallowed. "Thank you for sharing."

He liked her bravado. Most of the women he knew would be in need of major hand holding by now. "Let's give them a while. If we start needing food and water, I promise, we'll come up with something.

"So," he continued, thinking it best to move on from the scenarios he'd planted in her head. With the time being wasted just standing there, he would have thought he'd rather be anywhere else at the moment, too. Almost. "Why diving?"

It wasn't often that he met anyone he found particularly intriguing, much less anyone who truly surprised him. Never would he have imagined her wrestling air tanks and weight belts to play tag with eels off the Great Barrier Reef. As docile as she'd first seemed, he wouldn't have thought there was an adventurous bone in her slender little body.

"Because I like the way I feel when I'm doing it."

"How's that?"

"Free," Amy said easily. She no longer cared what he asked her while they waited. She was just grateful for the distraction he offered, and for his solid presence. Had she been trapped there alone, she might well be huddled in a corner by now. "I don't feel that anywhere the way I do in the water. There are no restraints. It's just you and this whole other world. It's all just so…different. So…natural." *So peaceful,* she started to add, only to go silent as awkwardness abruptly crept through her.

Describing the abandon she felt in all that unhurried quiet didn't seem as simple as telling him about goals that probably weren't extraordinary at all to someone who seemed as urbane as this man did. Even in the dark, she ducked her head. "It's hard to explain to someone unless they've been there themselves."

Moments ago she'd moved closer. Not by much, J.T. thought. Just close enough that every breath he drew now brought her subtle scent with it. He couldn't figure out what it was. It seemed too light to be perfume. Her shampoo, maybe. Body wash.

Already more aware of her than he wanted to be, he thought about moving himself. She was clearly growing more uncomfortable, though, and trying her best to mask it. So he stayed where he was. Despite whatever discomfort or awkwardness she felt, she also seemed to feel safer near him.

"You don't have to explain it to me." He offered the assurance as he turned from the back wall, edged to the wall adjoining it. She was right there, presumably with her back against the panels. With his arms crossed, he let his jacket sleeve rest lightly against her upper arm. She could move closer if she wanted. Or away, if she chose. "I know what you mean."

Though he sensed hesitation, she stayed where she was. "You do?"

"I haven't been diving in years," he admitted, wondering if he hadn't just felt her relax a little. He preferred to be on the water, pushing for speed and battling the wind for control. "But I sail for the same reason." Especially to an island that I want to build a home on someday, he thought, and overlooked the agitation that came with the idea of potentially losing access to it. "I haven't had time to indulge myself lately, either."

"Did your father teach you?"

That agitation seemed determined to be felt. She couldn't possibly know that his relationship with his father bore no resemblance whatsoever to what she'd apparently shared with hers. He just wasn't about to tell her how many times Harry had raised his preteen hopes about them doing something together, only to attend a meeting instead. How many times he'd fallen asleep outside his dad's office to show him something he'd made or a paper for which he'd received an exceptional grade only to have a housekeeper wake him and tell him his dad had left. Old Harry had been far too busy building his technological empire to bother with anything so mundane as what might matter to a kid.

"I learned with a friend. We borrowed his brother's boat and basically taught ourselves."

He'd been grounded for a week when Cornelia had discovered what he'd been doing and told his father about it. He'd been grounded for another week for risking his neck because Cornelia had insisted they could have capsized the boat and drowned. He'd never been worried, though. By the time she'd found out what he'd been up to, he'd become a pretty good sailor.

"How old were you?" he heard Amy ask.

"Twelve." He hadn't thought back so far in years. "I decided then that I'd have my own sailboat someday."

"How long was it before you bought one?"

The smile in her voice seemed to say that she didn't doubt his determination for an instant. Drawn by that, he might well have told her about the series of boats that had led to the forty-foot sloop he currently kept docked in Seattle. But even as he opened his mouth he remembered that he needed her and everyone else in the ad agency to think him a relatively average guy. He had no idea what she and her stepsister did or didn't share with each other, but he didn't want to say anything he wouldn't want repeated. He strongly suspected that a modestly successful architect wouldn't trade-in million-dollar sailboats the way most men did cars.

Grateful once more for the dark, he told her only that he bought a small one when he was eighteen. He wasn't sure why he was telling her any of this as it was. He wasn't in the habit of talking about his childhood to anyone. There'd been good parts and bad. He'd survived it. End of story. But he was spared having to wonder at how easily the young woman beside him had drawn him out when the elevator jerked.

Amy's breath caught as she grabbed for him. Jared's hands clamped around her upper arms. In the awful seconds while she waited for whatever would happen next, she didn't know if he pulled her to him to keep her from losing her balance, or if he was simply bracing them both. All she knew for certain was that he'd pulled her into his arms, that his body felt as solid as steel, and that she could do nothing but hang on.

With her heart battering her ribs, she buried her head against his chest.

Beneath her feet, the floor remained still long enough for her to become conscious of being surrounded by his heat—an instant before the elevator started to descend. Slowly. The way it always did.

Her pulse still racing, she opened her eyes, drew a quick, decidedly cautious breath. The scents of citrus aftershave and warm male filled her lungs as she blinked at the strip of cashmere between the soft wool lapels fisted in her hands.

The lights had come back on.

"Are you okay?"

His voice came from above her, the rich sounds of it a quiet rumble beneath the strains of the Muzak once again filtering through the speakers.

Looking straight ahead, all she could see was the wall of his very solid chest. She didn't want to move. For that unexpected, too-fleeting moment, she felt very safe where she was. Sheltered. Protected. She hadn't felt anything remotely resembling that alien sense of security since long before her father had died.

The feeling vanished with her next heartbeat.

Glancing up, her eyes met his. With her head tipped back, she was close enough to see shards of silver in cloud gray eyes, the carved lines bracketing his beautiful mouth. Already aware of the compelling feel of his arms, she nearly forgot what he'd asked.

He'd gone as still as stone. Or maybe it was she who failed to move as his glance skimmed her face and settled on her parted lips.

For one totally surreal instant, it seemed as if he was about to close the negligible distance between them. Yet, even as her heart nearly stalled at the thought of his mouth on hers, a muscle in his jaw jerked. His hold on her eased.

Releasing her grip on his lapels, she stepped back just as he did.

It was only then she remembered that he'd asked if she was all right. Considering the knotted state of her nerves, she most definitely was not.

"I'm…yes, of course," she murmured, jamming awkwardness beneath a thin layer of composure. He was watching her, rather curiously from the feel of his eyes on her as she scooped up her stack of mail while the elevator continued its descent. "I'm…fine. I'm just sorry you had to wander under the little black cloud that's been following me around all day. That's probably why I nearly ran you over in the office, and why you got stuck in here with me now." Refusing to consider what else could go wrong, she aimed a commendably calm smile at the cleft in his chin. If she'd learned anything from her years in advertising, it was that perception was everything. If you appeared in control, everyone thought you were. "The good news is that it's me, not you, and that bad days get better."

"What about bad weeks?"

"Those are the ones that build character." Or so her grandma said.

"Bad months?" he asked, and watched as her smile made it to her eyes. Something knowing shifted in those doe-brown depths.

"That's when you need to find something to do that takes you away from your problems for a while. Whatever you're dealing with won't go away," she warned him, "but for that hour or that day, you've taken away its power over you."

The elevator stopped. Even as her smile fell away, the doors opened to a lobby crowded with office workers. Before J.T. could ask what sort of thing she would suggest as an escape, or what else had happened to her that day, she'd slipped into the mass of people grumbling about having had to walk the however-many flights they'd taken to get to the ground floor, only to now have to wait for an elevator to go back up.

He moved into the crowd himself, stopping a lawyer-type in a three-piece suit to ask what had happened to the power. The man told him that one of the building's floors was being gutted and remodeled. A worker had apparently shorted an electrical line and tripped the building's main breaker.

J.T. had barely thanked the guy before he glanced back to see if he could catch a glimpse of short and shining brown hair. He saw no one familiar, though, as he moved through the surge of people and out the building's tall glass doors.

Frowning at himself, he stepped out into the early fall air. He was on the brick-paved transit mall. MAX, the commuter

train, rattled by on its light-rail line. A bus idled at the light on
the corner. He couldn't believe how close he'd come to kissing
her. With her mouth inches from his, her scent and the feel of
her coltish little body drawing him closer, he'd come within a
heartbeat of seeing if she tasted as sweet as she looked.

Sweet. He'd never met a female he would have described
that way.

He shook his head, plowed his fingers through his hair. He
really needed to focus here. He fully intended to get to know
her stepsister. Even if Candace hadn't seemed to be an excellent candidate for the hunt, Amy wasn't at all the sort of sophisticated, worldly female that normally attracted him. The sort of
woman who'd developed a certain cynicism about the opposite
sex herself. When he entered the game, he preferred an equal
playing field. The young woman he'd just spent the past hour
with probably didn't even know there *were* rules. One of which
had always been that a woman not get too close.

It occurred to him, vaguely, that the way he'd played for
years might need to change. For now, though, all he cared
about was that he'd caught himself before he'd done anything
foolish. Circumstances had pretty much thrown her into his
arms was all. With his first priority being to save his position
at HuntCom, he had more to worry about than a young woman
who possessed far more insight about his feelings for his
backup project than he was comfortable with.

Amy hurried past a curved, Plexiglas bus kiosk, her arms
wrapped tightly around her bundle of envelopes as she
glanced back over her shoulder. She saw no sign of Jared
Taylor on the tree-lined sidewalk. As tall and imposing as
he was, he would stand out in any crowd, but he'd already
disappeared.

She could still almost feel the strength in his hands when

he'd helped her to her feet back in the office—right after she'd plowed into him and scattered files at feet. Just as she could almost imagine that same warmth filling her whole body when he'd held her in the elevator—moments after she'd practically crawled inside his jacket when the elevator had lurched. When he'd let go of her, the way his broad brow furrowed had made it abundantly clear that he'd wondered what on God's green earth he'd been doing. At least he'd been gentleman enough to pretend nothing unusual had happened while she'd rattled on about having had a bad day.

She turned the corner to the post office, trying to shake off the entire unsettling encounter. She just hoped he wouldn't say anything about her to Candace. She especially hoped he didn't let it slip that she'd mentioned having to take care of her grandmother or make a comment about her having had a less-than-stellar day. The last thing she needed was to give Jill's admittedly beautiful, undeniably well-intentioned daughter any reason to caution her about maintaining professionalism with their clients, or to give her a pep talk about what she needed to do when things weren't going right.

Candace's solution for everything was either a new man or a shopping trip. While Amy loved to hit sales, the home where her grandma lived had raised its rates so her budget had become tighter than ever.

As for finding herself a man, she was beginning to think she might be in the home herself before that ever happened. It seemed as if every female she knew was married, engaged, involved or on the mend from a broken relationship and had sworn off for the duration. Candace always had a man in her life. She went out more in a month than Amy had in the past two years. It was just that Amy's obligations to Jill, the agency and her grandma—and the fact that her frequent visits to Edna seemed to be a turnoff for some men—had kept her from getting beyond a few first dates and casual friendships. Then there was what Candace called her totally naive belief in happily-ever-after instead of happy-enough-for-now.

She'd always wanted the fairy tale. She wanted a man she loved who loved her back. She wanted family to be as important to him as it was to her. She wanted to have children with him, to share with him, to grow old with him. As long as she was thinking about it, it also would be nice if the guy made her feel what she'd so fleetingly experienced with Jared Taylor. Even the pleasant sensations she'd felt from a couple of the more charming frogs she'd kissed hadn't touched her in as many ways as just being held by that man.

For now, though, she'd just take care of the mail, hurry to the printers to pick up the copies of the family photos she'd had made for Edna with the hope of jogging her failing memory—and promise herself that the next time she saw Jared Taylor, she wouldn't let preoccupation with her personal concerns embarrass her again. It had been worry about her grandmother distracting her when she'd so unceremoniously plowed into him by the reception desk.

Unfortunately, a little over a week later, that same concern had just compounded itself. She just didn't have time to deal with that worry at the moment. Fifteen minutes before he was to arrive for his preliminary presentation, she received a reply to her latest e-mail request for a routine credit check on their newest client. Like the other companies from which she'd requested information, this one claimed no credit, employment or academic history available on an architect named Jared Taylor.

Professionally, the man didn't seem to exist.

Chapter Three

"**Y**ou can't find *anything* on Jared Taylor?"

"Not a thing," Amy replied. She set a glass of water and two vitamin-C tablets on Candace's desk blotter. Candace had buzzed her moments ago, announced that her throat felt scratchy and that she could *not* afford to come down with a cold, and asked Amy to bring her whatever was available to fend it off.

Grabbing the glass, she downed the tablets. "That doesn't make any sense," she insisted, the moment she'd swallowed. "The man said he's been an architect for years. There has to be a record of him somewhere."

The Taylor file was open in front of her. Watching Candace's frown slip to the colorful logos the team would soon present, Amy picked up the empty glass herself.

Candace wore a new black suit today. She wore black well. With her pale hair brushing her shoulders, the contrast was stunning. So was the suit. The short jacket was fastened by half a dozen short, narrow gold chains. Small gold chains linked the buttons at the cuffs. Amy had noticed earlier that the new black sling-back heels she wore were embellished with gold-toned buckles. The look was polished, yet with just enough of an edge to make others take notice. With Jared Taylor on her schedule, she had clearly dressed to impress.

Amy was more interested in undoing the impression she was afraid she'd made on him. Determined to appear totally professional herself, she had chosen a black skirt to wear that morning, too, along with a tailored white silk, French-cuffed blouse that she never would have been able to afford had it not been on sale. She'd thought about wearing heels, only to ax the idea even as she'd reached for a pair of black flats. If she wore heels, not only would her feet be killing her by noon with all the running around she did in the course of a day, but everyone would want to know what the occasion was. Since the only other appointments that day were with a client and vendors who were frequently in and out of the office, Jared's presence would be the logical conclusion to draw.

No one knew she'd been stuck in the elevator with him. No one knew she'd been stuck at all. When she'd returned that afternoon, everyone had been buzzing about the power having gone out. Everyone had also seemed to assume that she'd already left the building and missed all the excitement.

That was fine with her. Especially since the last thing she wanted now was for anyone to think that he had made any particular impression on her at all. Most especially since Candace had staked her claim. She'd heard her on the phone with one of her girlfriends only an hour ago. Candace had declined an invitation to lunch because she had an "extremely hot" new client coming in and wanted to keep the time-slot open in case he suggested doing lunch himself.

Though they tended to be polar opposites of each other in interests, tastes and temperament, Amy had always been a little in awe of Candace. What the woman wanted, the woman usually got.

Not, Amy mentally insisted, that she was all that interested in Jared herself. She'd admit that not a day had gone by that she hadn't found herself reliving that hour in the elevator with him. Specifically, the moments when he'd held her and reminded her ever so briefly of the sense of security she so desperately missed. But mostly what she felt for him was a certain sympathy for whatever it was he was losing—or had lost—that had caused him to strike out on his own.

"I'm sure there's a record somewhere, too," Amy agreed. "I just need to know more about him to get it. Like I told you the other day, there are several Jared Taylors with various initials listed with Dun and Bradstreet, but none are architects. Same with the credit reporting companies," she continued, only half-focused on the conversation. Needing to return a call, she glanced at her watch, took a step toward the door. "If you'll get his full name and an address other than the post office box in Seattle that he gave us, I'll probably have better luck."

Pulling a small, compact mirror from her top drawer, Candace quickly checked her lipstick. "Will do. I'm not concerned about the agency getting paid," she insisted. "We already have his retainer. I've just never gone into a preliminary presentation without more background information on a client. I think we've done a great job considering what we had to work with," she concluded, confident as always. "I just wish we'd had more." The compact snapped shut as she rose to pace. "Did you check international? Maybe nothing turned up here because he works out of the country."

Obtaining background information on a client was

standard operating procedure for the agency. Aside from making sure the client could pay his bills, information about a client's business history, contacts and vendors could help better serve the client's needs. That was why Amy had fully intended to research the international possibility yesterday. The day had totally gotten away from her, though. Jill had decided to have her living room furniture reupholstered while she attended a weeklong industry conference in Hawaii. It had taken Amy all day to get her organized, procure samples of the fabrics she'd ordered to make sure the bolt colors still blended with her carpeting, and get her to the airport for her six o'clock flight. First thing that morning, she'd had to let the men from the upholstery company in to pick up a sofa, two overstuffed chairs and an ottoman.

The agency was also still without a receptionist until Jill found the sort of young and attractive candidate she felt personified the agency's progressive image—which meant Amy was doing her job and the receptionist's, too. And would be until after Jill returned.

There's no one I trust more to make sure everything will go smoothly, Amy remembered Jill telling her as the porter had unloaded luggage from Amy's trunk. *Sometimes I don't know what Candace and I would do without you.*

Amy had thought at the time that if she trusted her that much, she'd let her hire a new receptionist herself—at least a temporary one. But Jill didn't feel that temps had a place on their tightly knit little team. In her defense, the woman did have a real knack for finding the right people for the job.

"I haven't checked international on him yet. But I can't imagine I'll get anything more without a full name and address."

Her own curiosity about the lack of information on Jared was on temporary hold. The bulk of her interest that morning was with the director of the care facility where her grandma lived. The woman had called wanting to talk to her about something "unfortunate," just as Candace had buzzed for her the first time.

Amy'd barely had a chance to make sure that her grandmother hadn't fallen or had been otherwise harmed before Candace had come out insisting that she needed her to fix the projector in the conference room ASAP for the Taylor presentation. That had been an hour ago and she'd been running ever since.

"Your notes in the file only indicate that his work is in Europe and Asia," Amy reminded her. Both were rather large continents. "Which countries should I check?"

"I have no idea." Nervous energy now had Jill's daughter moving from her desk to the window and back again. "I know I asked where he was working, but the subject got changed somehow. I'll ask him again when I see him."

"Is that all, then?"

"Is the projector fixed?"

"The conference room is all ready for you."

"Can you pick up my dry cleaning on your lunch hour?"

"Sure," Amy murmured, too accustomed to such requests to consider the imposition on her personal time.

With a quick smile, Candace snatched her empty Kelton & Associates coffee mug and handed it to Amy to get it off her desk. "Oh, and when he gets here, give me a few minutes with him before you alert the rest of the team. I'll buzz you when I'm ready for you to call everyone else."

Holding the mug, Amy acknowledged the request with the lift of her chin, grabbed the water glass and headed into the hall. Another glance at her watch told her she had ten minutes before Jared Taylor's appointment. In theory that gave her enough time to make her call to the director now.

"Hey, Amy." Eric Burke, their electronic media director,

strode toward her, five feet ten inches of faintly flamboyant creativity in navy worsted and cranberry cable knit.

"Hey, Eric."

"Where are you going for lunch?"

"Martinotti's." It was closest to the cleaners.

He turned as they passed, still talking as he walked backward. "Bring me back a turkey on multigrain, everything but mayo?"

"No problem," she assured him, now walking backward, too.

"By the way, love the schoolgirl look you've got going there."

Schoolgirl? she thought. That was so not the image she'd had in mind for today. With a grimace she muttered, "Thanks."

Savannah poked her head out of her office, her sharp wedge of cinnamon-red hair swinging. "You're making a deli run?"

Amy barely noted the graphic artist's hopeful expression before her backward progress was halted by hands on her upper arms. Amber Thuy, one of Savannah's crew, stepped around her. "I'd love a salad, if you are. Which deli?"

"Martinotti's," Eric called, and disappeared into the supply room.

Glancing behind her to make sure she wouldn't back into anyone else, Amy kept going. "Write down what you want and I'll order it," she told the women. "Right now I need to make a call."

She got a thumbs-up from Savannah, a quick "Thanks" from Amber and hurried into the break room to deposit mug and glass in the sink. Reminding herself to wash them later, she headed to the front desk and punched out the number for Elmwood House, the facility her grandma lived in, before anyone else could delay her.

Kay Colman, the facility's director, immediately came on the line. Just as she did, the main office door opened.

Jared Taylor walked in, six feet, two inches of long, lean masculinity in a charcoal turtleneck and a tailored black leather jacket. His quicksilver eyes flicked from his watch to the clock on the wall. With the command of a man with an agenda to keep, he kept coming, his focus shifting to where she sat at the reception desk with the phone to her ear.

Her glance had stalled on his broad chest. Realizing that, she jerked her focus to his face to acknowledge him and turned her attention back to her call. Now was not a good time to think about how he'd held her there, next to all that hard, solid muscle.

"I'm so sorry," she murmured into the phone, "would you hold for just a moment please."

Suddenly aware of her heartbeat, she put the director on hold. She just wasn't sure if her pulse felt uneven because of the hesitation and concern she'd just heard in the director's voice, or because of the easy way Jared smiled at her as he walked up to her desk.

"How's the weather?"

"The weather?"

"The black cloud that was following you around. You said bad days get better," he reminded her, sounding as if he might have doubted her optimism somehow. "I just wondered if yours did."

A faint smile formed. "I think you witnessed the worst of it."

Torn between her need to get back to the woman waiting on the phone and wanting to know if he was feeling better about the venture that had brought him there, she glanced back to the telephone console. The line she'd just put on hold was blinking. Candace's line was lit.

"You're busy." Sounding as if he might have had something else to say, he nodded toward the hall. "Is she in?"

"She's on the phone." He didn't look any more enthused,

she decided. If anything, he just looked tired. "If you want to have a seat, I'm sure she won't be long."

The overhead lights caught the gray silvering the dark hair at his temples as he gave her a preoccupied nod. Preoccupied herself, she pulled her attention from his broad shoulders when he turned and reconnected herself with Kay.

"I'm sorry," she repeated, her voice hushed. "You said earlier that my grandmother is okay." Her voice dropped another notch. "If she is, then what's the matter?"

From the corner of one eye, J.T. saw Amy slowly rise from her chair at the curved Lucite desk. He didn't know if she was trying to keep him from overhearing what she said, or if what she'd just heard had just caught her off guard. Either way, there was no mistaking the disbelief entering the quiet tones of her voice.

"Close? The whole facility?" She paused, listened. "But you said drastic changes aren't good for her."

For a long moment she said nothing else as whoever was on the other end of the line etched concern deeper into the delicate lines of her face.

She had her back to the reception area. Her hand covered her face as she rubbed two fingers against her forehead. Even turned away from anyone who might have walked through, there was no mistaking the unease she couldn't quite mask. That disquiet was in the hushed tones of her voice when she spoke again, and in the furrows of her brow when she turned to write on a notepad.

It was feeling his own brow pinch that made J.T. aware of how blatantly he was eavesdropping on her conversation. He'd caught enough of Amy's side of it to realize something was going on with the grandmother she was working to support. Edna, he remembered, was the woman's name. She'd mentioned that while she was trying not to panic in the elevator.

There wasn't much he didn't remember about her. More, specifically, about their conversation. He just didn't want to think about how accurate her insight had been about the new company he might—or might not—start. Or about how he was now feeling the definite need to get on his sloop and disappear for a few days, thanks to how she'd so perfectly described the freedom he felt when it was just him and the water. He would overlook the fact that he'd found no peace in the solitude of the island the last few times he'd been there, and that the challenge of fighting the wind had...lacked. Those were aberrations, he was sure. As it was, he had no spare time to indulge himself. Not for at least a month. With as much as he had to do between now and then, that month felt as if it was a year away.

Telling himself that what he'd overheard was none of his business, he turned his attention to the Blackberry he'd pulled from his pocket and started to check his messages. He'd spent the past eight days in Seattle in conferences with Gray, avoiding Harry and shuffling personnel in his department to make sure the schedule for the warehouse expansions there and in Jansen, Washington, would be met. It was a point of pride with him to come in on time with every project he undertook. The more challenging the project, the better.

High-stakes anything had always attracted him. It didn't matter if it was sports, cards or real estate. He worked as hard as he played, and much to the bafflement of his infinitely more cerebral father, he freely admitted being drawn to just about anything legal that involved a risk. His reputation for being a player worked well for him in business. Anyone who knew him, knew him as the master of the deal, the man who never flinched. They also knew that where his professional obligations were concerned, he was ruthless in seeing they were met. As for personal obligations, he simply didn't allow them.

He'd felt let down too many times himself to want to disappoint anyone counting on him to be there for them.

With the Seattle project on track, his main focus now was the HuntCom campus outside New Delhi. The expansion there was scheduled for completion next year. Not that falling behind schedule might even matter. With his future hanging on him and his brothers finding brides, it was entirely possible he wouldn't see that or any other HuntCom project to completion.

Which was all the more reason he should have called Candace for dinner, he mentally muttered. He just hadn't had the time to come back to Portland until now.

"There's nothing you can do to get the funds?"

His focus sharpened on the distress in Amy's furtive tones as she asked how much the person on the other end of her line was talking about. He just couldn't hear what else she said in the moments before he realized he was eavesdropping again.

Giving up on his messages, he saw her nod as she murmured something into the phone. Her short hair feathered around her face. From what he could see of her profile, her dark eyes looked huge and worried. But it was the strain in her voice that truly betrayed her concern. She seemed more worried now than she had stuck ten floors up in an elevator.

Or so he was thinking when he heard her tell her caller that there had to be something they could do, that she would get back to her when she thought of it, then punched a button on the console to say, "Mr. Taylor is here. Would you like me to bring him back?"

With a quiet, "Okay," she hung up the phone and took a deep breath. As if totally accustomed to burying her concerns in the time it took most people to blink, she turned a calm smile in his direction.

"Candace will be right out."

He couldn't help wonder how often she was required to

make that sort of emotional transition. Suspecting from its ease that she'd had considerable practice, he hitched at the knees of his slacks.

"No hurry," he said, when he usually hated waiting.

He'd never been a man to sit and speculate when an answer was available. He wanted to know what was going on with her; what it was putting the strain in her pretty smile. Figuring the time they'd spent stumbling upon bits of each other's respective baggage in the elevator allowed him a little license, he was about to ask.

He'd barely approached her desk when Candace emerged in the hallway.

"Jared, I'm so sorry to keep you waiting. It's good to see you again."

His intent interrupted, he offered Amy a distracted smile of his own and moved toward her stepsister. The ad exec in the black designer suit moved with the long, leggy grace of a model. She had everything going for her. Beauty. Hair. Dazzling smile. Being male, he couldn't help but notice it all. Still vaguely preoccupied with her younger stepsister behind him at the desk, that was as far as his thoughts strayed.

"You, too," he replied, mentally shuffling priorities back to his plan. "You have my preview ready?"

"We have some ideas we'd like to share with you," she confirmed. "You understand this is all preliminary."

"Understood."

"Amy?" Candace arched one perfectly shaped eyebrow. "Will you have the team meet us in the conference room in five minutes, please?"

What J.T. figured would take ten minutes took twenty. The concept and design team presented him with options for logos, all of which were projected on a screen accompanied by an impressive power-point presentation of how each had been designed to make a different statement about him and his own designs. He was offered catch phrases, all incorporating variations of the buzzwords he'd liked when Candace had asked him if he had a mission statement.

He was asked if he would supply photos of buildings he'd designed and executed. Their Web master wanted to catalog them on the Web site he'd mocked up. The art director felt that taking a particularly unusual or impressive element from one of his structures would make a nice background for print copy.

There was more. All of it well done, considering how little he'd given them to work with, a point that was raised ever so tactfully by the quick, decidedly enthusiastic Candace. The woman was clearly a motivating force with her team. The collective effort of that team for the success of the client seemed to be what counted to her. It was also what impressed him most about her right then. He just found himself too distracted through much of the presentation to feel more than polite interest in the offerings. First by the way she dangled one high-heeled shoe from her toes. But mostly by the curiosity and the odd concern he felt for the young woman who was again on the phone when Candace finally escorted him back to the reception area.

On the desk in front of her, Amy had the Yellow Pages open to Realtors. From what he could hear her saying about needing to "get it on the market as soon as possible," it seemed she was arranging to sell a house.

Candace was talking, too. With his attention divided, he nearly missed the blonde's question about how long he would be in town.

"I know you have to return to the project you're working on in Singapore," she said, trying to catch his eye. "But I can have my assistant make the contract changes we discussed and have the amendment ready for you to sign first thing in the morning. If you'll still be here," she added, hinting.

Singapore. She had pressed, politely, to know where he was now working. Since he'd had to come up with a place, he'd mentioned the location everyone at HuntCom thought would be the next logical place to develop a presence. He'd been to that thriving city and he would, hopefully, start checking out potential real estate soon. So he'd let her and the team think he was working on a complex there for a client who didn't wish to be identified until the project was complete.

He hadn't wanted her digging around for information on him in India. He had no idea if his name had appeared in any of the business newspapers in New Delhi lately or what the translations would say if it had. There were employees in the company paid to keep track of any mention of HuntCom or those connected with it, but that wasn't the sort of thing he stayed on top of himself.

He also hadn't wanted to supply them with pictures of his former projects, all of which could be identified as HuntCom properties. But that had been easier to finesse. He'd simply told the truth; that the properties were designed under the name of the partnership he would soon be leaving. While the designs were his, they were owned by the partnership and he wasn't at liberty to use the images on his own.

Candace's people weren't happy about not having art. But then, he figured they were even. He wasn't too happy with the reason he'd had to come to them in the first place.

The reminder of why he was being forced to have a fallback company also reminded him he was losing time in his pursuit of a wife.

"I'm staying until tomorrow," he finally told her, switching gears from Plan B. A muscle in his jaw jerked. He wasn't at all comfortable with the subterfuge he was being forced to employ. "I have some other business I need to take care of here, so signing tomorrow works fine. If you're free tonight, I'll buy you a drink to toast the new campaign. If you're available I could meet you about seven."

She didn't hesitate. Tipping her head, she smiled. "Seven will be perfect."

"Can you suggest a place?"

"Where are you staying?"

He told her he was staying at The Benson, and caught the immediate, approving lift of her eyebrows at his choice of accommodations. He'd stayed at the beautiful old hotel with its venerable architecture and refined service the last time he'd been there. In one of their penthouses.

His accommodations weren't quite as spacious now, though. When he'd checked in before, he hadn't been thinking about the Bride Hunt or the rule about the prospective woman not knowing he had money. This time, he was in a decidedly more modest junior suite. Just in case he invited Candace up.

"There's a nice little lounge a block over," she told him. "How does that sound?"

That made it easy enough. He told her it sounded great, that he'd buy her a drink there. He made no mention of dinner because a drink could lead to dinner if things progressed. But "just a drink" left the bail-out option available if ending the evening early became a better idea.

He had operated that way for years. An hour with a woman over a glass of wine or a martini was usually all he needed to get an idea of how fast or slow she played the game, or if she was looking for a good time or a relationship. It felt odd to think that what would have sent him running before was what he was supposed to be looking for now. But all he concentrated on at the moment was that Candace impressed him as being sharp, driven and aggressive. She'd given him no clue how she felt about relationships, though, much less about marriage or having a child.

He just hoped she'd take the ball and run with it from there. All he knew about serious relationships was how to avoid them.

Or so he was thinking when Amy's voice drifted toward him once more.

"Tomorrow at twelve-fifteen," she said. "I'll meet you at the house then."

Candace spoke at the same time, her phrasing an odd echo of her stepsister's. "I'm looking forward to tonight, then."

His response was the vague lift of his chin as Candace turned to the desk. Amy's attention had fallen to the slip of paper she tore from a notepad.

He'd barely turned away before he heard Candace tell her stepsister—her "assistant" as she still referred to her— that there would be changes in his contract that she needed made as soon as possible. She also reminded her to not forget her dry cleaning, a moment before he heard Amy say that she'd take care of everything in a minute. Amy was then on the line asking whoever she'd phoned what kind of salad she wanted for lunch when he closed the door behind him.

He stood in the outside hall, his brow furrowed, his hand on the knob. She'd sounded fine now. A little rushed, maybe. But from what he'd seen of her in that office, "rushed" seemed to be her normal state.

He dropped his hand, headed for the elevator they'd been trapped in together last week. He should let it go. Not just the fact that she seemed to have a problem, but his inability to understand how she'd sounded so accepting of what she did for a living when it had so little to do with what she wanted for herself. With the possible exception of swimming with sharks, business and advertising had nothing in common with marine biology.

He'd be going back to India in two days. In the meantime, trying to juggle projects on both sides of the globe, he needed to focus on the reason he was in Portland to begin with. Of the dozen architects working under him at HuntCom, he knew of three he felt fairly certain would be willing to work for him if and when he opened his new firm. Depending on what happened with Harry's company, they might all need or want a different job, anyway. What he had to do now was find suitable office space for them—which was why he had an appointment with a leasing agent in half an hour to see what was available.

He glanced at his watch, the relatively inexpensive one he'd bought to wear whenever he came to Portland. He didn't want to be doing any of this. Amy had figured that out in no time at all—and called him on it pretty much in this very spot.

With a certainty that felt totally unfamiliar to him, he strongly suspected that she didn't want to be doing what she was doing with the house she'd been on the phone about, either.

That suspicion clung like barnacles to a pier. By the time the elevator reached the lobby floor, what little he'd overheard of her conversations could no longer be ignored. Without questioning why he couldn't let it go, he waved down a cab as soon as he hit the street, flipped open his cell phone after he'd given the cabbie his destination and called information for the number of Kelton & Associates.

Amy carried Candace's notes to the reception desk and dropped them on the other files she'd brought from her own office to work on that morning. As anxious as Candace was to impress their new client with their efficiency, she wanted

Amy to make the changes before she did anything else. Amy knew from what she'd caught of her and Jared's conversation that the changes in Jared's contract could be made anytime between now and tomorrow morning.

She had overheard him ask Candace out to celebrate. But that wasn't the reason she wanted to leave the office just then and walk off the anxiety sitting like a rock behind her breastbone. Taking precedence over the odd letdown she'd felt over that totally expected development was the situation with her grandmother.

The ring of the phone had her automatically reaching to answer it.

"Kelton & Associates."

"Amy, it's Jared. I heard you on the phone when I was leaving. What's the problem with your grandmother?"

With his deep voice in her ear, she closed her eyes, rubbed the spot threatening to ache behind her forehead. She hadn't realized how much of her conversation he'd overhead. "The place she's living has to close," she told him. "It's having funding problems."

"So you're selling her house?"

"Mine."

"You're selling *your* house?"

"I'm looking into it. The seniors' home needs money for repairs and improvements to keep its license," she said, her voice deliberately low. With her eyes closed, his voice so close, she could almost imagine him standing beside her in the elevator. Then, just by letting his arm touch hers, he'd ever-so-subtly let her know he was right there if she needed him. She didn't believe for an instant that he was letting her know he was there for her now, but the fantasy had a certain appeal. "The way values have gone up in my neighborhood, I may have enough equity to help them out."

She had no idea what to make of his heavy pause. Or of the frown that entered his voice. "What about your stepmother? Or Candace? Can't they do something about this?"

"I wouldn't ask them to."

"Why not?"

"Because I can't." She lowered her voice another notch. "I'm not in a position to talk about this right now."

Staring at the back of the driver's head, J.T. hesitated. Buying that house had been at the top of what she'd called her life list. Now she was actually thinking about letting it go.

He'd never in his life known any woman who would sell what he suspected was her only asset to help someone else. The women he'd known did nothing but take.

"Can I see the house?"

"What?"

"Can I see the house?" he repeated, touched by what she was willing to do when little touched him at all anymore. "I know someone looking for an investment property," he explained, improvising. "I might be able to help you out."

Amy hesitated, ambivalence flowing through her. An immediate sale would be a godsend. The thought of losing her home also doubled the size of the knot in her chest.

"When do you want to see it?"

"What time do you leave the office?"

"You want to see it today?"

"Works for me if it works for you."

"But it's not ready to show yet." The dining room was a mess. She had stacks of magazines by her bed, lingerie hanging in the bathroom. "I was going to clean tonight before the agent came tomorrow."

He started to ask why she didn't call her housekeeper and have the woman straighten up the place before she got there. But even as he opened his mouth, it occurred to him that she'd said she intended to clean that evening. Not everyone had always had a housekeeper.

"Is it in that bad a shape?"

"There's nothing fuzzy growing anywhere, if that's what you mean."

He chuckled. He liked that about her. Even worried, she could dig up a little sass. "Then give me your address. I'll meet you after you get off work."

Chapter Four

Amy threw the notes for Jared's contract changes into her briefcase with her laptop computer and raced out of the office at exactly five o'clock. On time for once, she grabbed the 5:07 bus to the neighborhood known simply as Northwest. Walking the block from the bus stop to her house twenty minutes later, she saw a taxi pull up to the curb in front of her tiny front lawn.

The area she'd chosen to live in was old, but full of young, upwardly mobile types who'd renovated the late-nineteenth- and early-twentieth-century houses. Some had been converted to shops, restaurants or boutiques. She'd become friends with many of the shop owners on the neighborhood's narrow, tree-lined streets. Her favorite place to spend Sunday morning was at any of the outdoor tables at the Starbucks on the corner.

The chill settling into the late Indian summer air had just reminded her that the incessant rains of fall and winter would soon drive everyone back inside when Jared stepped from the cab.

It was only then, with him looking up at her modest, white, two-story house with its charcoal shutters and Bristol-blue front door that she considered how very modest it was.

She had the feeling he was accustomed to finer things. Finer than she was used to, anyway. Everything about him—the quality of his clothes, the cut of his hair, the very way he carried himself—spoke of a man who had been exposed to a certain sort of prosperity. The exposure could have come through his clients. Companies and individuals who hired international architects to design their facilities and homes tended to have money themselves. Or, through his family, though she really didn't know enough about him to make that assumption. It was also entirely possible that he'd worked his way up from modest means himself. Yet, no matter how he'd acquired it, there was no denying the slightly intimidating sophistication she'd first noticed about him.

As much as he traveled, a person was bound to pick up a certain worldliness, she supposed. But she knew, too, that whatever assets he personally held were now tied up. She'd overheard him tell Candace he was putting every penny he had into his new business.

That venture seemed to be costing him everything he had. Or had left, anyway. Because he'd seemed so indifferent about what would have excited most people, she still couldn't help wondering if maybe he'd gone through a divorce that had been as much an emotional loss as an economic one. Or if there were financial problems within the partnership he was leaving and whatever he'd invested in it was gone. Whatever his situation, he apparently knew someone with the means to buy her house.

He must have asked the cabbie to wait. The Occupied light

on the screaming yellow vehicle remained on as the engine went silent.

Assuming Jared figured that a couple of minutes were all he needed, she watched him turn toward her with his hands in his pants pockets and waited for her to reach the short walkway.

She wasn't at all sure what he might think of her home. Rather wishing she'd put him off at least another fifteen minutes, she dug her keys from the oversize purse hanging off her shoulder and hurried past him. She'd leave him in the living room while she snatched the underwear she'd left drying over the shower door. Everything else would just have to stay where it was.

"I know you're in a hurry," she told him, thinking of his date with Candace, "so I'll make the tour quick." She took the three steps to the stoop at a jog. Moving past the blue pots of bright orange marigolds lining the wood railing, she pulled open the storm door. "Just keep in mind that it looks better straightened up. Okay?"

He held open the outer door while she unlocked locks. "You make it sound as if you had a poker party in there last night."

"Nothing that exciting," she replied, then remembered the nail polish and cotton balls on her coffee table. Her evening had consisted of going through old photos and giving herself a pedicure.

Pushing open the door, she stepped in and flipped on the entry light.

Behind her, J.T. moved into the small foyer and glanced up the narrow mahogany staircase that hugged a pale-blue wall beside him. Straight ahead, past an entry table and mirror, his focus caught on a tall, cylindrical aquarium of brightly colored tropical fish, then shifted to a painting of a huge, breaking wave. Beneath all those shades of aqua, a sand-colored sofa sat strewn with sea-foam-colored pillows.

With Amy leaving her coat over the back of an overstuffed wing chair, his perusal followed her to the tall candles and shallow bowl of seashells on the coffee table. A bottle of cherry-red nail polish sat on a paper towel beside cotton balls and polish remover. She snatched everything up before he could do much more than lift one eyebrow at the bold, bright color and follow her to the dining area on the other side of the open room.

Framed prints of sea coral flanked the tall, draped windows. The top of an old mahogany dining table had been obliterated by stacks of photo albums, photo boxes and an assortment of photographs. An album in progress sat by the only chair not holding shoe boxes.

"I'm putting some pictures together for Grandma," she murmured, motioning him through. "The kitchen's in here."

She led him into a neat space of refurbished white cabinets and blue Formica counters. Fresh herbs grew in tiny pots along the windowsill above the sink. A bouquet of yellow sunflowers graced a small breakfast table.

"The plumbing and electrical were all inspected when I bought the house three years ago," she told him while she tossed the paper towel and closed the rest of what she'd carried into a drawer of a built-in desk. "So there shouldn't be any surprises for a new buyer.

"It's three bedrooms. Two and a half, really," she continued, turning back to the dining room now that she'd shown him all there was to see of the kitchen. "One of the upstairs ones is really small, so I use it for storage. There's only one bathroom. It's back by the downstairs bedroom."

Moving past him, she apparently intended to lead him there.

"The whole place is about seventeen hundred square feet. Twenty four if you count the basement, but it's unfinished. There's nothing down there but cement floors and the furnace."

She'd made it as far as the cluttered dining table before he caught her by her arm.

"You can show me the rest of the house in a minute."

Aware of the faint confusion in her expression, more aware of the warmth of toned muscles penetrating soft silk, he eased his hand away. His glance fell with it. The slim little black skirt she wore skimmed her narrow hips. With her prim-looking white blouse tucked in, her waist looked small enough for him to span it with his hands.

"Right now," he suggested, jerking his glance back to her face, "why don't you tell me why you have to keep that facility going yourself. Can't you just move your grandmother some-place else?"

Her slender fingers curved where his had just been. The motion seemed as unconscious to him as the concern that entered the depths of her dark eyes.

"I'm going to have to if I can't help the home stay open. But that's one of the problems. Grandma needs to be in familiar surroundings so she stays oriented as long as possible. Change isn't good for her. The other problem is that the only facility the director will recommend is nearly two hours away. Everything closer with the atmosphere she's used to has waiting lists forever long. With the hours I work, I'd only be able to see her once a week."

"How often do you see her now?"

"Three times. Sometimes four."

J.T. was at a loss. He didn't see certain members of his family three times in an entire year. "Why so often?"

Suddenly looking self-conscious, her glance fell to the photos. "Amy?"

"So she won't forget me," she murmured. "So she won't forget any of us."

Her short nails were neat and bare. He noticed that when she touched one slender finger to a picture of a young woman who bore a striking resemblance to her cameolike features.

Hearing the disquiet in her admission, something unfamiliar pulled in his chest. A more recognizable need to protect himself from whatever it was pulled right back. "So don't sell your house," he said, focusing on what he understood. "Just use the equity."

"I can't afford the additional monthly payment."

"You wouldn't have one. You'd loan the home the money. In turn, they make payments to you and you send them on to the mortgage company."

"The home can't make any more monthly payments, either. Kay...she's the director," she explained, "said they can't acquire any more overhead without raising what they charge their residents again. Several of those ladies are on fixed incomes and their families can't afford to pay any more."

"So you're going to just give them the money?"

Amy turned her focus to the shine on his size elevens. She wasn't entirely sure what she was doing. She knew only that she couldn't put the only real family she had in a strange place miles away. If Edna needed her in a hurry, she needed to be there. It was the least she could do for the woman who had been there for her so often herself.

"What about going to Jill or Candace, then? The ad agency is successful isn't it? Could they come up with at least part of the funds?"

"I told you, I can't go to them with this. And don't ask me to explain why," she insisted, certain the question was coming. "You're a client and that's a...family...matter."

"Forget the client part," he muttered, wanting answers. "And don't tell me it's complicated. Family matters always are."

There was no mistaking the conviction in his tone. Or the edge behind it. That edge seemed to compound the faint tension she'd sensed in him before. As before, his tension only made her that much more aware of her own.

"Then you know that just because you could ask for something, doesn't mean you should. Or that you will."

"Understood," he agreed. "Completely." The lines fanning from the corners of his eyes deepened as his focus narrowed on her face. "So why won't you ask them?"

The man was as tenacious as a rat terrier with a bone. From the absolute certainty in his response, it also seemed he knew exactly how difficult certain situations with family could be.

"You won't repeat what I say?"

"Who would I tell?"

"Candace?" she suggested, wondering how he'd come by that understanding. "You are meeting her for a drink tonight."

"Trust me," he muttered, having momentarily forgotten about that. "Anything you say stays right here." A family problem was the last thing he wanted to get in the middle of. If Candace had issues with Amy, he wanted to know about it up front. "No family problems" was on his list of criteria for a future wife.

That rationale seemed easier to justify than the odd empathy he felt for her younger stepsister.

"So why won't you go to one of them for help?"

"Because mention of my grandmother tends to drop the temperature in the room about thirty degrees. Jill thinks Grandma tried to break up her and dad before they got married. Candace doesn't like my grandmother because she thinks she tried to sabotage her mom."

"Did your grandma try to break them up?"

Amy shrugged. "I'm sure she did," she admitted, because her grandmother had always had a way of letting her opinion be known. "Grandma lived with dad and me to help us out after mom died, so she felt she had a right to speak her mind about certain things. Especially when it came to me."

"How long ago was this?"

She had to think. She'd been eleven when she'd lost her

mom. Fifteen when her dad and Jill had started dating. "They were married when I was sixteen, so about nine. Dad and I had been really close. But when he took on Jill as a partner, he started spending more of his free time with her than he did with me. I know Grandma thought he was shortchanging me, and that she told him as much."

Her grandma had also thought Jill had what she called "airs."

She shook her head, reached for a photo of her and a grinning woman with a shock of short white hair. That way of speaking had been so much the way of her very Midwestern grandmother. Still was, for that matter.

"She was just looking out for me," Amy defended, because Edna Moore had always had her only grandchild's best interests at heart. "It wasn't one-sided. Jill didn't like being around Grandma, either. I think it was because she was a reminder of my mom."

"The woman your dad married first."

At the flat note in his voice, Amy glanced up from the photos. "You sound familiar with that sort of competition."

"I've been around versions of it. With my own father," he explained vaguely. "Distance is definitely better."

"Exactly," she murmured.

It almost had been as if Jill had needed to prove to Edna that she was as good a wife as her daughter had been. Then, there had been her grandmother's displeasure with the way she thought Jill wanted to turn Amy into a clone of herself.

Amy realized now that Jill probably hadn't been trying to change her, so much as she'd been looking for a way to relate to her. They'd had absolutely nothing in common except for her father. At fifteen, Amy had been perfectly comfortable in T-shirts and jeans and running around a soccer field. She'd also been a little overwhelmed and a lot intimidated by the energetic woman in the designer suits who insisted Amy would be so pretty if she'd just do something with her hair and dress more like a girl.

Jill hadn't said anything about her clothes in ages, but it was obvious from the way she regarded the understated style Amy had developed for herself, that she felt she could use a little more flare.

"So what happened when they did get married?"

"Dad sold our house and he and Jill bought one together," she said, slipping photos of her parents into an envelope. "I had a room there, but it wasn't home. Grandma had moved into an apartment, so Dad agreed that I could live with her as long as I went to the office with him on Saturday so we could spend the day together.

"That's basically what happened," she said, "and why I won't go to her now. Jill resents Grandma. Grandma isn't Jill's family," she also told him. "Since Dad died, technically she and I aren't family, either."

Jared's eyebrows had formed a single slash.

"What?" she asked.

"Where was Candace during all of this?"

"At UCLA working on her master's. She's five years older than I am, so she wasn't here while all that was going on."

"You two never lived together?"

"She didn't move to Portland until about four years ago. Her mom asked her to come to work for her the year after Dad died." Mindful of the cab out front with the running meter, and her need for some quick money, she set the envelope in an open shoe box and turned from the table. If he had questions about Candace, he could ask her himself. "Do you want to see the rest of the house?"

As if remembering the cab himself, or maybe what he remembered was his date, he held out his hand for her to proceed.

She promptly turned toward the hallway leading to the

back of her house. Even as she did, she could practically feel his curiosity burning into her back.

"So how did you wind up working there?"

Picking up a pillow that had fallen from the sofa, she plumped it, set it in place. "Jill needed someone to help her in the office after she found herself without a husband and business partner," she replied. "Dad had handled all the managerial stuff. Jill is more of a concept person, and very good at what she does," she allowed, because the woman's marketing ideas could be truly inspired. Jill had just never cared much for details. Or organization. "But she was having to do everything after Dad died.

"I'd worked for the agency during summers in high school and through my freshman and sophomore year of college," she explained, continuing on to the hall. "Since I knew how to do the billing and ordering for the office, she asked me to work for her full time until she could hire an office manager. I knew dad would want me to help her." She gave a shrug. "So I did."

The woman had been overwhelmed as much by her grief as the responsibilities she couldn't effectively tackle just then. Amy saw no need to mention that, though. Or how she'd been grieving herself. It hadn't mattered to her that she and Jill had never bonded in any familial way. The one bit of common ground they'd shared was love for Mike Kelton. Jill had really cared about him and, despite her grandma's disapproval of the woman, Amy knew she'd made her father happy.

It also had been about that time that she'd realized there was something more than simple forgetfulness going on with her grandmother. Focusing on the agency and keeping things obsessively organized had simply been a way for her to keep some normalcy in her life.

What normalcy she'd managed had suffered in the past week, though. As she'd gone through the boxes of old photos for her grandma, the memories of the awful insecurity she'd felt then had all been right there in front of her. Now she was actually considering selling the house she'd bought as security for them both.

Reaching the short hallway, she flipped on the overhead light.

"The laundry room is down here," she told the surprisingly silent man behind her. She motioned ahead of her, thinking she'd dart into the room she'd just passed while he poked his head inside. It would only take her seconds to pull her lingerie from the shower rod and stuff it somewhere. "The washer and dryer can stay if the person you mentioned is interested in buying it."

Instead of going on to the laundry room, he stopped by the bathroom door, blocking it. "Do you run personal errands for Jill, too?"

"Too?"

"I heard Candace ask you to pick up her dry cleaning. I just wondered if you do that sort of thing for her mother, too."

It was no longer simple curiosity she heard in his voice. Disapproval shaded his tone.

"It's part of my job."

It had become part of it, anyway. As overwhelmed as Jill had seemed without Mike around at first, Amy hadn't minded taking over certain personal tasks for her. When her daughter had arrived, she'd asked her to arrange her move into an apartment and teach her the office routine. What each had expected of her had slowly escalated from there.

"It didn't start out that way," she admitted, when the furrows in his forehead deepened. "But it's okay. I was going to leave a couple of years ago. When I had to move Grandma into Elmwood House," she explained, "her social security didn't cover the cost of her medications and the monthly fee, so I told Jill I had to find a job that paid more to meet the additional expense. Jill raised my salary by half to keep me on board."

Looking as if he now understood, he lifted his chin, gave a slow nod. "So she pays you well to take advantage of you."

Amy could practically feel her back stiffen. She didn't care for his phrasing. Mostly what she didn't care for was that, in some ways, he was probably right. Much of what she did for Jill, and for her daughter, was now taken for granted.

"I prefer to think that our arrangement is mutually beneficial. Jill needs someone to handle the things she doesn't want to be bothered with. In turn, she pays me far more than I could earn anywhere else without a degree. She knows what I use that extra money for."

"But she's benefiting most. How many hours a week do you put in? For her, the agency and Candace. On an average," he asked, because she seemed about to hedge.

"Fifty-ish."

"Ish?"

"Sixty."

His questions made her uncomfortable. The unexpected sympathy that slipped into his eyes simply confused her.

"I make my own choices." She tipped her chin, more conscious of him than she wanted to be in the confines of the narrow hall. "And for now, I'm comfortable with the choices I've made."

Not as comfortable as you'd like to be, J.T thought. There was steel in that delicate backbone. Strong hints of it, anyway. But he'd be willing to bet his sailboat that she was no happier about the choices she'd been forced to make than he was with those he was being forced to make himself.

He had a problem with people who pushed buttons or made demands simply because they knew they could. He had an even bigger problem with people who somehow used what was important to a person as a way to make them do their bidding. He didn't get the sense that she was being jerked around as ruthlessly by Jill as he was by Harry. And he, at least, had the option of starting his own company with his own considerable resources if he lost his position. But from what he'd just heard from Amy, it sounded as if the only option she felt she had was to put her life on hold for everyone else.

He decided to test that theory.

"You said you wanted to get your degree in marine biology," he reminded her. "When do you plan to go back and get it?"

She had no such plans. Not in the immediate future, anyway. He felt certain of that even before she glanced away.

"I'll get it. Someday," Amy assured him, sounding far more positive than she felt. Her goals were probably nothing but pipe dreams now. She'd planned to eventually borrow against the equity in her home to finance her education. Or take those once-in-a-lifetime diving trips she'd so naively thought might actually be possible. But that had been before her grandmother's care changed those plans.

She reached past him. "This is the bathroom," she said, and flipped on the light to change the subject. Totally distracted by the disquiet his questions brought, she'd forgotten the lacy teddies and bras hanging on the shower rod.

Jared's glance left the top of her head to sweep past a counter overflowing with lotions and makeup. It swung on to the swirls of cobalt and aqua covering a partially drawn-back shower curtain. His perusal immediately stalled on what hung next to it.

"There's a heat lamp overhead," she said.

With all the aplomb she could muster, she walked over the instant he glanced up and pulled down those entirely feminine bits of pink, peach and black lace. It seemed to J.T. that only the faint color heightening the natural blush of her cheeks betrayed the discomfort she felt standing there holding her surprisingly sexy underwear.

"And the shower has a spa showerhead," she continued, wadding everything up, hangers and all to hold against her middle. A bra had tiny roses embroidered along its straps. The legs of a teddy, lacy and high cut, dangled from beneath it. "I was going to put in glass doors when I redid the bathroom, but it wasn't in the budget."

The room held her scent, that elusive combination of body wash, lotion and shampoo from the bottles lining the edge of the porcelain bath tub. The fact that she'd redone the room explained why that tub, the sink and commode were all deep blue. Water-blue tile covered the counter and formed the backsplash. From the way she'd decorated the other rooms he'd seen with the serene shades of the shore and the sea, it was as clear to him as her unease with his perusal that she had a true affinity for the ocean and what lived in it.

He looked from the framed prints of dolphins underwater reflected in her mirror. There was no doubt in his mind that this house, this home, he corrected, was her sanctuary.

He stepped into the hall. As if hugely relieved to be out of that private space, she stepped past him, dropped her lingerie onto the top of the dryer and started toward a door at the end of the hall.

"The master bedroom is back here."

"I don't need to see it."

The concern that hit him again really wasn't familiar to him at all. The tightening of certain nerves in his body was far more explicable. With her scent surrounding him and the image of her in pink and black lace wanting to form in the back of his mind, the last thing he needed was to see where she slept.

Disappointment shadowed her eyes. Or maybe what he saw was the anxiety she felt at the prospect of having to sell at all. All he knew for certain was that she looked terribly fragile standing there while she crossed her arms protectively around herself—and more than a little lost.

"You don't?"

He shook his head, conscious of how tempted he was to reach for her, to touch the softness of her hair and tell her everything would be okay. But that assurance wasn't his to offer, and he had no business being tempted by her at all. Even if he didn't have a date with her stepsister, he wasn't comfortable with the thought of offering comfort to a woman. Since he'd never really done it before, he wasn't even sure he knew how.

"I've seen all I need to see. You need to keep your house," he said, as her glance faltered. "Don't even think about selling it."

Amy's unease shifted to incomprehension. She'd thought for certain that he'd found her home lacking. What was lacking was his appreciation of her situation.

"But it's the only way I can think of to raise that money. It's not just Grandma I'm worried about. It's the nine other little old ladies who are going to be displaced right along with her. There's no way they can all go to the same facility," she told him, wanting him to understand just how disrupted their lives would be. "They'll lose contact with all the people they've come to think of as family. Some of them don't recognize their own relatives, but they know the staff and the people they live with. Sometimes, anyway," she hurried on. "I need to sell this," she stressed. "I don't have anything else."

"Which is exactly why you need to hang on to it."

Exasperation tugged hard. "Jared," she said, her tone utterly patient. "I don't think you're getting this. What I need doesn't matter right now. These women live in a very small world. Most of them are going to be confused and frightened by such a drastic change. I know Grandma will be. Depending on the sort of day she's having, she can get upset with herself for not remembering a doorway was where she thought it was."

"I get it." J.T. fairly grumbled the assurance. He didn't understand a thing about dementia, other than that people forgot things. Until then, he hadn't even realized the scope of her concern. But he did understand how important her home was to her. There wasn't a house on it yet, but he felt that way about the island. "I'm an architect," he reminded her. "Maybe I can figure out a way to make the improvements the place needs that won't cost so much."

Amy opened her mouth, closed it again. Tipping her head as her eyes held his, she finally said, "You would do that?"

"If you don't mind introducing me to the director."

For a moment she just stood there, looking at him as if she couldn't believe he was actually willing to do what he'd just offered. Yet, instead of asking him why he wanted to help, which he halfway expected her to do, her lush mouth curved with a smile that lit her eyes and seemed to drain the strain from her face.

It was just a smile. Women had smiled at him before, with varying degrees of effect. But something about hers just then, the soft, sunshine warmth in it, seemed to ease the restlessness always lying in wait and touch something buried deep inside.

That unexpected sensation had barely washed over him before practicality replaced the pull of her pleasure at his offer. He had to meet Candace in an hour. He didn't have time to stand there wondering at her former stepsibling's effect on him.

What he did need to do was focus and prioritize. "I need to get going. Candace," he explained, taking a step back. "See what you can work out with the director for tomorrow."

With a quick nod, Amy watched him move into her living room. The reminder of his date had her feeling enormously grateful that she hadn't just embarrassed herself by hugging him. For a moment, that was exactly what she'd wanted to do. She didn't know how much cutting costs would help, or if it would help at all. It just relieved her to know that someone with some expertise was willing to lend it.

"I have to work tomorrow. And you have an appointment in the morning to sign the contract I need to revise tonight," she reminded him. "If I can arrange it, could we do it on my lunch hour?"

"Would that give us enough time?"

She grimaced. "Not really. It's twenty minutes from here. Thirty from the office."

"Tell you what," he said, moving into take-charge mode as he passed the dining table. "Mail the contract to me at my P.O. box. I have my mail couriered from there twice a week. I'll tell Candace about that tonight, and that you'll be late in the morning because you're taking me to…"

"Elmwood House," she supplied as he turned to her in her entryway.

"…to see if I can save them some money. Charity work is good PR for a business new to a city, anyway. We even talked about it as a way to get my name out in the right circles."

He saw the light in her eyes die even as she blinked. He hated that he'd killed it. But having her think he was acting from a business angle felt infinitely safer than the odd protectiveness he'd somehow begun to feel toward her.

He kept his focus on her suddenly guarded features. She had a real knack for hiding whatever was going on inside her. Was actually pretty good at it from what he'd seen. Most of the time, anyway. At the moment there was no denying her disquiet.

"I can't do that. I mean, I can't be late."

"Will this cause a problem for her with you?" he asked. "Because it's for your grandmother?"

"Candace knows I take care of Grandma. What will cause the problem is me doing something for her on office time. Jill is out of the office until next week, and we're down a receptionist. If I'm late, there's no one to open the office and answer the phone."

"We'll go before work, then. What time do you have to be there?"

Before? "I usually get there at eight, but the office doesn't open until nine. That's pretty much when everyone else arrives."

"Is the address for the home in the phone book?"

"It is."

"Then set up a meeting for seven o'clock." As if totally accustomed to people arranging their schedules around him, he reached into the pocket of his jacket and pulled out a business card. It was one from the hotel. Slipping his hand into the jacket's inside pocket, he withdrew a pen that looked suspiciously like real gold. "If the director can't do it then," he said, writing on the back of the card, "call me on my cell phone or leave a message for me at the hotel." Pocketing the pen, he held out the card. "Otherwise, I'll see you there."

Amy took the card, studied the numbers. The discipline of his profession had become so ingrained in him that even the quickly written figures revealed a passion for precision. The bold slash underlining them, though, struck her as oddly…defiant.

As the contradictions registered, she folded the card into her palm. She didn't care how complicated the man was, or what motivated him to help. She didn't care that he messed with her heart rate simply by standing there. She was just grateful for whatever help he could give.

J.T. could see that gratitude in the small smile she offered before she told him she'd take care of the arrangements. Smiling back—because she made smiling easy—he let himself out her door.

Chapter Five

Amy was not a morning person. It usually took a shower, two mugs of French roast and being jostled on the bus to get her body up and running and her brain engaged. Her habit of arriving at the office before everyone else was simply a way to make sure she was fully functional before she had to have an actual conversation.

Since she'd had to rise over an hour earlier than usual to be at the home by 7:00 a.m., she'd feared that her alertness level would be in the subbasement. She realized she needn't have worried. Watching Jared come up the walkway to the lovely old Tudor-style house effectively erased any possible trace of lethargy.

He hadn't bothered with a jacket. A cream, cable-knit sweater that made his shoulders look impossibly wide and tan cords were all he wore against the dawn chill. If he had a problem with morning, she saw no evidence of it in his easy, athletic stride, or the set lines of his handsome features before she stepped from the window and opened the front door.

The moment he noticed her, he turned to where the cab he'd taken still sat at the curb. With a wave from him, it pulled onto the quiet street of other Tudor revival-style houses with their lovely lawns, neatly trimmed hedges and dogwood trees growing in their deep yards.

"I figured you could give me a ride back to town," he said by way of greeting as he walked in. "You don't mind, do you?"

He smelled of soap and shaving cream. Of spice and fresh air. Pulling her focus from his smoothly shaved jaw, she skimmed her glance over his broad chest and closed the door. "Of course not. You're doing me a huge favor."

"I haven't done anything yet."

"You showed up," she murmured.

In the back of her mind had been the nagging thought that maybe he and Candace had been out late, and that he'd oversleep. Or that he would simply forget because her problem was hardly his priority.

"We can go on back to Kay's office." She didn't want to think about him and Candace. All she wanted was his help. "It's right through here."

She started from the small parlor, glancing back to see him taking in the beautiful molding along the ceiling. The room with its overstuffed sofa and chairs was small, and used for visitors who had no need to be admitted to the more intimate heart of the home.

It also served as a discreet sort of double security for residents.

An intercom was in the wall by a closed interior door. The moment she pushed its brass call button, a female voice responded with a quiet, "May I help you?"

"It's Amy. Mr. Taylor is here."

With an electronic buzz, the lock on the door unlatched. That same buzz had Jared's forehead pleating in a faint frown.

"What's with the interior lock?"

"It helps keep residents from wandering out the front door and getting lost." Stepping into a short hallway, she waited until the door latched behind him before turning into the main part of the house. "The other doors have similar safeguards or open to the backyard. It's completely fenced back there."

"Wandering is a problem?"

"It is for some of these ladies. That's why I finally had to bring Grandma here. I thought we were doing okay until she started wandering off and getting lost while I was at work. There's staff on site here 24/7 and the residents all wear alarm-activating bracelets. That way they have their freedom around the property but staff is alerted if they go beyond where they're safe."

They passed an archway opening to a large living room.

"Is it always so quiet?"

"It's early. Everyone is either still asleep, just getting up or helping make breakfast."

Even as she spoke, the home's director came from the kitchen ahead of them.

Somewhere in her midfifties, Kay Colman wore her wavy, dark-blond hair in a low ponytail. She didn't bother to dye out the gray. She didn't bother with makeup, either. Wearing one of her customary tunics, a denim skirt and a smile of greeting, she looked exactly like who she was. A no-frills earth mother with a nurturing spirit and a kind heart.

Moving toward them, her eyebrows lifted ever so slightly at the man by Amy's side. Amy imagined Jared got that a lot; that unconscious reaction to his rather imposing presence.

"Amy," she said by way of greeting. "Hello," she added to Jared and motioned to a doorway beside her. "Let's go in here."

Her office was small, neat and filled mostly with a desk and filing cabinets topped with pots of robust ferns. All three of them ignored the formality of taking the chairs in front of and behind the desk as Amy introduced Jared to Kay as the architect she'd told her about.

"Mr. Taylor. It's a pleasure."

"It's Jared," he corrected easily, shaking her hand while Amy finished the introduction. "Thanks for meeting us so early."

"It's not a problem at all. I live here." Strain shadowed her kind expression. "I'm usually in the kitchen by six to help our cook, or with the aides checking on our residents. We have some early risers." Her expression turned decidedly apologetic. "I'm just afraid I've wasted time for both of you."

"Amy, I should have called you back last night. I'd intended to," she admitted, "but one of our residents had a problem, and it was nearly midnight before we got her settled down.

"I went over the numbers again after you called," she continued, sounding as if she'd hoped to find something there that she hadn't before. "I told you we need about forty thousand dollars. Even if we can cut the cost of the repairs in half, that won't keep us open." The apology in her eyes deepened. "I'm truly sorry that my grasping at straws inconvenienced you and your..."

"Client," Amy supplied when the woman hesitated. "Jared is a client of the agency."

"I'm sorry," she repeated, with the rueful shake of her head. "You told me that last night, didn't you?"

Forgetting that detail seemed perfectly understandable to Amy. Especially with everything else the woman had on her mind. She would have mentioned that, too, had Jared not already been talking.

"Why won't cutting the costs help?"

The woman who'd been a geriatric nurse for thirty years and resident director of Elmwood House for the past five, glanced from him to Amy and back again. Apparently realizing that Amy had already shared their predicament, since he was standing in her office, she indicated a file on the corner of her desk.

"As I told Amy, our mortgage is behind. We need over twenty thousand dollars to bring it current." Stifling a sigh, she crossed her arms. "Has Amy shared our history with you?"

"All I know is that she doesn't want her grandmother to have to go anywhere else. She doesn't want anyone else here to have to go, for that matter."

Her glance shifted to Amy. "I truly appreciate that. No one who has a relative here wants to move her, but no one has been able to come up with the means or a method to keep us all together."

Her focus moved back to the man in front of her.

"This home was started about thirty years ago by an older gentleman who couldn't find the kind of care he wanted for his wife. His elderly mother needed care, too. As did the mother of a friend. He bought this house, brought in nurses and support staff who understood his vision for nurturing the entire person and endowed the home in his will. In the will, he appointed a niece back East as trustee. She kept it going by hiring directors like myself over the years. The way the home was to be run was made very clear, but it's become more expensive each year to maintain his standards.

"I support those standards a hundred and fifty percent," she insisted, "but to meet them we've had to use the principal he invested on upkeep and to subsidize what we charge our residents. The endowment has now run out. The trustee says no one in the family has the means or the interest to re-fund it, and we've borrowed as much of the equity as we can on the property.

"The bank owns us now," she told them. "As its representatives continually point out to me, it's not in the elder care business. They're going to foreclose before much longer. In the past several months, I've contacted residential care management companies to see if anyone is interested in buying us and taking over, but we're either too small and our operating costs are too high to turn the kind of profit that for-profit corporations want, or too expensive for a not-for-profit operation to manage. The only people who are interested want to buy the house and turn it back into a private residence."

J.T. glanced from the utilitarian furnishings in the room to the woodwork around the doors and windows. He could see why a private buyer would be interested in the place. From the outside, the old, two-story house with its steep gabled roof, ornamental half-timbering and rows of mullioned windows had excellent bones. Nothing about the exterior betrayed it to be the care facility it was. When the cab had first pulled up, he hadn't even been sure he had the right place. At least, he hadn't before he'd noticed Amy and her quick, hesitant smile when she'd appeared in the doorway.

The taupe trench coat she wore against the outside chill had been buttoned and belted then. Now, in deference to the warmth of the house, she opened it to reveal a slash of a chocolate vee-necked top that turned her skin golden. A simple silver necklace dangled between the gentle curves of her breasts.

He wondered if she was wearing the bit of peach satin he'd glimpsed when she'd pulled down her lingerie—only to promptly force his mind back to business.

"What kind of work does the house need?"

"The biggest items are a new furnace," Kay replied, refocusing his attention on her, "and a plumbing problem. The plumbing in the entire house is old, but there's a leak somewhere between the upstairs bathroom the resident staff uses and the basement. The inspector for the state licensing agency wants it repaired before there are mold issues. The repair involves tearing out walls to get to the pipes.

"On the minor side," she continued, "we need one of the wheelchair ramps to the backyard rebuilt. We haven't been using it because we don't have any residents in wheelchairs right now. I'd also hoped we might be able to expand our sunroom back there someday and figured the ramp would be torn out anyway. But as long as it exists, the inspector said we have to keep it in repair."

"Mind showing me where this plumbing problem is?"

Kay's expression seemed to say she really did hate wasting his time. It was his to waste if that was what he wanted, though.

"This way," she murmured, and motioned him toward the door.

Snagging her coat around herself, Amy followed. As busy as the man was, she had no idea why he was bothering to look at the place when he knew that what he could offer wouldn't be enough. He gave her no clue, either, as he walked with the home's beleaguered director through the quiet living room with its comfortable sofas and chairs, game tables and console television. Someone had turned on the TV and tuned it to the morning news. The drapes had been opened on the windows, revealing the spacious backyard with its vegetable and flower gardens, fruit trees and greenhouse. But other than the voice of the newscaster, the room remained empty.

Other voices could be heard, though. They drifted through the doorway of the efficiently arranged kitchen and the large, brightly lit dining area beyond.

Jeanette, the copper-haired cook with wide hips and a wider smile, stood at the double ovens, removing muffins that filled the air with the scents of apples and cinnamon. Her attention immediately caught on the long, lanky male invading their midst.

At the island in the center of the room, three stooped, gray-haired ladies stood with a young brunette, one of the aides, wrapping silverware in paper napkins to be carried to the table. Tina Ives, the aide, and the elderly Edith Ross looked up. The even older Arlene Newcomb kept wrapping and going on about whatever it was she was talking about.

Oblivious to them all, white-haired Harriet Bower kept wrapping and humming to herself.

Kay included them all with her quick smile. "Ignore us, ladies. Mr. Taylor is just going to look at the plumbing."

Edith scowled through her trifocals. "What'd she say?"

Arlene's head came up. "What did who say?" Her voice held a hint of a tremble. "I didn't hear anybody say anything. Young lady," she prodded, apparently having forgotten Tina's name. "Did somebody say something?" she asked, only to narrow her rheumy eyes on Jared's retreating back. "Who's that?"

"Mr. Taylor," came the aide's patient reply. "I think he's with Amy."

Arlene looked even more confused. "Mr. Who?"

"Oh, for Pete's sake." Harriet leaned toward her fellow resident and raised her voice. "Where are your hearing aides?"

Arlene's hands reached up to cover her ears. From the look on her face, she apparently hadn't remembered to put them on.

Tina touched the woman's arm. "We'll go find them."

"Is my grandma up?" Amy asked on her way by.

Tina, a licensed practical nurse and mother of a three-year-old son, left her charges to their wrapping. With a smile and a surreptitious thumbs-up for the exceptional specimen of masculinity Amy had brought with her, she told her that Edna was in the dining room, added that she seemed to be having a good morning and walked off with the woman with the dowager's hump to retrieve what the older woman had forgotten.

A dozen steps later, Amy had moved into the sunny-yellow

space filled with four oak tables for four that overlooked one of the gardens.

"Grandma," she said.

The smile in Amy's voice had J.T. turning from his perusal of the walls and ceilings for cracks and water stains that would indicate signs of settling or leaks. At one of the tables behind him, an elderly lady with a head full of steel-gray curls and dressed in shocking pink sat with a silver walker at her elbow. A woman he assumed to be one of the aides stood beside her, curling the resident's gnarled hands around a mug as if reminding her how to hold it.

Amy's smile had settled on the only other person in the room, a small, white-haired lady in a purple jogging suit who looked up from where she was setting plates on the farthest table.

He'd never had reason to be around old people much. Or children for that matter. From what little he'd seen of both, they now struck him as remarkably similar. Their conversations were nearly indecipherable, they favored bright colors and certain of them required more assistance than others.

Realizing that the woman in purple was Edna, he stopped Kay to tell her he wanted to meet Amy's grandmother.

Amy saw Jared motion toward them. Most of her attention, however, remained on her grandma. The seventy-nine-year-old had once worn her short, snowy hair fashionably spiked. Amy helped her keep it short by taking her to the salon every six weeks. But now, because her grandma no longer bothered with gel, or remembered to, her hair hugged her head in flat, feathery layers. Behind her rimless trifocals, pale-blue eyes met her own.

"I'm helping with breakfast."

"I see that." Amy quietly searched her expression. Sometimes her grandmother knew her. Sometimes, lately, she didn't. "Do you know who I am, Grandma?"

The older woman's brow pinched. Confusion at the question settled over the wrinkles fanning from her eyes, cut into her forehead, her cheeks. With one arthritic hand curled against one hip, she said, "Well, of course I do." More wrinkles formed. "Is it the weekend? You're here early."

She seemed lucid today. Relieved by that, thankful for it, Amy brushed her soft, cleansing-cream-scented cheek with a quick kiss.

"It's Thursday," she told her. "I brought someone over to see where you live," she decided to say. She saw no sense in mentioning things like repairs or the home being in trouble. Part of what she tried to do for her grandma was protect her from upsets. Considering how the woman had always been there for her while she'd been growing up, the trade was only fair. Some days her grandma had enough to deal with simply remembering that she no longer lived with her. The days she wanted to go home were hard. Especially when the home she wanted to go back to was the one Amy's dad sold when he'd married Jill. She just didn't remember that having happened. Amy was no longer sure she even remembered that her dad had remarried.

Jared stopped where they stood. With his big body all but blocking her view of the other women openly watching them, Amy introduced him to the woman staring up at him.

"Mrs. Moore," J.T. said, finding surprising strength in her frail-looking hand when he took it. "It's a pleasure to meet you."

Her voice held surprising strength, too. "Jared is it? Is that a family name?"

J.T. opened his mouth, promptly shut it. He didn't honestly know. He didn't know of any Jareds on his father's side. And he hadn't a clue about his mother's. All he knew about his name was that somewhere around third grade he'd decided he didn't like it. He had no idea now what he'd thought was wrong with it, but that was when he'd insisted he be called by his initials. He didn't bother having to respond to Edna's question, though. She seemed to have forgotten what she'd asked.

"Amy, dear, I think we should sit down and have coffee. Oh, wait," she insisted. "I stopped drinking coffee, didn't I? What is it I drink?"

"Herbal tea."

"Then that's what I'll have." Patting Jared's arm, she murmured, "Coffee agitates me. I'm not supposed to mix it with my heart medicine, anyway." Her brow pleated. "Or is it my diuretic?"

Not sure what else she was about to share, Amy drew the woman's hand into hers. "Grandma, I'm sorry. We really don't have time to visit. I'll come back…"

"You bring your boyfriend to meet me and you don't have time to visit?"

"He's not my boyfriend…"

The wrinkles in her forehead deepened. Looking up at the man who towered a foot above her, she seemed to study the strands of silver at his temples, the lines of character carved into his face, the breadth of his shoulders.

Apparently finding him worthy of her granddaughter's interest, she wanted to know, "Why not?"

Amy swore she could feel heat rising from her neck. Putting her hand to her throat to conceal it, she struggled for a response that wouldn't embarrass her or Jared and would put an end to that particular course of conversation.

That struggle lasted three seconds before her grandmother piped in again.

"Is he married?" Her eyes narrowed on Jared's. "Are you married?"

It was Jared's turn to hesitate. "Ah…no, ma'am. I'm…not."

"See?" Edna challenged.

Amy didn't "see" at all.

"Come sit," her grandmother insisted to him over the clatter of an empty muffin tin hitting the sink. "Tell me about your family. Your mother," she said, as if she intended to start there. "Do you get along with her?" The curiosity, so often missing from her eyes lately, cut to where Amy drew a deep, discomfited breath. "A man who gets along well with his mother usually makes a good husband," she informed her. "You should know this."

She turned her attention back to the man towering over them both.

Before she could say anything else, Amy's voice fell to nearly a whisper. "Grandma, please," she began, only to hear Jared's voice over her own.

"I never knew my mother, Mrs. Moore. She left me with my father when I was two."

The unexpected admission put a few more wrinkles in the older woman's brow. "Then you were probably better off without her," she announced flatly. "Did your father remarry?"

Amy caught the twitch of a muscle in Jared's jaw. Torn between quieting her grandma and needing to hear what else he might reveal, she remained silent herself.

"He did," he said with a tight half smile. "I'm sorry, Mrs. Moore, but we really can't stay much longer. I need to check out something back there." He hitched his thumb toward the doorway behind him. "And Amy needs to get to work soon." Clearly not wanting to be rude, but having no intention of facing further interrogation, he gave her a polite nod and stepped back. "You two visit. I'm going to go with the director now."

"Thank you, Jared." Amy murmured the words as they walked past the dew-dampened shrubs at the front of the house to where she'd parked her little black Honda Civic in the driveway. With the belt of her coat now tied rather than buckled, she started digging in her briefcase-size purse for her keys. "I really appreciate you taking time to come out here. I know Kay appreciated it, too."

They were a dozen steps from her car. Before Jared could head around the slightly dented front fender and make her wait even longer to say what she really needed to say, she reached out her hand to stop him.

Beneath the heavy knit of his sweater, the muscles in his arm felt like rock. Trying to overlook that the muscles of his chest had felt that way, too, she glanced past the slight dimple in his chin, past the carved shape of his beautiful mouth and met his inscrutable gray eyes.

In the crisp morning air, the breath she took left her lungs in a trail of fog. "I'm sorry about what happened with my grandmother. About her questions, I mean. She's always spoken what's on her mind, but she used to be a little more discreet about it. Now, she just blurts out whatever she's thinking. The doctor said she's lost the ability to judge what's appropriate and what isn't in social interactions."

That loss was part of what he'd called her disease process. Amy was about to offer that in her grandmother's defense when she realized she still held his arm.

Aware of his heat penetrating her palm, conscious of the funny flutter it put in her stomach, she let her hand fall.

"It's not a problem. I know someone else like that."

"You know someone with dementia?"

"No," J.T. admitted, watching her curl her fingers between her lapels. He knew mental aging wasn't what was going on with Harry. According to Justin, their dad's cardiologist had said their old man was still as sharp as a blade. "The guy I'm thinking of is perfectly fine. He just doesn't have any sense of when he's crossed a line." As near as J.T. could figure, his highly intellectual father had always been seriously out of touch where other people were concerned. Harry wanted people to be logical, predictable. Like the computer languages he wrote. J.T. hardly held himself up as an expert on relationships, but he at least knew there was little predictable about them. "And, no apology necessary."

"Still," she murmured. "I am sorry." She tipped her head. "About your mother, too. I thought losing my mom was hard. I can't imagine what it's like for you to have never known yours."

There was sympathy in her eyes, something soft that told him she put his loss on the same level as her own.

He didn't deserve that. What he'd felt for the woman who'd chosen money over him had more to do with disdain than loss.

Before he could mentally withdraw from her generosity, she walked to her modest little car and opened the driver's-side door.

"It's just too bad there isn't anything you could do for Kay."

"I didn't say there wasn't."

He'd already walked to the passenger side. Over the low black roof, he watched Amy's head pop up.

"What do you mean? You told her the estimates she got were pretty solid."

He opened the passenger door, motioned for her to get in. Climbing in himself, he pushed the seat back as far as it would go. "They are," he confirmed, as she slid in herself. "Twenty thousand, give or take a little, seems about right. A furnace is expensive, and the plumbing that needs to be repaired involves some major deconstruction. A contractor might get a little off the price of the furnace and the materials for the plumbing repair, but he still has to pay for labor."

Unless a contractor donated that labor, he thought, over the thuds of doors closing. Or, if he could do some of the work himself.

Seat belts clicked into place.

"But even if you could save a few thousand dollars on labor," she said as she started the engine, "there's still the cost of the furnace, the materials and bringing the mortgage up to date."

"That's short term."

She glanced behind her as she backed out of the drive. Having noticed the dent in her front fender, so did he.

"To keep this from happening again," he continued, "she needs to re-fund that endowment."

Her glance caught on his, only to sweep back toward the windshield as she straightened out and headed up the awakening street. "And knowing the home needs even more money is helpful how?"

"Just bear with me for a minute."

With the lift of one hand, she indicated the digital clock in the dashboard. "You can have all the minutes you need. Traffic will be hideous right now."

The digits glowed 7:41 in neon amber. Rush hour at its peak.

She was going to be late.

"Do you really think she and the rest of those women will suffer if they have to go someplace else?"

"Absolutely."

"How? I'm not trying to be inconsiderate here, but, Amy, a couple of the ladies they brought in for breakfast didn't really seem to know where they were. Or to care, for that matter."

She kept her eyes straight ahead, her grip firm on the wheel. "I understand that some of them don't," she admitted. "As for how a move would affect them, I can't speak for all the women. My experience with all this has only been with my grandmother. But from what I've seen, change confuses and agitates her even more. I've been told it's the same with the other ladies. They may not be able to articulate their thoughts, but if something is different, or if they're moved, they'll know something isn't right. Different can be frightening to them."

Her brow pinched, her focus still on the curving road. "I see how the staff interacts with all of them and I can't help but think they're slowing the process somehow."

"The process?"

"I'm losing my grandma in stages, Jared. Right now she's where the women you saw in the kitchen are. At the middle stage of Alzheimer's. Sometimes she seems almost fine. She's functional. Other times she needs help dressing and can't express what she wants to say.

"That obviously wasn't the case today," she muttered, "but there are things she no longer does at all. She can't play bridge. Numbers seem to be gone for her. She can't sew. She doesn't seem to remember the women she volunteered with at the senior center. She can still cook, though, as long as someone is there to help her with measurements and around the stove. And she loves to garden.

"It's the gardens and greenhouse in back that keep her going. Gardening is something she's always loved and it's keeping her mind active and focused. The staff encourages anything that will keep her and the others involved in the activities of daily living. It gives them purpose, makes them feel part of what's going on around them. It's not easy finding a home that has all that."

If he remembered correctly, she'd said the nearest one the director would recommend was nearly two hours away. "And those other women? The one's that didn't seem…all there?"

"They're farther along," was all she would say.

He remembered the pictures scattered over her dining room table.

She was losing her grandma in stages, she'd said.

She was doing everything she could to preserve the memories of her small family. For herself, because it seemed to him that she really only had Edna left now. And for Edna, before those memories forever slipped away.

He focused on the red brake lights glowing ahead of them. Traffic on the highway she'd just pulled onto was bumper-to-bumper.

His first instinct was to simply write her a check. The only problem there was that Jared Taylor wasn't supposed to have that kind of money. And J.T. Hunt wasn't supposed to use his own wealth.

He'd never been in the position of being unable to do what he wanted where his money was involved. Not caring for that situation at all, the rebel in him instantly surfaced. He could have the money sent anonymously—then plead innocent if someone suspected he must have had something to do with the mysterious appearance of funds. He was one of only a handful of people at that point aware of how much trouble the home was in.

Part of him didn't want the solution to be that quick, that…neat, anyway. Part of him suddenly, badly, wanted the escape Amy had no idea she'd just offered him.

Bad days get better, she'd told him the afternoon he'd first met her.

Bad weeks built character.

But when a person was having a bad month…

That's when you need to find something to do that takes you away from your problems for a while. Whatever you're dealing with won't go away, but for that hour or that day, you've taken away its power over you.

The jaw-grinding resentment he'd felt in the days following the delivery of Harry's ultimatum had only intensified once he'd actively started playing by the old man's rules. He'd thought that by working to put his backup plan in place and adding his own criteria for a wife, he would still be in control.

Yet, Harry still had the upper hand. Because of those rules, he was having to hide who he was while working to keep his projects current in case Harry didn't sell everything off. He was also having to build an architectural firm that might never materialize. It felt as if everything he did might well be for nothing. And he had nothing ahead but nine months more of the same.

Unless he did what the unexpectedly wise young woman beside him did and he focused on something short term. Something that had a relatively quick resolution and nothing at all to do with anything causing the churning uncertainty in his life. Not HuntCom. Not his backup plan. Not the beautiful woman who, over drinks last night, had seemed fine with the idea of him being a guy who, she thought, had a small condo in Seattle, the prospects of his own architectural firm and who'd said she totally understood his passion for his new venture because her career was hugely important to her, too.

At the moment he wasn't thinking of how Candace's dedication to her career fit exactly with what he wanted—or of how completely wrong she was about his attitude toward what he was doing there. His thoughts had ventured in a totally unexpected direction.

He and Amy might well be able to help each other out.

As much as he enjoyed turning the concept of a building into blueprints, getting his hands dirty with actual construction appealed even more. Tearing something apart first sounded like an especially fine idea to him just then. If he could do some major juggling with his schedule, he could even knock off the plans for expanding the sunroom the director had wanted.

"Someone I know is familiar with charities," he said, going no further with who that someone was. His half brother Alex, as head of the Harrison Hunt Foundation, would know how to raise the money. "I know he's been involved in fund-raisers," he continued, because he'd heard Gray complain about Alex having roped him into yet another one. "Would you be interested in going that route?"

"A fund-raiser?" Her thoughts clearly distracted from her driving, her glance shot to him. "What do you have in mind?"

He hadn't a clue. He did, however, know she tended to not pay attention to where she was going when she got preoccupied.

"You want to watch the traffic?"

With the quick widening of her eyes, her focus jerked to the car ahead of them. Red taillights blinked on.

She hit the brakes.

He reached for the dashboard.

"I don't know anything about them. But I'll ask," he offered, more concerned with having just avoided being part of the commuter traffic report than in what he'd just agreed to do. "In the meantime, see if Kay can get the bank to give her a little more time. It might if there's the possibility of funds out there. If that's a go," he added, "I could get someone in to start on the plumbing repair. That's the least expensive part of all this…and something I could help with to keep the costs down."

"You'd do that?"

His shrug didn't feel anywhere near as indifferent as it looked. He wanted this. "I need to start working with the local trades. Now's as good a time as any to start."

Amy was already digging in her purse. Coming up with her cell phone, she started punching in numbers with her thumb. With one hand on the wheel, her attention was not-so-evenly divided between the traffic and the touch pad.

"I didn't mean this second," he muttered, when she put the phone to ear.

"It's already ringing."

"Then, I'll ask her. I'd rather you just drive." Slipping her phone from her hand, he put it to his ear, instead. "I've seen your front fender."

"Kay Colman, please," he asked, since the line had already been answered. Feeling his own smile form, he murmured, "Sure. Jared Taylor."

At his front fender remark, Amy's eyebrows had merged once more. "How do you know someone didn't hit me?"

"Did they?"

She clamped her mouth closed.

"Well?" he prodded.

"It was a bad day."

"So how's today going?" he asked, not sure if he should be worried.

"Good," she murmured. Her eyes smiled into his. "Really good."

Chapter Six

Amy dropped Jared off at his hotel with the promise to call as soon as she heard from Kay, then navigated her way to the office where she managed to get the lights and the coffee on before the crew started straggling in. By the time Candace arrived a little after nine o'clock, she'd printed out the contract she'd changed last night on her laptop computer so she could have it ready when Jared stopped in to sign it at nine-thirty. Since they'd gone to the home before office hours, he'd kept his appointment with Candace.

She saw him only long enough to tell him that Candace was waiting for him, and missed him completely when he left because she'd been helping Eric clear a jam in the copy machine. She knew he'd been in a hurry, anyway. He'd told her he had a meeting an hour north of Portland at eleven and that he'd be going back to Seattle that night. In the morning he was heading overseas.

He hadn't said a word to her about his date with Candace last night. Not that she'd thought he would. His personal business was none of hers. Candace had said nothing to her about their date, either. But then, Jill's daughter rarely shared her personal life with her, unless there was something she needed Amy to do that was somehow related to it. Candace had always been fairly free about announcing when she was seeing someone after work, or that she had a date for this or that event. But with those in the office, she kept the particulars of her social life to herself.

As far as Amy was concerned, she hadn't had to say anything, anyway. It seemed apparent enough from the way she walked around smiling to herself after he'd left that she'd be seeing him again.

Without letting herself dwell on why, Amy felt enormously grateful to have been spared details. It also relieved her to know that Jared hadn't mentioned having met her at her house last night or at the home that morning. If he had, Candace certainly would have mentioned it herself. Until Amy knew whether or not his friend could suggest how to raise the needed funds, she saw no reason to subject herself to Candace's inevitable questions about how he'd gotten involved in the first place.

Kay called her a few minutes before three o'clock.

Twenty minutes later, navigating pedestrian traffic on her way to the printer's, she was on the phone to the man whose unexpected kindness had been on her mind all day.

J.T. pulled his ringing cell phone from his pocket. Expecting calls from a supplier holding up construction in Seattle and the company comptroller about releasing more funds for the New Delhi project, he was about to answer with his usual "J.T. Hunt" when he noticed the area code on the digital display.

"Jared," he said, instead.

"Hi. It's Amy," came the quick greeting. "Am I catching you at a bad time?"

"I'm just leaving my meeting." The number on the display wasn't familiar. "Where are you calling from?"

She seemed to hesitate. "My cell phone. I won't keep you," she hurried on, the smile in her voice edging into excitement. "I just heard back from Kay. She said the bank agreed to postpone foreclosure proceedings for an additional month if we can show we have a means of raising funds underway. That gives us ten weeks," she told him over what sounded like traffic noise. "What do we do now?"

"Hang on a minute."

Pulling off his hard hat, he set it inside the door of the Jensen facility's construction trailer. "I'll find out," he told her, walking back across wheel-churned dirt. "If you don't hear from me in the next couple of hours, I either didn't get hold of the guy I need to talk to or I got tied up."

For a moment he thought the call had been dropped. Then, he heard what almost sounded like a sigh.

"Thank you, Jared. So much. You have no idea how much this means…"

"Save that for when I've actually done something." Her gratitude made him uncomfortable. If this worked, he'd benefit as much as anyone. "I'll call you later."

With that, he broke the connection. Scanning the collection of vehicles nose-in to the cyclone fencing surrounding the expansion site, he headed for the SUV he'd rented in Portland. On the way, he scrolled through his phone book to find Alex's cell phone number.

His brother answered just when J.T. thought the call would go to voice mail.

The distant beeping of a backup horn preceded a terse

"Hold on." Brushing sounds joined a thud before the noises faded and Alex came back on the line. "If you're calling me at work, there must be a problem."

"'Work' is eighty miles north of here. What you're doing is…what are you doing, anyway?"

"Filling orders."

"Right. Look," he said, knowing now was not the time to get details. "There's no problem. I just need to talk to you. I'm over at the expansion site…"

"You're in Jansen?"

"I just finished a site inspection with the construction foreman. Which warehouse are you in?"

"Don't come over here. If somebody recognizes you, they might recognize me. I get off at four. Meet me at my place at four-thirty."

"Where's that?"

The directions Alex gave him seemed easy enough to follow. It was his warning to not be surprised by the place that he didn't understand. At least he didn't until he got there.

Alex's newly rented apartment was on the second floor of a two-story complex in a decidedly working class neighborhood not far from HuntCom's Jansen distribution center. As J.T. climbed the outside stairs he couldn't help thinking that *nondescript* didn't begin to describe the lack of character about the place.

The building's gunmetal-gray paint nearly matched the overcast sky. A peephole and unit number provided the only embellishment on any of the apartment's doors. There were no interesting curves or angles in the plain wooden railing. No landscaping to speak of, either, other than for a line of junipers dividing the row of low open parking spaces from the ground-floor walkway.

He hesitated when he reached Alex's door. Rather than knock, he pushed his hands into the pockets of his khakis and drew a breath that made his shoulders rise beneath his navy crew-neck sweater.

He rarely went to a member of his family for anything. Anything not work related, anyway. Even though he trusted his half brothers as much as he did anyone, in many ways they were all strangers to him.

He supposed he wasn't the only one who'd felt that way. Justin hadn't come to live with them in the Shack until he was twelve. J.T. had been fourteen at the time. Already well into his rebellious phrase, he'd had little in common with a kid who'd come straight from a cattle ranch, and whose passion continued to remain with those wide-open spaces.

J.T. figured he probably now had the most in common with Gray, but only because his older brother was as driven as J.T. himself. He was pretty much the opposite of Alex, though. Not that he knew him all that well. What he did know was that Alex truly believed that having too much money and power corrupted those who possessed them. It wasn't as if the guy didn't appreciate quality. He just held a definite disdain for wealth, the sense of entitlement it brought and the way it could be used to buy a person's loyalty or affection. Or to buy them off.

Personally, J.T. had never had a problem owning the finest, the fastest and the best. He even thought power a good thing, as long as it wasn't being used to jerk other people around the way their father was doing with him and his half brothers. As for buying people off, every one of their mothers had abandoned them for a piece of Harry's action, so he knew exactly where Alex was coming from there. He also knew that giving away money was what Alex loved best.

J.T. didn't want money. He just wanted Alex's expertise.

The door opened within moments of Jared's knock.

"Hey, Alex," he said, stepping in as his brother stepped back.

"Hey, J.T."

Alex wore work boots, jeans and a flannel work shirt. His hair was nearly as dark as his own, though where J.T.'s was straight, Alex's fell in a slight wave over his forehead.

"How's the expansion here coming?"

"We're on schedule," replied J.T, closing the door behind him. "We had to change subs on the electrical, but the new company came right up to speed."

Alex's eyes didn't quite glaze over, but J.T. strongly suspected his brother wasn't at all interested in the day-to-day business of HuntCom. At least, not unless it somehow affected funds coming into the Foundation. By asking about the expansion, he was just making conversation.

Not caring to bore him with further details, J.T. glanced around the decidedly downscale space. "When Gray said you'd taken a job at the warehouse as a cover for this bride-thing, he didn't mention that you'd moved in with the masses."

Alex laughed. "When in Rome…"

"In Rome, they at least live with some color."

J.T.'s thoughtful frown moved from the breakfast bar that separated the small kitchen from the living area. A beige sofa, coffee table and black leather recliner formed what there was of a seating area. An inexpensive television sat on a low cabinet. The whole place had to be a far cry from Alex's apartment in downtown Seattle. J.T. had never been in it. But he knew the trendy, high-end address.

"You could seriously use some art here," he observed. "Did the furniture come with the place?"

"I bought it at a discount store. If anyone from the plant comes over, I don't want them to suspect anything."

"Any luck there? Meeting an appropriate woman, I mean?"

Alex gave a guarded shrug. "I've only been there three weeks."

The evasion immediately caught J.T.'s attention. "Then you've spotted a prospect?" He did not want to be in this alone. As far as he knew, Justin hadn't made any moves on the mother of his child. Gray didn't have anything going yet, either.

"It's too soon to tell.

"I don't have much of a liquor supply," Alex continued, not bothering to be subtle about the change of subject. "About all I can offer you is a beer." He nodded toward the kitchen. "Do you want one?"

J.T's eyes narrowed. "Let me guess. You bought it in on sale, three ninety-nine for a twelve-pack."

The good-natured teasing met with a smile that would have looked sheepish on anyone but a six-foot, three-inch, thirty-six-year-old male. "There are a few things I still spurge on. I have Beck's or Black Sheep Ale."

"Surprise me."

"So," Alex said on his way past the espresso maker and a collection of olive oils and vinegars he'd splurged on, too. He swung open the refrigerator's door. "Why do you need to see me?"

"I need some advice."

Alex turned from the refrigerator, a bottle in each hand and one eyebrow arched. "From me?"

The concept clearly seemed unusual to him, too.

From where he remained on the other side of the bar, J.T. frowned across the beige Formica. "You're the only person I know who knows anything about fund-raisers."

Utensils rattled. "What makes you think I know anything about fund-raisers?"

"Hell, Alex. You go to them all the time. And you have to raise money for the Foundation somehow."

"That shows how little we know about what each of us does," Alex muttered. "You're right about one thing. I've attended a lot of fund-raisers for different charities or organizations, but the Harrison Hunt Foundation doesn't raise money that way." He popped off caps with a bottle opener, held a bottle out for J.T. "We use the interest from Harry's money to fund our causes." His dark eyebrows pinched. "Why do you want to know about them?"

"The short version is that I want to help someone raise some money."

"And the long version?"

J.T. took a pull on the beer. He'd had the feeling he wouldn't get off that easily.

"This Bride Hunt thing," he began, because it was responsible for his immediate problem. "Because of Harry's rules, I can't just write a check. Or," he added with a half smile, "go to my brother and ask the Foundation to do it. If I did that, I'm afraid she'd figure out the money had something to do with me." The smile died. "If she did, I could tell her I just happened to know someone with connections, but I don't want to raise any red flags."

Looking curious, Alex rounded the counter and pulled out a bar stool. Motioning for J.T. to take the other, he asked, "You've found a potential wife?"

J.T. gave him an uncomprehending frown. "How did you get that from what I just told you?"

"You're talking about helping a woman. You said you can't because of Harry's rules. I'm not the math genius in the family, but it's pretty much one plus one, J.T."

Except that, in this case, the math didn't add up that way.

"I've found a woman with the potential to be a potential wife," he qualified, thinking of Candace, wanting to talk about Amy. "The woman I want to help is her assistant." She was also her stepsister, he could have added, but certain aspects of the situation were feeling complicated enough as it was. "Her grandmother lives in this home that's going to have to close if the director can't come up with about forty grand."

Both of Alex's eyebrows lifted this time. "That's not the kind of money you can raise selling calendars. You need an event, and a corporation or two to underwrite it. Like I said, we don't organize fund-raisers," he reminded him, "but I know people who do. One of the women on the Foundation board chairs an annual luncheon and fashion show that makes a mint for the Seattle Opera Guild. Maybe your girlfriend's assistant could do something like that in Portland."

Hearing Candace referred to as his girlfriend made J.T. more than a little uncomfortable. He really barely knew the woman. He let the reference go, though, along with that uneasiness. He could design manufacturing facilities and office complexes from the subbasement to the fortieth floor if he had to. A fashion show was completely beyond his comprehension.

"Would you talk to her for Amy? Ask what she needs to do?"

"Amy's the assistant?" Receiving a nod, Alex shrugged. "Sure. She'll probably have other ideas, too."

"Let me run this by Amy, then. If she thinks she can handle something like this, I'll get back to you."

"Not a problem." Alex lifted his bottle. "You hungry?"

"Getting there."

"I'm starving. How about I throw us something together to eat?"

"What do have in mind?"

"Paella," he said, heading back into the kitchen. "I picked up shrimp and sausage at the market last night." He opened a cupboard. "I have saffron, nutmeg, paprika. Rice," he muttered, rattling off more ingredients as he went through his inventory. "That sound okay?"

"You can do that?"

The droll look in Alex's expression matched the wry note in his tone. "Yeah," he replied, turning the word into three syllables.

J.T. could grill with the best of them. He was okay with pasta, too, as long as the dish didn't require over a few ingredients and he had a glass of a good Barolo to nurse while he was putting it together.

He hadn't realized that his brother possessed any interest in cooking at all, much less the culinary skills to pull off one of his favorite dishes. But then, until now, he'd never realized that maybe they had a little more in common than he'd thought.

He had Amy to thank for that.

"Then it sounds great."

Instead of eating alone that night, he had dinner with his brother.

He had Amy to thank for that, too. He just didn't mention it to her when he called her on his way to the airport in Portland at eight o'clock that night.

"Jared," she said, obviously pleased to hear his voice. The quick welcome in her tone turned to caution. "Did you talk to your friend?"

"I did." He liked that the welcome had been there. He rather liked the soft way she'd said his name, too. "He said he can find out what you need to do from a woman who does fund-raisers for the opera in Seattle. She does a lunch and fashion thing every year that apparently raises the kind of money you need. He thinks she has other ideas, too. What you need for certain is a corporate sponsor. Or two."

"A luncheon and fashion show?"

Oh, yeah, he thought, that was how he'd said it. He was about to tell her that, too, but he never got the chance.

"Jared, that's brilliant! I knew it would have to be something major, but all I could come up with is a raffle or an auction. We'd still have to get things donated for a fashion show, but at least I have connections there. I know the marketing director at a high-end department store and the owner of a fabulous boutique hotel. If I can convince the store to loan the clothes and models in exchange for publicity and the hotel to cut a deal on the cost of the lunch for the same, we'll be in business."

"You will?"

"Oh, I hope so." She all but sighed the words. Her mind, however, still raced. "We'll need runway lighting and sound people," she hurried on. "I know a DJ from a hugely popular radio station we work with. I'll ask him to do the music…"

"Amy."

"Maybe the station would come on board as a sponsor. You said we need corporate sponsors," she reminded him. "The radio station is owned by our biggest newspaper. That would be huge."

Her energy was infectious. So was the animation in her voice as she went on to speculate about who else sponsorwise they could bring on board. She was clearly accustomed to organizing on short notice. She also seemed to think nothing at all of taking on tasks of slightly gargantuan proportions.

He truly hated to burst her little bubble. Partly because he liked the way she was making him smile. Mostly because he knew how much this all meant to her. But she was in serious need of a reality check.

"Amy," he said again.

"…do it before the holidays. Once we get past Thanksgiving, people's whole focus changes…"

"Amy!"

"What?"

"Slow down, will you? That all sounds—" like a huge amount to accomplish on such short notice, he thought, "—great," he said. "But what are the chances of you getting that kind of sponsorship for something that will only benefit a handful of people? Even if you could get a couple of corporations to underwrite your expenses," he said, willing to give her the benefit of the doubt for the moment, "you'd need over three hundred people at $150 a plate to meet your goal."

Details apparently didn't deter her. "I've helped promote charity events before. Through the agency," she explained. "And I've seen advertising for functions for no-kill animal shelters and to save the spotted owl. Groups have raised funds to help with organ transplants and transplanting seedlings for trees. It's not always the cause that brings in the money. It's the value. The see-and-be-seen factor," she explained, "and the entertainment that makes people show up. You can never underestimate the power of a certain demographic wanting to be where they think everyone else will be."

For a moment Jared said nothing. As his headlights bounced off the airport exit sign, he was struck by a number of things at once.

When he'd first met Amy, he never would have suspected her to be so absolutely determined, so business savvy or so…passionate, he supposed.

"If you think you can pull that off," he said, telling himself he had no business wondering how deep those passions ran, "then I'm good to go on the plumbing. I'm leaving in the morning, but I'll make some calls while I'm gone and see who I can get out there to start."

"You'll make calls from Singapore?"

He hesitated. He'd all but forgotten that was where she thought he was headed.

"The company doesn't mind if I use its phones to call the states."

"That's a nice perk. When are you coming back?"

"I'm not sure," he replied, glad she'd moved on. "I'm scheduled for a few weeks. I'll see what I can do about cutting that short."

Forty minutes later, carrying his black Gucci overnight bag up the port-side airstairs of HuntCom's corporate jet, the animation he'd heard in her voice still intrigued him. Or maybe what intrigued him was simply the woman herself. He'd rarely met any female who seemed to care the way Amy did about other people. He doubted she'd know a selfish agenda if it bit her. And for reasons he couldn't begin to fathom, when he was with her, talking to her, he didn't feel the restiveness that even now was slowly creeping back.

He managed to delay the worst of the feeling by wondering where she was going to find the time to do all she'd said needed to be done. That subtle agitation promptly shifted direction when he realized that Candace and her mother probably would not be too pleased to have Amy enlisting the aid of a client.

"Our goal is to raise forty thousand dollars to keep the home open. I know it's only one home," Amy said, clutching her phone as she absently fluttered the pages of the notebook on her cluttered desk. She was in her own office. On her lunch hour. "But it does great things for the women who are fortunate enough to live there. When their cognitive abilities completely fail, a different type of facility needs to be found for them, but they seem to maintain those abilities longer in the environment the home provides. Elmwood House has helped over a hundred women since it opened thirty years…ago…"

It wasn't that Amy had suddenly forgotten what she wanted to say that caused her to falter. She'd repeated the information so many times in the past few days that she practically had her appeal memorized. What had her going quiet was the odd feeling of being watched—and the realization when she looked up that Jill had opened her door and poked her head inside.

Now she watched the woman with the smart gray bob and silver hoop earrings slowly swing the door wide. Tall and slender as a willow, she looked like an ad for middle-aged chic in her winter-white pantsuit.

She also looked decidedly unhappy. Clearly, she'd heard much of what Amy had just said.

"My office, please?" she asked.

Amy watched her go, then tried not to sound rushed while she finished her call to the florist that Eric in electronic media had suggested she contact. In less than two minutes, Eric's friend told her he'd be happy to meet with her to discuss table arrangements and that, depending on what she had in mind, he might be able to do the work for just the cost of the flowers. Since his shop was only a year old, he'd love the exposure.

She made an appointment with him for the following Saturday, thanked him profusely and was about to head out the door before she could indulge any of the hesitation she felt about Jill's summons when Jill walked back in.

The woman who had been her father's business partner for six years and his wife for four, had returned to the office yesterday. Other than for the usual conferences and conversations catching up entailed, she hadn't said anything to Amy that wasn't business related, except to ask how long it would be before her reupholstered furniture was delivered.

Now, looking unusually guarded, she stepped inside the small office with its bright-blue filing cabinets, potted palm in the window and sticky notes plastered over numerous surfaces, and quietly closed the door.

Jill had never impressed Amy as an impatient person. Exacting, professional, a little demanding at times, but never particularly impatient. She definitely seemed that way now.

"May I see that?" she asked, indicating the open notebook on Amy's desk.

Without giving Amy a chance to do much more than step aside, she slid on her turquoise-rimmed reading glasses and started flipping pages.

Inside that notebook were lists of vendors, checklists, call lists, a time line, weekly schedules, and an agenda that was still a work in progress for the luncheon and fashion show that had now been slated for earlier than Amy had wanted. The second Saturday in November, however, had been the only date she could get from the hotel. Because of the timing, the fashions to be shown would be geared for the upcoming holidays. A sort of preseason kickoff had been the inspiration of the marketing director at the department store. Calling it FashionFest had been Amy's idea.

"I saw Jennifer Radmacher at the Chamber of Commerce luncheon a while ago," Jill said, still turning pages. "She told me you were organizing a luncheon and fashion show at the Kensington."

Amy's brow furrowed. "I haven't talked to Jennifer." She hadn't gotten that far on her list. Jennifer was the chamber chairperson and would be a huge asset when it came time to sell tickets.

"Paul Erickson mentioned it to her."

Paul owned the theatrical lighting company the hotel used for special events. Part of Amy was thrilled that news of the event was spreading that quickly. Another part, at the moment…wasn't. She'd worked hard for so many years keeping what she did for Edna separate from her work life. In her mind, this project had been no different. Or so she'd thought.

"How long have you been working on this?"

"Four days."

Jill's eyebrows rose. "You put this together in four days?"

"I put most of the lists and schedules together in one evening." That had been the easy part. "I'm still working on the contacts and commitments. But I'm doing them on my own time," she hurried to make clear. "I've been making calls on my lunch hour or meeting people after work." Which meant she hadn't seen her grandmother since the weekend.

An injured look crept into Jill's expression. "You could have told me what you were doing."

"I didn't think you'd want to know," Amy admitted. "This is a personal project. It has nothing to do with the agency."

"It has everything to do with the agency." Totally overlooking Amy's disclaimer, disbelief appeared to join displeasure. "I've always considered you one of the most responsible people here. Yet you're approaching our clients and asking them to donate their time and their money to help Edna. Aside from the fact that you know she is not my favorite person, do you realize how it makes me look that you feel you had to go public to help your grandmother rather than coming to me?"

Bright spots of color bloomed on the woman's cheeks while the knot in Amy's stomach doubled. It had never occurred to her that Jill would think she would approach her with this, much less that she would inadvertently bruise the woman's image by failing to do so.

"It's not just for Grandma," she insisted, grabbing at the first of the claims demanding to be addressed. "It's for the other residents, too. And those who will come after."

"That's not the point," she cut in. "The point is that you didn't come to me. I wouldn't have been able to help you with the money. Everything I have is tied up in real estate and this agency. But I wouldn't have had to hear about what you were doing from someone else."

And that, in a nutshell, Amy realized, was why she was so upset.

"I'm sorry if I embarrassed you, Jill. I really am." She meant that sincerely. She just didn't know how to explain what she'd done without getting into the one issue they both tended to avoid. Avoiding it now, however, took more creativity than she could manage on such short notice.

"I didn't mention this to you because I know how you feel about my grandmother," she told her, feeling defensive, trying not to sound it. "The other reason I didn't ask—" the more selfish one, Amy thought "—is because I didn't want you to do what you just did and point out how much you dislike her.

"It's not like you ever just let it go at that," she hurried on. "Grandma's name doesn't come up that often, but when it does, I get a day or two of the deep freeze from you because you remember how she tried to come between you and Dad. I didn't want that, either."

Jill opened her mouth, apparently to protest the "deep freeze" remark. Not denying the irrefutable, she clamped her lips shut again.

In the sudden silence, Amy considered remaining silent herself. If she said nothing else, the status quo would remain. Yet, despite her assurance to Jared that she was fine with her arrangement with Jill, fine with all the choices she'd made, there were certain aspects of the status quo that she hated. Jill's attitude toward her grandmother was one of them.

"I know you resent her," Amy said, because they'd never get past where they were if she didn't speak up now. "I'd have issues with someone who tried to come between me and someone I cared about, too. But it's been years," she stressed. "I just wish there was some way you could let your dislike of her go. I honestly don't think she even remembers what happened between the two of you, Jill. I don't mean this as an insult," she prefaced, fearing it could sound that way, "but I don't know that she remembers you at all. There are days when she barely remembers me."

Her stepmother had the grace to look disquieted. Amy just

couldn't tell if that was because of what she'd just admitted, or because of her wish that Jill could drop the hostilities. What did seem apparent as Jill's glance faltered was that she knew the embarrassment she'd felt learning secondhand of the event for Elmwood House was as much her own fault as Amy's.

Years of holding onto her grudge didn't allow her to let it go easily, though. Instead of even acknowledging it, she did what she always did when she no longer cared to discuss an issue, and simply moved on to something else.

"I still can't have you imposing on our clients. I don't want them feeling they have to be involved in your project," she explained, seeking the safety of addressing business concerns, "and I certainly don't want any of them to feel we now owe them a favor. That's not how Mike did business. It's not how I do it, either."

"I haven't approached anyone I don't know personally. I went to school with Rob Schumann…"

"Who?"

"The Whip. The morning DJ on KISS," Amy explained. KISS was their client. Had been for years. Rob had been a friend far longer. "I asked him if he'd donate his time for the music and he offered to ask his station to come on as a sponsor."

Apparently unable to find fault there, she continued on. "And the Kensington Hotel?"

"I called Keith Adler."

"Who just happens to be the owner and one of this firm's oldest clients."

"He was one of Dad's best friends," she reminded her. "He's known me most of my life. He knows Grandma. His own mother is in an assisted-living facility. He was happy to help."

Looking somewhat appeased, but mostly—oddly—guilty, she glanced toward the notebook, back to Amy. "Just make sure that what you're doing doesn't take time away from the office," she told her. "We have four major campaigns in the works and a dozen proposals out. Next month will be busy."

As if that was all she'd come to say, she walked out without another word.

Jared had departed for India the morning after he'd returned from Portland. The trip took roughly twenty-six hours on a commercial airline. Thanks to HuntCom's state-of-the-art, fifty-million-dollar, ultralong-range business jet with its added forward fuel tank and ability to fly at Mach .85, he could make it there in twelve to fourteen, depending on the head- or tailwinds.

He'd arrived at 9:00 a.m., New Delhi time, which was 7:00 at night according to his body, since Seattle was still on daylight savings time. Over the years, he'd learned he experienced less jet lag if he just went with whatever the local time was and dove into his day. Armed with the blueprints and reports he'd studied during the flight, he'd headed for HuntCom's fifty-acre campus. By midafternoon, he'd been briefed by his second-in-command and discovered that the weather had delayed a cement pour. The results of a ground compaction test were also still needed before ground could be broken on a new dormitory to house employees.

He pushed through the meetings, drank more coffee than he should have and, as usual his first night there, even with all the caffeine, he slept the sleep of the dead.

Within forty-eight hours, though, the restlessness a screwed-up body clock tended to overshadow was back.

That restiveness seemed as ordinary to him as breathing. It was also what made it so easy for him to pick up at a moment's notice and head for some other place he needed to be. Movement was good. Changes of place, faces, duties, kept him focused pretty much on the present. Yet, in the couple of weeks since Amy had made him aware of just how little enthusiasm he'd come to feel for whatever he found himself engaged in, that quiet, constant tension had taken on a sharper edge.

Amy.

He'd found himself thinking about her with disturbing regularity before he'd left. He thought about her even more now as he wondered what sort of progress she was making on her fund-raiser, if she got the dent in her fender fixed, if she was doing okay with Jill. Those odd thoughts hit mostly at night while he paced between his bed and his view of the spotlighted palm trees outside his hotel waiting for return calls from those whose day was just starting in Seattle.

He stayed up every night until 1:00 a.m. reviewing and approving, or sending back for redrafting, all the plans that would be needed for the next phase of campus expansion. He was back at it by eight every morning, reviewing invoices, authorizing payments, delegating, assigning. By the time he was on the jet heading west once more, he'd jammed three weeks of work into two.

Within minutes of takeoff, he unfastened the seat belt on one of the plane's eight, caramel-leather passenger seats and moved to the office area outside the bedroom with its queen-size bed and full bath. Tossing his day planner onto the conference table's burl wood surface, he settled into one of the leather chairs bolted to the floor and opened the pages to month-at-a-glance.

He now had the next six days free. He'd planned to spend the following week in Seattle and Jansen, but decided now to just make day trips if something arose that couldn't be handled by phone, courier or e-mail. The week after that was the one he'd blocked out to go sailing in the Bahamas, since the weather tended to be too iffy in the San Juans at the end of October. He'd now spend that time tearing out walls. Or, possibly at that point, putting them back in.

Wanting to see what he'd scheduled for himself the week he'd originally planned to return, he flipped to the pages breaking down the month into weeks—and sat slowly tapping his pen against the table's shiny surface.

Candace's looping handwriting stared up from a yellow sticky note he'd slapped on the page. She'd written "Call Candace" on it and handed it to him after they'd set an appointment for the end of that week for her team to present its finalized initial campaign to him. The note had been to remind him to call her if he had time to get together before then.

At the time, he'd thought he would call her. That he should, anyway. Now his only thought was that there was no need for her and her team to push to make their presentation that soon. He knew what it was like to stress over a deadline. In this case it was unnecessary. He wouldn't need his ad campaign for months, so there was no need for her to rush to get it finished. Aside from that, he didn't want to take time out to deal with Plan B while he was working on the home. The whole idea of taking that break was to get away from everything Harry had pushed him into.

He glanced at his watch. It would be a little after eleven in the morning in Portland. Reaching for the phone mounted below the edge of the conference table, he removed it to punch in the numbers for an international call.

Amy answered on the second ring.

At the sound of her voice, he actually felt the tension in his shoulders ease.

"Still no receptionist?" he asked.

He could have sworn he heard a smile in her tone. "Not yet. But Jill is working on it." She paused. "Where are you?"

"In the air. I'm on my way back."

"You are?" she asked, trying not to sound so obviously delighted by his news.

He couldn't help the chuckle he tried to mask at the pleasure he felt at her unguarded response.

"I am. I'll be in Seattle in the morning and in Portland on Wednesday."

"You must be using one of those phones. In the seatback in front of you," she clarified, obviously thinking of the sky phone in commercial craft.

He hesitated. "Amazing where you can make a call from, isn't it? Look," he continued, hating how he had to hedge with her. "I called Kay last week to make some arrangements. Once she told me you'd set a date for the fund-raiser, I contacted the Construction Contractor's Board and lined up a couple of plumbing contractors to talk with Wednesday afternoon. If you'll meet me at the home after work, I'll tell you what I've worked out. Are things still progressing on your end?"

"Still progressing," she echoed.

She was at the office. Considering that, there might be things she wasn't in a position to share. Certain she would have told him more had she been able to, a smile slipped into his voice.

"I'll get details when I see you." He would enjoy that, he thought. He'd enjoy seeing the animation he'd heard in her voice when she'd launched into her verbal list of things to do to get the project rolling. "In the meantime, is Candace available? I need to talk to her."

Amy seemed to hesitate. "Of course," she murmured, her tone suddenly losing some of its energy. "Have a safe trip home, Jared. I'll put you right through."

Chapter Seven

Five minutes after Amy put Jared's call through to Candace, the light on the console indicating that Candace's phone was in use went out.

Amy had consciously kept her project limited strictly to her own time and out of earshot of office personnel. Jill hadn't said a word about it since their discussion nearly two weeks ago, so it seemed she was pretending the event didn't exist. The ostrich approach worked just fine for Amy. The less confrontation, the better. She just didn't know what Jill had said to Candace about what she was doing. Candace hadn't mentioned it at all.

She was about to, though. There wasn't a doubt about that in Amy's mind when the tall blonde in the jersey wrap dress and chunky necklace walked up with her coffee mug in hand and stopped just short of the desk.

"Do you have a minute?" she asked, and turned back down the hall before Amy could say a word.

The quick, letdown sensation Amy had felt when Jared asked to talk to Candace had already been buried. Now, adjusting the wide, low-slung belt she wore with her knit sheath, she headed down the hall herself.

Candace walked into the break room with Amy right behind her.

"Jared called to change the date of his presentation." Looking every bit as casual as she sounded, Candace crossed the small space with its colorful molded chairs and two round tables. "We were scheduled for next week, but he told me he didn't need the campaign that soon and didn't want me to feel I had to rush." Smiling as if she thought his consideration very sweet, she stopped at the stainless steel coffeemaker on the back wall counter. Apparently, she was getting her coffee herself. "We rescheduled for the fourteenth of November. That gives us another month."

"I'll make that change on the office schedule."

"You'll do a memo, too?"

"Of course."

"He's coming back sooner than he'd planned," she continued. Pulling out one of the two carafes, she poured coffee into her mug. "But I'm sure you already know that." The carafe clinked back into place a moment before her puzzled eyes met Amy's. "You never mentioned that Jared was working on your fund-raiser with you."

There was no accusation in her expression. Only a certain incomprehension that made it clear she didn't understand why Amy had failed to mention that she was working with this particular client. A client Candace seemed to expect her to know she was interested in on more than a professional basis.

Rather than ask why she'd thought mention was necessary, since Candace hadn't discussed Jared with her at all, Amy spared herself hearing what was so obvious to the entire office. Anyone who'd seen Candace with him, overheard a conversation with her girlfriends, or seen her after she'd talked with him on the phone, knew she was verging on serious lust with the man.

"He's not working on the fund-raiser with me," Amy replied, not caring to consider what she felt about him herself. Gratitude she could deal with. Anything beyond that felt a little too…futile. "He's working on the plumbing."

At a loss to see the difference, Candace's confusion increased. "Did you ask him to do that?"

"He volunteered."

"That's what he said." Apparently trying to understand why he'd done such a thing, her beautifully arched eyebrows pinched as she left her mug on the counter. "We'd talked about charity work being beneficial for a corporation new to an area. But when I mentioned him getting involved in the community, I had something more visible in mind. Had I known about this, I'd have steered him away from helping where your grandmother lives.

"It's not that I'm opposed to what you feel you need to do for her," she admitted. "I know you're torn when it comes to Mom and Edna. I just don't want their issues involved in my dealings with him."

"Why would they be?"

"Because I can see Mom encouraging me to discourage him from what he's doing."

"She hasn't discouraged anyone else who's working on the event." Not that Amy knew of, anyway. "And he's a big boy. The decision about who and what he wants to help is his. Not hers."

The flat conviction in Amy's tone drew a faint frown. "Of course it is. And I'll handle it if Mom says anything," she insisted, as if the advice had been unnecessary. "Right now,

I'm just trying to figure out how he knew the home needed help if you didn't tell him about it."

Amy didn't hesitate. "He overheard me talking about it on the telephone," she said with more ease than she felt just then. She had nothing to hide here. There were just certain details that were no one's business but hers. If Jared cared to share, that was his prerogative. But the evolution of their…friendship, if that was what it was, shouldn't require explanation. "He asked what the problem was and I told him."

That was the nutshell version, anyway.

Candace lifted her chin and breathed out a little. "Ah. So he asked you about it himself." As if his motives might be coming into focus, her eyes narrowed. "Was that before or after he'd asked me out?"

"After."

The word was no sooner out of her mouth than Amy mentally winced. She could have at least given the appearance of having had to think about her response. She remembered far too much about him. What he said. When he said it. She'd really rather Candace didn't realize that.

The faint arch of those perfect eyebrows seemed to indicate only that she'd just confirmed whatever conclusions the woman was drawing.

"Well, he's obviously a very practical and generous man. A soft touch, too. I really hadn't suspected that about him." She offered the admission thoughtfully, processing the new information. "He seemed a little too focused and driven to me to be that aware of things on the periphery. Not that being focused and driven is a bad thing. I want that in a man," she insisted, reaching for her mug with her French-manicured hand. "But what he's doing at least makes sense now."

It does? Amy thought.

"I think he probably feels bad for those old women." She

tipped her head, looking as if she found his concern rather appealing, too. "And by helping out there, he has an excuse to spend some real time in Portland."

"Why would he need an excuse?"

"Oh, Amy," she murmured, humoring her. "If you can't see what he's doing, then you really do need to get out more."

"Excuse me?"

"Get out. Get a boyfriend. Date," she emphasized. Entirely missing the point of the question, she slipped immediately into the mentor mode she sometimes adopted with her and the younger women in the office. Her expression brightened. "I even have someone for you. I met a really nice junior stockbroker at the Downtown Association meeting last week. He gave me his card. Why don't I set you up with him?"

Amy could think of several responses to Candace's truly well-intentioned offer. For starters, "junior" anythings tended to be barely out of business school, out only to prove their prowess in their field and in bed and possessed the maturity and attention span of a gnat. She also strongly suspected that the guy had given her his card hoping Candace would call to go out with him herself. She really wasn't interested in being seen as a disappointment.

"That's very generous of you, but I think I'll pass. And I know what getting out means. What I asked," she stressed, "is why does Jared need an excuse to be here?"

"It's simple." Her tone went indulgent. "If he just wanted time to get to know the area, he could do that without anyone thinking anything of it. But the way male minds seem to work, when a man is really interested in a woman, he needs an excuse to hang around. If he's here working on that place, it'll give him more time to get to know the area. And me. He didn't quite *say* that," she qualified with a little laugh. "But it makes perfect sense. Especially since he knows we're stepsisters."

What Jill's daughter seemed to see as evident made little sense to Amy at all. Confused, suddenly uncomfortable, she looked away from that feminine, knowing smile.

A bit of paper lay on the gray carpet. Amy picked it up.

"I can't imagine what our relationship has to do with anything."

"It's obvious isn't it? He's doing something nice for you."

And what better way to make points with a woman than to do something nice for someone she knows.

She didn't say the words. She didn't need to. As Amy tossed the paper into the trash, they simply hung in the air along with the scent of rich French roast and Candace's exquisite perfume.

Amy drove to work on the days she visited Elmwood House. She had to pay to park her car in the office garage, but she saved travel time and that gave her longer to spend with her grandmother. Seeing her grandma when she first arrived Wednesday evening, however, had to wait.

The moment she was buzzed in and she stepped inside, Kay wrapped her in an antibacterial-soap-scented hug.

"That man is amazing. He hired a contractor this afternoon. And he's paying for him out of his own pocket. He's still downstairs tearing out the laundry room wall."

"The contractor?"

"Jared." The resident director set her back by her shoulders. "I can't thank you enough for bringing him here."

Before Amy could do much more than feel her pulse skip, knowing she would soon see him, the wiry woman pulled her to the island in the kitchen to show her the rough sketches he'd given her of ideas for an expanded sunroom. The only reason she stopped going on about what a godsend he was, was because one of the slower residents to finish her supper in the dining room called out that she was stuck and needed help getting up.

"Edna went to her room after supper," Kay told her on her way across the kitchen. "Come get me after you've seen her and I'll take you downstairs. Jared wants to see you before you go."

Amy had known all day that she would see him tonight. And all day she'd battled the little fantasies that had started creeping into her days and invading her dreams at night. Fantasies about being with him again in the dark, hearing his deep voice in her ear, feeling his strength wrapped around her. Fantasies about him having kissed her when she'd been in his arms instead of pulling away as he had.

· Fantasies about him wanting her.

She really needed to kill those needy and erotic indulgences. Or at least not think about them when she was minutes away from seeing him again.

Luckily she had the buffer of seeing her grandmother first.

With that reprieve in mind, she headed into the house's back hall— "the speedway," as her grandma had first dubbed the long, wide space where little old ladies with walkers passed each other between their respective rooms.

Halfway down that well-lit corridor, Amy knocked on the wall beside her grandma's partly open door and poked her head inside.

Edna's private space smelled like the rose-scented lotion she always wore. Sweet. And comforting. Keeping things familiar for her grandmother had become even more important in the past few years. That was why this room echoed the rooms she'd lived in before. Edna's own bedroom set and her overstuffed easy chair took up most of the space. Family photographs sat on her dresser and night stand, and the walls were adorned with collections of wildflower and Audubon prints that had always graced her bedroom and dining room walls.

Edna sat in her pink cabbage-rose-print chair, her attention on the small television set in the corner. She looked up when Amy came in, but there was no recognition in her weathered features. At least, it didn't seem to Amy that there was, until, staring hard, the older woman finally gave a small nod.

"Hi, child," was all she said.

Relieved that she still knew her, for today, anyway, Amy bent to give her a hug. When she'd seen her last weekend, it had been nearly an hour before recognition had come. "How are you feeling, Grandma?"

"Tired," was all she said.

"Do you want me to help you get ready for bed?"

"Maybe after."

"After" apparently meant after the game show that had the bulk of her attention.

"We can talk after the show, then?"

"After I've had my supper."

She'd already had her supper.

Disappointment tugged hard. Her grandma was confused tonight.

"Okay," Amy murmured, and kissed the top of her head.

Her grandma didn't move. She didn't pat her hand as she sometimes did. Or reach for another hug. She didn't seem interested in anything other than watching the wheel on the screen being spun.

Amy had hoped to talk to her. About the ads they were putting together for the local symphony because her grandma loved music. And about the author readings at the bookstore around the corner from her house because she'd once loved books. But mostly to see if there was any insight she could share about how to stop being attracted more by the minute to someone else's prince charming.

With that wisdom unavailable to her just then, that left Amy with nothing to do but tell her grandma she'd be back after the show to help her into her nightclothes. Leaving her coat on the old hope chest at the foot of the bed, she headed back down the hall.

She felt totally ambivalent at the prospect of seeing Jared. The unsettling effect of her fantasies aside, until a couple of days ago, she'd hardly been able to wait to tell him how quickly everything was coming together. It was as if the Fates had decided that this home and those who staffed it needed to continue their work no matter what obstacles were thrown in their path. Thanks to The Whip and his huge popularity, the radio station was already getting calls for tickets that hadn't even been printed yet.

Her desire to share all that with Jared had been tempered greatly, however, by Candace's conversation with her. Those few minutes in the break room had served as an in-her-face reminder that he was not there simply because he wanted to help. He had his own agenda. Even as kind as he had been to her, it was hard to imagine him really interested in hearing all her little details.

She'd never been in the basement before. It was a "staff only" area closed off by two separate doors from a storage area off the kitchen. Unlocking the doors for her, Kay told her where the laundry room was, asked her to let her know when she left so she could make sure the doors were locked behind her, and left her on her own to find Jared.

Fluorescent lights hummed overhead as she reached the bottom of the wooden steps. Off to the left loomed the large, hulking furnace that needed to be replaced. From the looks of the boxes, furniture odds and ends and a row of empty cabinets standing in the middle of the space, the bulk of the basement served as storage.

Taking a deep breath, she headed to the open doorway on the right.

The large room had been painted with white enamel. Long florescent lights illuminated two washers and dryers, a sink and a long folding table. The air smelled of laundry soap and fabric softener and was warm from the heat of a running dryer.

Not far from a trio of large hot water heaters farther down the wall, Jared stood with his back to her. Both hands gripped a chunk of the wall he was already dismantling. Beneath heavy cotton, taut muscles shifted as he gave a jerk and pulled off a sizable section of drywall.

He tossed it to the pile behind him. Dust rose in a little puff. As it did, he caught sight of her watching him from the doorway.

A smile moved over the tired lines of his face. "Hey," he said.

"Hey," she replied, wishing her heart wasn't beating so hard.

The cobalt color of the shirt stretching over his broad shoulders turned the flecks of silver in his gray eyes to shards of pale blue. His jeans had been worn white at the thighs, the pockets and alongside the fly covering his zipper. Realizing where her glance had stalled, her attention darted to the thick black pipes and two-by-fours he'd exposed behind him.

"You've been busy."

"Had to be." His eyes shifted slowly over her face as he walked toward her. "The plumbing contractor I hired only has a two-week window starting next week. I need to get fans on this first thing in the morning so the wood can start drying out. That could take a few days."

"You're doing this yourself?"

"I'm doing it with Mike. The contractor," he explained, his eyes on the faint confusion in hers. "I'll do the tear-out to keep costs down. He'll find the leak and fix it, then I'll bring in a drywaller to help me with the rebuild."

"You plan to be around for the whole project, then?"

"I'll have to make a few trips up north, but, yeah," he said, looking at her with a little frown. "That's my plan. I told you I'd take care of the repairs."

She knew he had. But even when Candace had talked about him spending some real time in Portland, she hadn't considered that he intended to do so much himself. He'd mentioned hiring someone. And helping. It hadn't occurred to her that he had planned to stay and oversee. He'd obviously told Candace that, though.

Just be grateful for what he's doing, she insisted to herself, and gave him a hesitant smile. Crossing her arms over the trim sweater tucked into her simple narrow skirt, she indicated the wall with a nod.

"That's where the problem is?"

Needing to not be so close to his scrutiny, she moved to look up at the tiny trickle of water leaking down the pipe, then down at the wet wood and concrete.

"That's the result of the problem. We have no idea where the leak is coming from." Jared looked from where the pipe disappeared through the overhead boards to the delicate, decidedly guarded lines of her profile. "It could be any of a dozen connections between here and the upstairs bathroom. Or a section of pipe could be cracked."

Over a period of weeks, months probably, he told her, that tiny leak had dampened the studs in the basement wall nearly three feet up and soaked through the drywall. The reason no one who worked in the home had noticed it was because a storage cabinet had blocked the damage.

He told her that, too, then watched her give him the merest hint of the sunshine-bright smile he'd hoped to see.

He'd thought that she would like his help. She'd sounded so grateful for it on the phone. Not that he wanted gratitude from her. All he wanted was the ease he'd felt the last time he'd been with her, the times they'd talked on the phone. Yet, instead of seeing enthusiasm or the warmth in her eyes that had seemed to soothe him somehow, she seemed strangely withdrawn.

"Are you okay?" he asked.

Her glance moved to his, then slipped away. "I'm fine," she replied.

He wasn't buying that. Something wasn't right.

"Is everything going okay with your event? Kay told me how fast the hotel signed on, and that you already have a commitment from a department store for models and clothes." Amy had even said herself that things were still progressing when he'd talked to her a couple days ago. "Have you run into a problem?"

"Not so far," she said. "Everything is going unbelievably well."

He wasn't going to get details. He wasn't going to see that smile, either. Feeling oddly cheated, a little surprised by how much that mattered, he took a step closer.

"How is Jill with what you're doing?"

He watched her brow pinch.

"I'm not really sure."

"Is she giving you a hard time about it?"

"Actually," she murmured, "she's not saying anything about it at all."

"How about your grandmother, then?" he asked, trying to think of what could have her so subdued. "Is she all right? I didn't see her when I got here."

"She's in her room. I think she's a little tired." And I'm not sure she really knew it was me tonight, Amy thought, but she didn't want to go there right now. Not with him looking at her with all that concern etched in his handsome features. Every time she saw her grandma, she missed the woman that much more. She couldn't talk to her the way she once had, couldn't get the advice that she hadn't always followed but valued nonetheless. Talking about that would only make the void feel that much bigger. And then, she'd want his arms around her that much more.

Ducking her head at the thought, she shoved her fingers through her hair, turned away from all that solid muscle.

She really needed thicker armor where he was concerned. Every time she talked to him, saw him, thought about him, she found herself falling just a little bit harder for the man she wanted to think of only as a rather unlikely…friend.

"I was just thinking about what you're doing here. The help you're giving these women," she explained, utterly determined to find a way to keep from falling even more.

"I know charity work will be good for your new business. And this is a great opportunity to get to know some local contractors. You're even in a better position to spend more time with Candace," she continued, because her stepsibling's conclusion had made sense and she didn't want him thinking she had any illusions about him herself. None that he needed to worry about anyway.

"I think you'd have made more points with Candace working on something more mainstream," she continued, forcing a lightness into her voice that she didn't feel. "But whatever your reasons, I think what you're doing for this home and these ladies is enormously kind."

Conscious of the distance she'd deliberately put between them, Jared watched her across six feet of bare concrete floor. He had no idea what to make of the way she'd just recapped the excuses he'd given her about why he was helping out. He wasn't sure where the part about Candace had come from, either. All that interested him at the moment was the disquiet she was trying hard to mask.

The need to relieve that unease tugged hard. So did the need to correct one glaringly erroneous assumption.

"I do have my own reasons for being here," he admitted, preparing to strip his motives to the basics. "But they have nothing to do with trying to make points with anybody. I'm not even thinking about my business right now." A muscle in his jaw bunched. Other than to temporarily escape its necessity, he wasn't thinking about the Bride Hunt, either. "I'm just looking for some downtime."

Disquiet merged with caution. "I don't understand."

That made two of them, he thought. He wasn't totally sure he understood all that was going on with him himself. "I'm at a crossroads," he decided to call it. "I'm literally going in two directions at the same time, and I feel nothing but resentment either way I turn."

The caution in her pretty face slipped into her voice. "Does this have anything to do with why you aren't more into your new business?"

"Between you and me," he muttered, because she'd already picked up on his ambivalence, "it has everything to do with it."

He shoved his fingers through his hair, restlessness spiking straight up his spine. If he felt like this now, he could only imagine how he'd be come next July. "I want a break, and you need help here. You said that when you're having a bad month, you do something to get your mind off things for a while. That's what I'm doing. Getting my mind off what's going on before the Fates decide which road I'll take."

He'd remembered what she'd said that day in the elevator. The thought would have left Amy momentarily speechless had it not been for the rest of what he'd said.

"What are you talking about?" Confusion moved to conviction. "A man like you doesn't wait for fate, Jared. You make your own decisions. You decide your own destiny."

He should have felt flattered by her unguarded opinion. Or maybe humbled by it. Yet what touched him just then was the utter lack of guile in her expression. Her eyes searched his, her fragile barriers falling unheeded. She looked as if her faith in him was absolute.

"Like you've decided yours?" he asked, not wanting her to be that vulnerable. Not to him. Not to anyone. It left her with no protection, no way to defend herself against those who might take advantage of her.

"You know it's not that easy, Amy. You know that whenever people who can pull your strings are involved, your wants end where theirs begin. You've put off your whole future because of what other people need or want from you. So you know how little what you want yourself can matter sometimes."

Amy opened her mouth. Rather than try to refute what he'd just said, she drew a deep breath and closed it instead. With his eyes steady on hers, she couldn't begin to deny what was probably obvious to everyone she knew. Those who knew she'd had other dreams, anyway. What he couldn't possibly know was that those dreams where changing, unbidden, to include a man she knew next to nothing about. A man who'd only held her once, but who had given her a glimpse of feelings she'd never felt before. A man who had insisted there had to be a way to help this home without selling her own because he'd somehow sensed what her home meant to her. A man whose need for escape had him ripping holes in walls.

She could find a way to protect her heart from him later. Right now, all she wanted was to know why that need was there.

"You know why I've made the choices I have. And, yes," she admitted, because denying it was pointless, "in some ways I feel as trapped as you seem to." She couldn't let herself think about that, though. If she did, she might start to feel the resentment practically radiating from his big body. That wasn't something she wanted to deal with at all. "But we're not talking about me."

When his only response was a deep breath, she quietly

asked, "Who's pulling your strings, Jared?" He'd told her grandmother he wasn't married. That didn't mean he couldn't be having problems with an ex-wife. "Do you need to move back to the States because of a bad divorce?"

He shook his head. "I've never been married. It's nothing like that."

"Are you having trouble with a partner, then?"

An edge entered his voice. "We're not partners. And it's not that I'm being forced out." Not in the literal sense, anyway, he thought. "Certain terms of an agreement we have are just...causing complications."

"Is this the person who doesn't have any sense of when he's crossed a line?" Seeing his brow pinch, she added, "You mentioned him when we were leaving here a couple of weeks ago. When we were talking about Grandma's inappropriate..."

"I remember," he murmured. "And, yeah. That's him."

"I take it you can't talk to him."

She offered the conclusion quietly, empathy shading her tone. For a moment, Jared said nothing. He just stood there letting the quiet concern in her expression wash over him. He didn't know if he was getting old, or if he was just tired from having pushed himself so hard lately. But something about this woman seemed to touch him in places he didn't know existed.

The realization felt as compelling as it did dangerous. She also had a way of getting too close to things he couldn't talk about. Things he didn't want to talk about. And that felt more dangerous still.

"I could talk, but he won't listen."

"Does he...?"

"Just leave it. Okay?"

He watched her lips part an instant before her glance dropped from his. With the blink of her dark lashes, she took a step back. She looked as if he'd just slammed a door in her face.

Swearing to himself, he reached for her before she could move any farther. With his fingers curled around her upper arms, he felt her slender muscles tense.

"Amy, don't. I'm sorry." He hated how he'd killed the light in her eyes. He hated even more that she wouldn't look at him now. "Things are just really complicated. I'd explain if I could, but I can't."

She didn't understand. She couldn't possibly. Yet, she gave a little nod anyway. She just wouldn't look at him while she did it.

"Amy."

"It's okay," she assured him. "And I'll leave it," she promised, echoing his phrasing. "I didn't mean to…"

"Look at me."

"…step over any lines…" she continued as he let go of one arm.

Slipping his fingers beneath her chin, he tipped her head toward him as she kept talking.

"…myself."

Her last word was little more than a whisper as his thumb touched the corner of her mouth. Hearing her soft intake of breath, feeling the softness of her skin beneath his fingers, he also promptly forgot whatever it was he'd meant to say.

Her eyes met his. He'd expected the wariness he saw in those dark and lovely depths. What he hadn't anticipated was the quick awareness she didn't have time to mask, or the heat he felt at that unguarded response to his touch.

Her breath shuddered out. Beneath his fingers her skin felt like warm satin. Her unadorned mouth looked lush, sensual, inviting. He'd once come within inches of tasting that compelling softness.

With her breath quickening, his body tightening, he was within inches of lowering his head now.

He was not a selfless man. When he wanted something, he went for it. Especially when it came to women. But this woman was different. As he let his hand slowly slip away, he didn't bother considering what those differences were. He considered only that she deserved far more from a man than he could ever offer.

"Would you rather I get someone else in here to do this?" he asked.

She was shaking her head even as she stepped away herself. As if unconsciously holding in his touch, her hand covered the spot on her arm where his hand had been.

"No. No," she repeated, pulling composure around her like a cloak. He'd seen her do that before. Bury whatever was going on inside as if she couldn't let it matter. "I don't want you to go. You're helping the home keep its license. And if doing this will help you, too, then this is where you should be."

A ghost of a smile tugged at her mouth. It was the vulnerability in her eyes he noticed most, though. She wasn't anywhere near as immune to him as she wanted him to think.

That was dangerous knowledge for a man to possess.

"I should let you get back to doing whatever it is you need to do to finish here. I told Grandma I'd help her get ready for bed."

Amy watched him push his hands into his pockets, give her a small smile. "Say hi to her for me. And tell Kay I'll be out of here in about ten minutes."

"Sure."

"And, Amy?" he said, as she started for the door.

She hesitated, turned back.

"I'm sorry."

She wasn't exactly sure what he was apologizing for. For not caring to confide in her? For not being attracted to her? Not that it mattered. Either way, his apology only added more embarrassment to what she already felt as she hurried up the stairs and on to her grandmother's room. Confusion and humiliation hurried right along with her.

She'd wanted him to kiss her. He knew that. She'd stood there with her heart pounding, waiting for him to do what she so desperately wanted him to do, and instead he'd let her go.

Scrambling for composure, not at all sure she achieved it, she opened the door to her grandmother's room.

Edna was already in bed.

The aide who'd made sure she'd taken her medication and helped her with her nightgown was just on her way out. Her grandmother had apparently forgotten that she'd said she'd be back to help her. If she'd even remembered that she'd been there at all.

All things considered, it seemed to Amy like a perfect evening to curl up in front of something mindless on TV with a pint of chocolate caramel ice cream. So that was what she did. That and promise herself that the next time she saw Jared Taylor, he wouldn't have any idea that he mattered to her at all.

Chapter Eight

"I don't think we want anything that heavy. I love what you came up with on the second menu. The mixed greens with raspberry vinaigrette is perfect. So is the tasting plate with the salmon mousse, the leek wrapped asparagus, and the wild-mushroom-stuffed chicken roulade. The women are going to be watching all those skinny models in those great clothes while they eat. The last thing they want is food they know will go straight to their thighs.

"Except for dessert," Amy continued, holding her cell phone to her shoulder while she untied her coat. "Like you said, a few bites of something decadent would be wonderful. Something chocolate. And something vanilla or caramel. We can serve it with the champagne Elk Cove Vineyards is donating." She passed behind Harriet Bower, who was rocking and humming to herself in front of a picture on the community room wall. "Their sparkling wine with anything caramel is a truly sensual experience.

"I'm sorry, Alaina," she said into the phone. "Could you hold for just a second?"

With the catering manager for the Kensington Hotel on the other end of the line, Amy smiled at an aide near the temporary wall that cut six feet off the communal space.

"Is my grandma in her room?" she quickly asked, then offered a "Thanks" and a smile before she turned back to the call that had come just as she'd been buzzed in. She'd been waiting all day to hear from Alaina Tyler. As busy as the woman was, and with the hotel donating everything but the cost of the food, which the radio station was underwriting, she didn't want to ask if she could call her back.

"Sorry, Alaina. Where were we? Oh, yes," she said, laughing a little when the former chef reminded her they were talking about sensual experiences. "You're the expert with food, and you know we're going for a feel-fabulous, rock-your-garters-off girl thing here. So does that sound all right to you?

"Oh, thank you," she replied, relieved. Unbuttoning her coat, she nodded to the ladies ensconced in front of the television. "Then, that's what we'll do. I'll get the contract back to you as soon as you fax it to me."

With that she flipped off her cell phone and rounded the corner of a temporary wall. That wall jutted into the room like a big plywood box. It was itself walled on both ends to keep residents safe from the construction mess on the other side.

"Garters?"

The deep voice that came from behind her sent her heart to her throat a moment before she turned with what she hoped was a passably easy smile. Jared stood just inside the doorway of the temporary structure. The sleeves of his chambray shirt were rolled to the middle of his strong forearms. Worn denims hugged his narrow hips. Beneath the dark hair tumbling over his forehead, his carved features looked almost as guarded as she felt. Only the way his mouth curved at one corner relieved that heavy caution.

She hadn't seen him in well over a week. Partly by circumstance. Partly by design.

"It's just an expression," she murmured.

One dark eyebrow arched. "Sensual experience?"

"That's a…marketing term."

"I thought you were just feeding women and showing them clothes."

She'd wondered all week what would happen when she saw him again. If he'd be polite but distant. Or if his attitude toward her would recede to the businesslike manner she'd never totally managed with him herself. Yet, amazingly, mercifully, he seemed to be doing exactly what she'd hoped she could do; act as if nothing had happened at all.

For him, nothing probably had. Or so she self-protectively reminded herself before she could respond as she would have if he had not, not kissed her.

"Therein lies the difference between women and the male of the species." Indulgence slipped into her tone. Except for the jolt of unexpectedly seeing him, she felt good tonight. Better than good. A local women's group had just come on board to cover the last of the costs. Anything made from ticket sales would now go straight to the home to reduce its debt. "A fashion show is about image. About possibilities. A woman will look up on the runway, hear the beat of the music and picture herself in the gown or the suit being modeled and think, 'Yeah, I want that. I want that confidence. I want that gown. With them, I can conquer my little corner of the world.'"

"A woman gets all that from clothes?"

"What's a man doing when he picks out a red tie?"

J.T. watched the smile in her eyes settle into his. He'd wondered if she'd ever look at him like that again.

"Got it."

More relieved by that smile than he would ever admit, he motioned to her cell phone.

"Kay said you've really been running. You've only come by twice this week." According to Kay and the rest of the staff, Amy had been on her cell phone when she'd walked in both of those times, too. Kay and the staff clearly adored her for what she was doing. They also soaked up every detail she so freely shared with them and shared them with him.

"There's a lot to do," she replied, understating considerably. "We only have two weeks left." Dropping her cell phone into her purse, she crossed her arms over her open coat. "Why are you here so late? Kay said you and Mike are usually gone by five."

The self-protectiveness in her stance didn't go unnoticed. Preferring to ignore it, along with the way she no longer seemed interested in sharing details with him herself, J.T. motioned behind him. He'd just finished nailing fresh plywood over the gaping hole in the pale-green wall.

"I wanted to get that covered. I have to go to Seattle in the morning, so I won't be working this weekend." Since he'd begged off the trip to the Bahamas with his sailing buddies, he would use the next couple of days to take care of his own boat. The weather was supposed to hold over the weekend, a miracle this time of year in the Northwest. He would winterize *Renegade*, as he'd christened his forty-foot sailing sloop, and button her up for the season.

A canvas tarp covered the carpet where he stood. He saw Amy look from the power- and hand tools scattered over it to the boards hiding black pipes and studs.

"Are you almost finished?

"We're about halfway. We've replaced the cracked pipe and resealed all the joints, but we won't be able to do a final test for leaks and start repairing the walls until next week. It's doubtful anyone would unlock the door, but Kay didn't want to take any chances on one of the ladies getting in here and getting hurt."

He didn't want to take that chance, either. Amy felt certain of that as he looked toward the six silver-haired ladies more interested in watching them than *Jeopardy*. They were presently discussing whether to raise or lower the volume on the television. Harriet Bower still hummed at the picture of a forest on the wall, the aide at her side.

Apart from them, Edith Ross sat in a chair with a magazine in her lap.

It was Edith who received a quiet smile from Jared that would have melted most women's knees. The elderly woman was wearing only her reading glasses, though, so she wasn't able to see that far.

Amy looked back to the handsome lines of his profile. Edith had made him oatmeal cookies. Kay had mentioned that when Amy had come by Sunday. Tuesday evening she'd heard that several of the women, the cook included, had taken on his care and feeding.

"I hear you've been adopted."

His eyes met hers, silver-shot gray and suddenly, surprisingly uncomfortable. "Yeah," he murmured. "It's been…interesting. I've never had anyone think I'm their son-in-law or grandson before."

J.T. watched her peach-tinted lips curve. Frowning at himself, he pushed his hands into his pockets and forced his glance in the direction she'd been headed. Standing there thinking about how incredibly soft her mouth looked was not a particularly good idea. Especially considering what thoughts of that softness on his skin could do to the fit of his pants. Most especially with her watching him back.

She seemed okay with him. As uncomfortable as he'd made her with him the other night, he hadn't thought she would be. He wanted to keep it that way.

"You came to see your grandmother. I won't hold you up."

As if suddenly conscious of how she'd been studying him, Amy glanced over her shoulder, promptly looked back.

"Does she remember you? From the day you met her, I mean?"

He wasn't sure what he saw in her lovely brown eyes just then. Hope, maybe. Concern, for certain.

"What?" she asked, when he hesitated.

"She doesn't seem to."

He wished he could have offered a different reply. Hope had faltered. Still, she lifted her chin, gave him a brave little smile.

"I'll have to reintroduce you," she told him. "Just not now. She's tired in the evenings. That makes it harder for her to remember."

"Next time."

His eyes held hers.

"Next time," she echoed.

For a moment it looked as if there might be something else she wanted to say. Whatever it was, though, was dismissed when the sound of audience applause on the television was joined by the warbling tones of Arlene Newcomb's voice insisting that someone turn up the volume.

"Have a safe trip," she said quietly, and turned away, digging out her cell phone when it started ringing again.

She was halfway down the long hall when he saw her stop and turn with a smile that lit her entire face. Giving him a thumbs-up, she lowered the cell phone to her shoulder, said "We got Jeremy Walker," and lifted the phone to her ear once more.

He couldn't hear what she was saying as she continued down the hall, but there was no mistaking the animation in her body or in her smile when she glanced back toward him just before she disappeared inside her grandmother's room.

There was far more to Amy Kelton than first met the eye. Aside from the totally unexpected physical effect she had on him, that became more apparent to J.T. every time he came in contact with her. Out of her comfort zone, she seemed quiet, unremarkable, unassuming. There was still a certain innocence about her at times, but that vulnerability was belied by a kind of strength and quiet wisdom that went far beyond her years.

He'd also come to see in a hurry why Candace and Jill relied on her so much. In her element, she seemed relentless. Give her a project, she got it done. It didn't matter how much else she had to do, or what else was weighing on her. In the midst of everyone else's crises, she was the eye of calm competence. To them he suspected she was the glue they relied on to hold everything together. The people here now seemed to think of her that way, too. To him, she was more like a breath of fresh air.

He was halfway to Seattle the next morning when his curiosity got the better of him. He strongly suspected it was his own fault Amy wasn't talking to him about the fund-raiser. He'd made it clear he was there for his own purposes, which could easily make her think he didn't care about anything else. But he cared about what she was doing. And he didn't want information secondhand. Just because he intended to keep his hands to himself when he was around her, didn't mean they couldn't talk.

He punched her number into his cell phone. With his ear bud in his ear to keep both hands free, he passed a line of semis heading north on I-5. He'd expected Saturday-morning traffic to be lighter.

She answered on the third ring.

"Who's Jeremy Walker?"

He heard Amy laugh, the sound a little sleepy, but easy nonetheless.

"Just one of the best-known faces in Portland," she told him. "He anchors the evening news. He agreed to emcee the fashion show."

Jared glanced at the clock on the dashboard of his rented SUV. The carbon-gray Ford Explorer was a good, solid working-man's vehicle. With its Washington plates, it was easy to pass off as his own. He did actually own an SUV, a black Escalade that sat in his private garage next to his silver Jaguar and a classic blue Shelby Cobra he'd bought at a car auction last year for twice what it would have cost to rescue the home.

The clock read 8:36. "Did I wake you?"

"That's okay," came her sleepy reply. "I need to get up, anyway. I didn't mean to sleep so late. It was just nearly four when I got bed."

He hadn't seen her bedroom the day he'd gone to her home. Still, he could easily imagine her stretching beneath her sheets, shoving the long bangs of her short hair out of her eyes. The thought of the top sheet slipping away to reveal whatever it was she slept in threatened to put his imagination into overdrive.

Reaching for the coffee he'd picked up at a Starbucks drive-through, he lifted the container from the holder in the console. Imagining the shape of her breasts beneath cotton or silk honestly hadn't been what he'd had in mind when he'd placed the call.

He took a sip of the richly scented brew and nearly burned his tongue. Sufficiently distracted, he asked, "What kept you up so late?"

"Just stuff for the fund-raiser."

"Can you be more specific?"

"You want details?"

"That's why I called." One of the reasons, anyway. "I have a thing about wanting to know the details for something I helped inspire."

He'd been on the other end of the phone with her when the whole idea had been born. He was about to remind her of that when a rustling sound on the other end of the line made him think she might be propping herself up.

"In that case," she qualified, and went on to tell him that Eric, from her office, had been there working with her on the graphics for the event's ad campaign. Print ads for the newspaper, tickets. That sort of thing. Eric was donating his time away from the agency, she told him, but she needed to get the tickets printed. She just wasn't sure about approaching the printer the agency used.

Because he wanted to know why that was, she then explained Jill's initial concern that clients would feel the agency owed them a favor by coming on board to help with the fundraiser. That was when he learned that Amy hadn't asked anyone to help who she hadn't known personally.

"I'd wondered how that conversation had gone," he admitted, impressed by the scope and loyalty of her friends. "Is she still okay with what you're doing?"

"I don't know that she's okay with it so much as she's just ignoring it."

"As long as she's not making things harder for you."

"She's not," she replied, her voice softening at his concern. "I don't know what happened, but after we talked the other day, she didn't seem as resentful as she usually does of Edna. I don't mention the fund-raiser at work, anyway, so everything there is business as usual."

"Chaotic?"

"It's only semi-chaos. Some of the staff has been pulling all-nighters to meet deadlines, and Jill is finally interviewing receptionists. Oh, and Candace signed a major account she's been trying to land and they want everything yesterday." Her voice dropped as if she hadn't meant to get so chatty. "But you probably already knew that."

"Actually, I didn't."

He had only spoken with her stepsister once since he'd arrived in Portland. Candace had called last week while he'd been moving his bags and his laptop into the modest executive suite hotel that would have made his brother Alex proud. She'd told him she had names of property managers for some waterfront office spaces, and that she'd be happy to look at them for him since he hadn't found one he liked. She'd also given him the name of a designer to interview about pulling the space together and told him she'd be happy to set up the meeting for him, if he was interested.

His first thought had been that he didn't want to deal with Plan B for the next few weeks. Right on top of that had come the quick certainty that he didn't want her taking care of anything unrelated to the business he had with her. Outside the context of the ad campaign itself, he didn't want her doing anything that would make him feel he owed her somehow.

He hadn't bothered to wonder why that feeling was there. Going with his gut, he'd just explained that he'd put his office search on temporary hold for a while, said he'd be sure to call the designer when he needed one and asked her to please not use her time running around for him.

"Congratulate her for me, will you? So," he continued, feeling bad that the woman had gone to the trouble of tracking down the names of the property managers, "what's left to do to get your fashion show on the road?"

If Amy thought the change of subject abrupt, nothing in her

tone indicated it. Sounding almost relieved to move on herself, she told him the only things she could think of had to do with collecting what had been donated for the silent auction they'd added and the actual setup and run-through of the show. It was then that she went quiet.

"What?" he asked when her silence stretched.

"I was just thinking it sounds crazy, but I'm actually going to miss this."

"The constant running and demands on your time?"

"It seems I hardly have time to think, but, yeah."

"So why do you think you'll miss it?"

"I have no idea."

"Maybe it's because of that," he suggested. "Because you don't have time to think."

Her response was several long moments in coming. "Maybe," she conceded, though she didn't seem to care for the thought. Caution crept into her voice. "This is what you do, isn't it? Constantly stay on the run, I mean."

Put that way, he wasn't sure he liked the sound of it himself. "Pretty much."

"Do you like doing that?"

"It has its advantages."

She seemed to hesitate. "I can't decide if that's good or bad."

Not so long ago, he'd have immediately concluded that a hectic pace was a good thing. Even now he spent his evenings on his laptop working on whatever HuntCom problem had arisen that day and on the blueprints for the sunroom. Yet there was a subtle difference in all that activity. Working on those blueprints felt more rewarding somehow. And he found working with his hands during the day almost cathartic.

"Maybe it's neither," he said.

The rustling sounds came over the line again. "Well,

whatever it is," she insisted, lightness returning. "I hope you enjoy what you're doing this weekend."

"I'll do my best. I'm going sailing."

"You are?" Pure pleasure filled her tone.

He liked that about her; the uncalculated way she responded when something pleased her. Especially since she seemed so pleased for him now.

"Basically I'm just moving a boat that needs to be winterized," he told her, skimming past whose boat it was. "But I'll have a few hours to take it through the islands."

"If you see any orcas, say hi for me."

He chuckled, told her he would. Then spent the rest of the trip wishing he could have taken her with him so she could have seen the whales herself.

The next week passed in a blur for Amy. Midnight became her normal bedtime. Her cell phone felt like a permanent growth on her ear when she was outside the office. She didn't know what was going on with Jill, but the woman hadn't asked her to run any personal errands for her at all. She'd even arranged for her reupholstered furniture to be delivered herself, then stayed home the Saturday it was delivered to meet the truck rather than have Amy do it on her day off.

She still hadn't said anything about the fund-raiser, but Candace began casually asking how it was progressing. More specifically, she wanted to know how the repairs were progressing at the home.

Her interest would have seemed uncharacteristic to Amy had she not been so aware of the reason. She just didn't understand why her stepsister didn't ask Jared herself how much longer he thought the repairs would take—until she figured out that Candace was only trying to find out how often in a week Amy saw him herself.

She told Candace she hadn't seen him lately at all, and that she'd only spoken to him about the fund-raiser by phone. Because Candace's response had been a totally unenlightening "Oh," Amy had no idea what was going on with the two of them. She didn't want to know, either. It was none of her business.

What she did want was to keep her heart out of whatever her relationship was with him because it was entirely possible he could be around for a while. He was a client. The agency hoped to keep him as one, so he would be in the office on occasion. If he and Candace got serious, he could be around more often than that. She wouldn't have to worry about socializing with him, because she and Candace hardly ran in the same circles. But it was getting harder all the time to see him, which made no sense because, for the most part, he was so easy to talk with.

Unlike everyone else she knew, he knew that her job was something she did because she felt she had to. He knew her concerns about her grandmother increased every time she saw her. He knew about her life list, and that was something she'd never told anyone else about before. It as if he really knew her, really listened to what she said.

He'd called on his way back from Seattle to tell her he hadn't seen any orcas. It was the end of October and their migration season had pretty much ended. He'd seen a humpback at a distance, though. He'd taken a picture of it on his cell phone and wanted her e-mail address so he could send it to her. They'd spent over an hour talking about the different whales and their migration patterns, and about a wooded island he knew of where, every summer, a person could see a pod of orcas breeching a half a mile out. It was off that island that he'd seen the huge whale he'd photographed from one of its coves.

He'd also told her he had a problem with a project, so he wouldn't be back from Seattle until the middle of the week.

She hadn't doubted him for an instant when he'd said he needed a break. Yet, it seemed to her as the week wore on that he was working just as hard as he probably had before. Kay mentioned him getting calls on his cell phone that left him pacing the hall while he talked about work orders, moving personnel and rescheduling meetings. She didn't know when he worked on the blueprints for the sunroom, possibly on the evenings when he was in town, but Kay said he was still drafting them, too.

He'd already left Elmwood House when she stopped in Halloween night to bring her grandma her favorite chocolates. He'd worked the following Saturday to catch up from being gone, but that was the biggest single chunk of time she had all week to devote to the fund-raiser, so she hadn't seen him then. His SUV was there, though, when she rushed in Sunday morning to see her grandma while the older woman was still resting.

"Edna is in the greenhouse," Kay told Amy as they walked past the freshly drywalled wall in the community room. "She wanted to take in the mums from the side yard. I told her they would be fine in the ground over winter, but she insisted they'd all die. It was easier on her to let her dig them up and pot them in the greenhouse. She'll probably want to replant them outside tomorrow.

"Illogical behavior is normal. Just go along with her," she encouraged, aware of Amy's concern at the new development. "She's not hurting herself or anything else. She's happy. That's what's important."

It was cool outside and damp from the rains that week, but the sun was shining through the clouds and the golden and crimson leaves of the oak and hawthorn trees. Along the sides of the yard, chrysanthemums in yellow, rust, bronze and purple filled the beds below bushes of hydrangea and azaleas that wouldn't bloom again until spring. The deep lawn stretched like an emerald carpet to a small orchard of fruit trees.

Beneath an apple tree, one of the aides picked its red fruit with two gray-haired residents.

Uneasy with what Kay had told her, Amy tossed the end of her rust-colored scarf over the long sweater she wore with her jeans and low-heeled boots, and started along the concrete path that led to the glass greenhouse. She'd only taken a few steps before she noticed her grandmother by the sunroom extending from the back of the house. Wearing her pink gardening hat and a green sweat suit, she knelt on a pad in a flower bed by the hedgerow fence.

Amy had barely cleared the sunroom when she saw Mike the plumber by a load of wood near the sunroom stairs. A few feet away, Jared rested on his haunches looking under the wheelchair ramp.

Mike lifted his hand in greeting. She smiled back. As if he sensed rather than saw her, Jared went still a moment before he pushed himself to his feet.

She didn't know what Jared said to the middle-aged man in the baseball cap and flannel shirt. All she knew for sure was that she needed to ignore the way her pulse skipped when he started toward her.

"You have Mike working on the wheelchair ramp?" She watched him push his dark hair back from his forehead. He'd had a trim since she'd last seen him. Despite his work clothes, or maybe because of them, he still looked like an ad for *GQ*. Apparently, his stylist was in Seattle. "I thought he was a plumber."

"He is. But his wife split a few months ago, and Jeanette makes chicken and dumplings on Sundays. Helping me is his excuse to get a home-cooked meal."

She was sorry to hear about his wife. He seemed like a really nice guy. "He's working for food?"

He shrugged. "Not just any food. They feed us well here." His brow pinched, an odd hint of caution in his eyes as they moved over her face. "Aren't you supposed to meet the lighting guy this morning?"

"Not until eleven," she told him, wondering why that caution was there. "I thought I'd come see Grandma first."

The woman in the pink hat continued to dig in the dirt twenty feet behind him. A wheelbarrow sat beside her, along with a dozen containers filled with plants.

"She's been busy this morning," he told her.

"So I hear." Pulling her glance from the faded Seattle Mariners logo on his sweatshirt, she felt a smile form. "I also hear you've become the nonresident handyman."

J.T. watched her mouth curve. The breeze tugged her hair across one cheek. He pushed his hands into his pockets to keep from nudging it back. She looked tired to him. Pretty. But tired. Yet that weariness looked like more than the simple fatigue that came from the long days and nights he knew she'd been putting in. What he saw as he stood there with his eyes on hers was the kind of fatigue she was usually much better at masking. The kind that went clear to a person's soul and left her feeling alone even in the middle of a crowd.

He recognized that awful drain on her spirit only because he'd felt it so often himself. He'd never bothered to question why it plagued him. But he suspected why it taunted her. Even surrounded by people she was always there for, he didn't know of a single one who was always there for her. Her grandmother would have been had she been able, but after his conversation with Edna that morning, he knew the older woman was slipping even further away.

That knowledge only made him feel even more protective of her granddaughter than he already did.

"They were minor repairs," he conceded. "No big deal."

"They were a big deal to Kay."

"Young man?" Edna called.

Hitching his thumb behind him, he edged from the gratitude he truly didn't want. He was getting as much out of the deal here as anyone. "I'm being summoned."

Distracted by her grandmother, he watched Amy push back the hair from her cheek and fall into step beside him.

He truly hadn't done that much at all. Kay had mentioned a door that kept sticking and was difficult for the ladies to open themselves, so he'd shaved off a little wood. End of problem. A bookshelf had broken so he'd fixed that, too. Mike had helped him repair a couple of leaky faucets. He honestly didn't mind being their handyman while he was there. He liked the work he did at a drafting board, but he'd always enjoyed working with his hands. The more he worked with them now, the more he itched to pull out the plans he'd designed for the house he someday wanted to build on Hurricane Island. Before, he'd always thought he would contract out all the work. Now he found that he wanted to do what he could of it himself—if Harry didn't end up selling off the island to someone who wanted it for their own escape.

Shaking off the unwanted thought, he moved to where Edna pulled off her gardening gloves. Planting her hand atop the upside-down bucket beside her, she worked herself upright and started loading containers of plants into her wheelbarrow.

"Is that load ready to go?" he asked.

"It is," she said, setting a plant in with the others.

Amy's glance bounced from Jared to where her grandmother now narrowed her eyes to look intently at her. No sooner had Amy smiled and stepped forward to give her a hug, than that concentration faded and Edna turned her attention back to her plants.

"I used to have these at my house," she said, talking to

neither of them in particular. "My daughter loves the yellow ones. Even when she was little, yellow flowers were always her favorite."

Amy gave her a hesitant little smile. "You mean my mom, Grandma? My mom's favorite flowers were yellow?"

Behind her silver-rimmed trifocals, consternation flitted through her pale-blue eyes. Then, just as Amy thought she might do what she often did and get upset with herself for not remembering something, she lifted the flowers in both hands.

"These are as pretty as you are," she said, either changing the subject from her memory lapse, or having already forgotten what she'd been talking about. "Don't you think, young man?"

"Grandma…"

"Definitely," she heard Jared reply. "They're both very pretty."

"Are you her beau?"

"I'm her friend," he said without a moment's hesitation. "Let's get these into the greenhouse."

Without another word, her grandmother brushed at a streak of mud on her pants, handed him the plant she held and headed off, full-steam, for the glass greenhouse on the other side of the yard.

Amy reached toward the ground for two of the plants her grandmother had carefully split and repotted. "You've been helping her this morning."

Jared took the plants when she straightened and set them in the wheelbarrow with the others. "The aide over there has been helping the most. All I've done is provide muscle and answer questions."

"What kind of questions?"

"Just little things."

"Like what?"

"First, she wanted to know what day it was."

That wasn't unusual, Amy thought. Not as unusual as the way she'd just referred to her mother. "She's had a problem with that for a while. What else?"

Giving her a sideways glance, he added the last of the plants to the wheelbarrow. He didn't seem overly anxious to reply.

"Jared?"

"She wanted to know if her daughter was coming today."

"My mother?"

Amy didn't know what he saw in her expression as he carefully studied her face. Whatever it was caused a muscle in his jaw to jump a moment before his voice dropped. "Yeah. I thought I should warn you."

It seemed her grandmother had forgotten that her daughter had been gone for years.

"What did you tell her?"

"That she'd have to ask her granddaughter."

Amy lifted her chin, drew a long breath of the crisp fall air. She'd been warned that this sort of lapse could happen. She'd read about patients who forgot that people had died, or who mistook one relative for another. Intellectually she knew there would be more little losses. Losses that could come gradually or all at once. She knew there could be times when memory could return with amazing clarity, only to disappear the next hour. Or minute.

She just never seemed to be prepared when those losses or little gifts snuck up on her. Just now her grandmother had looked straight at her while she'd spoken of her only child. Yet, she obviously hadn't connected who Amy was.

Bracing herself, she gamely asked, "Anything else?"

The breeze feathered her dark hair across her cheek once more. Seeing all that quiet courage, thinking she looked badly in need of a pair of arms, he lifted his hand and tucked the strands behind her ear.

The softness of her skin had barely registered when he realized how instinctively he'd reached for her. He just wasn't sure if the need to touch had been there for her or for himself in the moments before he let his hand fall.

The breath she'd drawn at the contact seemed to ease out as her eyes shifted from his.

"Are you okay?" he asked

"I need to get used to things like this with her. So, sure," she said as if she had no choice anyway, "I'm fine…depending on what else she had to say."

"Nothing much, really." To keep from reaching for her again, he grabbed the handles of the wheelbarrow. "She just said she wanted to show her daughter the flowers," he told her on their way across the lawn. "By then Mike had come over to tell me he was going to the hardware store. She noticed his hat and wanted to know why it had a mountain embroidered on it."

Asking whatever was on her mind sounded just like her grandmother, Amy thought. Taking what comfort she could in that thought, she tried to not think too much of the gentle way Jared had just touched her. What he'd done was simply the gesture of what he had called himself. A friend.

"What did Mike tell her?"

"That the hat was a trophy. He bought it after he'd made the summit a few years ago on Mount Hood. I didn't know he was into climbing, so we got to talking about mountain-versus rock climbing and she seemed to forget everything but digging in her flowers."

"You like to climb?"

"You know how you've written down all the places you want to dive?" he asked. "I have a list of all the rock faces I want to scale."

"How many are on it?"

"A couple hundred."

Ahead of them, Amy saw her grandmother open the greenhouse door and disappear inside. "And you've climbed...?"

"About half of them."

Her glance moved to his profile and down the length of his hard, honed body. She'd seen pictures of rock climbers dangling from outcroppings hundreds of feet in the air, climbing like spiders, fingers and toes anchored in invisible nooks and crannies. She could only begin to imagine the sort of mental and physical conditioning such climbs must take. What she couldn't imagine was why anyone would want to subject themselves to such risk. One slip and the only thing between him and the ground was a rope and air.

At least diving, she could swim or float.

"You actually enjoy scaling cliff faces?"

"Love it."

"Why?"

Her total lack of comprehension brought a knee-weakening smile. "Because I can't think about anything but what I'm doing when the only things keeping me from breaking my neck are my own strength and a length of woven fiber." Seeming totally unimpressed with what he chose for a challenge, he nodded ahead of them. "Do you want to get the door?"

Still frowning, she pulled the door open so he could push the wheelbarrow inside the room-size space. It felt warmer inside the building from the sun shining through the glass, and humid from the hundreds of vegetable plants that crowded the long, waist-high tables like rows in a field. Her grandmother stood at an empty spot at one of those tables, waiting to direct the unloading of her uprooted mums.

Only half of Amy's attention fell on the woman who truly did look happy to be tending her little green charges. The rest remained on the man every member of the home's staff seemed to regard as kind, gorgeous and generous, but who, according to Kay, said very little about himself.

They probably had no idea that the man helping save the home and their jobs was an adrenaline junkie. He had to be to actually like the idea of dangling over a cliff. But she had the feeling from his response that there was far more to his search for adventure than the thrill of surviving it. He loved to sail, too, and to her sailing was both adventurous and peaceful. The dichotomy actually suited him. Either could be an escape for something missing from a person's life. Or, possibly, escape from whatever it was he'd told her he couldn't talk about.

She didn't want it to matter so much that he didn't feel he could confide in her about whatever that was. Especially since she'd confided so much in him. Already feeling at a distinct disadvantage where he was concerned, she really didn't need to stand there wondering if he'd unburdened himself to her stepsister.

"I'll take care of these," she told him, taking the plants he held out to her grandmother. "Thanks for helping her. And for telling me…" *about your conversation with her,* she wanted to say, but let the words trail off instead. She didn't want to talk about her grandmother with the woman standing right there.

"No problem," he said, seeming to understand, anyway.

Sensing she wanted time alone with her grandmother, or maybe just to gain distance from him, J.T. stepped back. "I have to take care of something in," New Delhi, he almost said, "Singapore," he explained, quickly catching himself. "So I won't see you before Saturday. Good luck with the fund-raiser."

A shadow of disappointment shifted over her face.

"Thanks," Amy said softly, masking the sudden letdown she felt. She hadn't thought for a moment that he'd be interested in attending the mostly female event. Still, part of her had wanted badly for him to see what he'd inspired.

Stifling that little wish, along with the infinitely larger ones she tried not to think about, she turned toward her grandma, then looked back to him. "Have a safe trip. Okay?"

He told her he would—and jammed his hands into his pockets before the weariness he'd seen before in her eyes had him doing something to mess up the status quo.

He was actually sorry he wouldn't be there to see what she had pulled off. In the past week, though, the New Delhi project had hit a bump that would be easier to smooth out on-site.

He left the women to their flowers, then left the home later than afternoon.

By eleven o'clock that evening, the corporate jet was waiting for him on the tarmac at Portland International.

It took nearly a week of wrangling over inspections and approval delays to get the project back on track, but the unmarked jet touched back down in Portland at 1:25 the following Saturday afternoon. Amy's event had started at 11:30.

At 2:00 p.m. sharp, he walked into the grand ballroom of the Kensington Hotel.

Chapter Nine

Music pumped energy into the air as J.T. stood at the back of the dimly lit ballroom. The room was filled with round, cloth-draped tables. With the eyes of the three hundred women seated at them trained on the runway slicing through the middle, no one noticed him looking for the woman who'd pulled the show together.

On the elevated runway, bright strobes of amber, orange and green flashed on a tall brunette in high boots and a skinny turtleneck dress. With a flip of her lengthy plaid scarf, she turned at the end the long platform.

Over the beat of music to strut by, the tuxedoed emcee at the podium waxed poetic about the colors of fall moving right into the holidays. As he did, the model disappeared through a tall wall of gauzy curtains behind him. The strobes on the curtains turned them from gold to shades of icy blue.

Checking out the backs of women's heads for short, dark

hair, he was about to ask a white-shirted waiter by the door if he knew the person in charge of the event when the curtains opened again.

Strolling out this time was a striking, middle-aged model in a shoulder-baring, green velvet dinner dress. With one hand on her hip and a glittery evening bag clutched in the other, she headed down the runway.

It had barely occurred to J.T. that the model looked familiar when he realized the woman was Jill. He recognized her from the photos he'd seen on Candace's office wall.

He wouldn't have been more surprised had the feathered mascot for the Seattle Seahawks been up there smiling his little avian heart out. She had to be the last person he would have expected to see here.

Or so he thought before she did an expert turn at the end of the runway, the curtains opened again, and Candace walked out. The tall blonde with the killer legs also wore a dress. Hers was low cut, red satin and hugged every curve. The way she was smiling, too, he almost expected mother and daughter to do a high five when they passed each other. Not that he could honestly imagine either of the sharp, sophisticated women actually doing that. But with the lights pulsing in time to the upbeat music, all eyes on them, they were clearly in their element.

Jill disappeared through the curtains. Another beautiful, long-haired brunette, this one wearing silver and looking all of seventeen, strutted out to that same beat.

Applause rose from the tables, nearly drowning out the emcee as the finale continued.

J.T. abandoned the thought of finding Amy. He had no idea what was going on with Candace and Jill being there, but as he moved to a set of closed double doors, he had the distinct feeling that his presence could easily interfere with whatever it was. He'd just wanted to make sure everything had gone okay, anyway, and maybe lend a little moral support if it hadn't. Since Amy clearly didn't need him around just then, he'd call her later.

By five o'clock that afternoon, he'd unloaded his bags, rolls of blueprints and his bulging briefcase from his SUV and moved himself back into the modest All-Suite Inn halfway between the home and downtown. He'd also dropped off his laundry at the cleaners, picked up what he'd left there the week before, and hit the grocery store for milk, cereal and antacids. He'd just left the inn for the car wash when he called her cell phone.

Aside from wanting her take on the fund-raiser, he wanted to make sure she'd be at Elmwood House tomorrow. The envelope on the seat beside him was for her. It held curriculum catalogs he'd asked his assistant to order from the universities closest to Portland with oceanography departments. Amy had said she was going to miss the demands on her time once her event was over. He didn't doubt that she'd find a way to fill that time doing something for someone else—or that someone else would fill it for her. But as protective of her as he was feeling, he hoped she would use whatever free time she now had to do something for herself instead.

He also had to admit to a more selfish motive for suggesting she take online classes or go to night school. He hated the thought of her being stuck at Kelton & Associates. He knew she needed the money she was paid. But he would take care of Edna's financial needs himself. In eight months, give or take a few days, his fate would be decided as far as staying with HuntCom or opening his own firm. Either way, he would no longer have to hide who he was and he could use his money however he saw fit. He'd drawn a blank on how to convince Amy not to worry about the money part right now, but he'd think of something. In the meantime, if he knew she was working toward her degree and would eventually be doing work she loved for a living, then he could leave her alone.

When she answered her cell phone, she sounded faintly breathless.

Music beat in the background. "Are you still at the hotel?" he asked.

"No. No," she repeated, the volume going down on the music. "I just got home."

"So how do you think today went?"

She sounded as if she might be grinning. "If you were here, Jared, I'd open this champagne," she said, apparently holding a bottle, "and toast your friend for his idea and you for talking to him to begin with."

For the first time in days, he felt a real smile form. "That good, huh?"

"That good," she echoed, sounding torn between relief and elation.

"So who are you celebrating with?"

"No one right now. I'm supposed to meet some of the people who helped me with everything in about an hour. I just came home to drop some stuff off and change clothes."

He glanced at the envelope on the seat. He could take it to her now. "Are you serious about the champagne?"

"Absolutely. It's still chilled."

"Then grab a couple of glasses. I'm five minutes from your house. In the meantime, tell me how you got Jill to model for you."

The quick silence on the line held a hint of surprise. "How did you know she did?"

"I saw her."

"You were there?"

"For the last few minutes of the show," he told her,

changing lanes to catch the next turn. The car wash could wait. "I left before it was over, but the place looked packed. Back to Jill, though. I wouldn't have thought she'd want any part of what you did."

Amy wouldn't have thought so, either. She told him that as she set down the bottle of champagne she'd just pulled from the box of silent auction bid sheets, extra programs and the thick notebook that, over the past several weeks, had become her bible.

If they hadn't been talking about what had happened with Jill, she might have paid more attention to the voice in her head reminding her that she needed more distance from this man, not less. But the need to share her little victories with him felt infinitely stronger just then.

There was no one else she could tell who would appreciate the size of the wall that had just crumbled. The people she'd be meeting for dinner had no idea that the wall with Jill had even existed.

"The show coordinator from the department store called yesterday to tell me two of the store models she'd lined up were down with the flu. Her backups were unavailable for a variety of reasons," she explained, on her way into the kitchen. "We were looking at huge gaps between clothing changes. The whole timing of the show was going to be ruined.

"Anyway," she continued, snagging a chair from her little bistro table on her way by. "I knew Candace would be perfect, if she was willing. But I didn't think she would be because she wouldn't want her mom unhappy with her. I knew Jill would be perfect, too, so I asked her if she'd ever done any modeling before I met her. To make a long story short, she never had, but she seemed flattered that I'd thought she might have. When I asked if she'd even consider modeling for the fashion show she said she'd be happy to."

"Just like that?"

"Not exactly." She climbed up on the chair, opened the cabinet over the refrigerator. She didn't own champagne flutes. Thinking wineglasses would have to do, she took two from the high shelf and set them on top of the fridge. "She asked if I really thought Edna didn't remember her," she told him, stepping down.

"I'd mentioned that probability to her," she explained, then went on to tell him about the conversation she and Jill had when Jill first learned of the fund-raiser. While she spoke, she moved the glasses to the counter and put the chair back. When that was done, she grabbed the bottle of leftover champagne a waiter had handed her and stuck the bottle in her refrigerator to keep cold while she searched for something to use for an ice bucket.

"After I told her I really believed that she doesn't have any memory of her, Jill didn't say much for a minute. She finally said she still hated what Edna had done, but that she wasn't hurting anyone but herself by holding on to her resentment."

Jared didn't sound at all impressed. "She's wrong."

"Excuse me?"

"She's wrong," he repeated, his tone utterly flat. "She's wasn't just hurting herself, Amy. What about how she's hurt you?"

Amy hesitated, wondering at the gruff note in his deep voice. "She acknowledged that. In her own way," she qualified, pacing now. "I was on my way out of her office when she stopped me at the door." Remembering, her voice softened. "She told me she was sorry Edna was losing her memory of me, too."

Those quiet, unexpected words had told Amy far more than that her stepmother felt bad for her. They'd said that Jill had really listened when Amy had admitted how badly she wished Jill could somehow let her bitterness go. Not only listened, but considered what she'd said.

"She owes you more than that."

"She doesn't owe me anything." The help she'd given her that day had been invaluable. She would have told him that, too, except he was talking even as she opened her mouth.

"Will this change your working relationship with her?"

"I can't imagine that it will." Outside, she heard the muffled slam of a car door. "She's already said that now that I have my life back, I can take care of a few things for her. The first item on her list is for me to get painting estimates for one of her rental properties." Because she had a feeling she knew what was coming, her tone turned insistent. "I know what you're thinking," she informed him. "And I'm not going to let you ruin my mood by getting into how much you think she's taking advantage of me. We've had that discussion."

"Discussing it now will ruin your mood?"

Leaving the glasses, she headed out of her kitchen. "Definitely."

"I wouldn't dream of discussing it, then."

Three short raps sounded on her door.

"Promise?"

"For now," she heard him say as she pulled the door open.

Jared filled the space on the other side of the glass storm door. A heavy crew-neck sweater stretched across his broad shoulders. Beneath it peeked the unbuttoned collar of his button-down shirt. With his cell phone to his ear, his eyes held hers. "So. How much did the fund-raiser make?"

She couldn't help but smile. "You'll never believe it," she said, talking to him through her own phone as she unlocked the storm door. "*I* can't believe it," she insisted, letting him pull the door open.

She stepped back, lowering her cell phone. He stepped in, snapping his shut.

Closing out the damp, late-afternoon chill, his eyes narrowed on her face. "Wow," he murmured.

The appealing sound of her laugh was soft, melodic. "Exactly. But I haven't even told you now much we made."

J.T.'s glance dropped to the belted black pantsuit defining her narrow waist, down to the pointed toes of the heels that put the top of her dark head level with his chin. Her face drew his focus once more. Smoky eye shadow turned her dark eyes sultry. Her already flawless skin looked as perfect as a porcelain doll's. Whatever she wore on her lush, pink-tinted mouth made it so shiny it looked wet.

"I meant you."

"Oh, this," she murmured, still smiling at she touched her cheek. "The models got hold of me. One of them said I needed cheekbones. Another said I needed to do my eyes. They started in, and this is how I wound up."

She liked how she looked. Loved it, actually, especially with the way Jared looked at her now. She just didn't love it enough to mess every morning with the dozen or so products the girls had stroked, patted and smoothed over her skin. As semifunctional as she was before she actually reached the office, eyeliner, mascara and lip gloss were all she cared to deal with before she headed out the door. The fairy godmothers who'd worked the little transformation had written down what they'd used, though. She'd asked for their ingredient list in case she ever conjured up a hot date.

Not about to bore him with all that, her attention caught on the large manila envelope in his hand.

"Ignore this. We'll talk about it later," J.T. said. He tossed the envelope on the entryway table. He wasn't about to dampen her mood, or rob himself of the warmth in her smile. She was the best thing that had happened to him all week.

"So how much?" he asked.

Her fragile features looked almost too perfect. Untouchable. But her warmth was back with the smile that seemed to light her from within.

"Nearly fifty thousand."

"Fifty?"

"Can you believe it?"

For a moment he almost thought she might launch herself into his arms. It was that kind of animation in her face as she self-consciously tucked her arms around herself and turned away. She made it to her living room with its cool blues and tall cylinder of tropical fish quietly bubbling near the sofa before she turned back.

The CD player she'd been listening to had been turned so low that all he could hear was bass.

"It was the silent auction that put us over the top," she told him as he walked toward her. "We had wonderful donations. There were actual bidding wars for some of the hotel getaways and the Botox and Thermage treatments. I haven't done a final tally on the walk-ins," she admitted as he stopped in front of her, "but we did it, Jared. We made enough to bring the mortgage current and pay for the repairs and the furnace. The home will even have a financial cushion for a while."

Casually pushing his hands into his pockets, he pulled his glance from the vee of soft-looking skin between the lapels of her jacket. "Have you told Kay?"

"I called her on the way home. She's…thrilled."

"I have the feeling you're understating considerably."

She shrugged, still smiling. "Maybe."

"Did she tell you you're amazing?"

The unexpected praise had her glance shifting from his.

"She should have," he told her. Caving in to the need to touch, he pulled one hand from his pocket and tipped up her chin. "Because you are."

Amy's breathing stalled. She should move, she told herself. It seemed there were a number of valid reasons why she should, too. With his tired gray eyes searching hers, the tips of his fingers slowly tracing the line of her jaw, she just couldn't remember what those reasons were.

"It's not like I did it alone. People were so generous with their time. And their expertise," she added, finding it hard to think with him touching her as he was. "Then there's what you and your friend did."

"None of it would have happened without you." He doubted she had any comprehension of the impact she had on people. It was an even bet that she didn't appreciate the impact she had on him. Just looking at her could make his whole body go tight. "So, when I say you're amazing, don't look at me as if the word couldn't possibly apply to you. Just say, 'Thank you,' and 'Yeah, I am.'"

The smile reappeared, only faint and with an embarrassed edge to it. "I can't do that."

"Sure you can." His thumb skimmed slowly over her bottom lip, drawing off the shine, leaving only softness. Hooked by her scent, by her, he felt inexorably drawn toward the temptation of her seductive mouth. "Just say, 'I'm amazing.'"

"Okay." With her pulse scrambling, Amy all but breathed the word. "You're amazing."

He went still. The instant he did, her heart stopped. Yet, instead of pulling back as he'd done before, his mouth curved inches above hers.

"Don't be obtuse," he murmured, and covered her mouth with his.

Her heart restarted with a jerk.

The feel of his lips was featherlight, the merest touch of skin against skin as he cupped her face in his hands. He had a beautiful mouth. It just had never occurred to her that something that looked so carved and hard could feel so exquisitely soft.

He brushed her lips again, her own parting to draw a shivery breath.

She never would have suspected, either, that the touch of his tongue to hers would literally rob the strength from her bones. Liquid heat seeped through her, pooling low in her stomach, melting any possible thought of doing anything other than leaning toward him. Needing him for support, she fisted his sweater in her hands.

Her breath escaped with a sigh as he gathered her closer. With one arm across her back, the other low at her waist, he drew her against the hard, honed length of his body.

She was finally where she'd wanted to be, where she'd fantasized about being since the moment he'd first held her. Except, what she'd imagined in her fantasies was nothing like the reality of being wrapped in his strength while their breath mingled and their bodies drew closer still.

She'd acknowledged before that she'd felt more being held by him than she had being kissed by any other man. In his arms she'd felt safe, protected. What she felt now was a kind of unfamiliar desire that might have felt a little dangerous had he not had her craving more.

A moan of longing slipped from her throat as she kissed him back.

J.T. drank that small sound and swallowed a guttural groan of his own. He hadn't expected the sharp need that had ripped through him at the tentative feel of her tongue tangling with his. He hadn't anticipated that one taste of her would annihilate his determination to overlook how badly he wanted her in his bed. With her curvy little body flowing toward him, her soft mouth responding to his, there was no way he could even begin to deny that in bed was exactly where he wanted her.

The admission barely registered before he felt tension slipping through her supple muscles. Lifting his hands back to her face, he eased his mouth from hers.

Confusion clouded her eyes in the uneasy moments before she lowered her head.

The quiet bubbling of the fish tank filtered through the pulse beating in her ears as Amy waited for her heart to slow. She felt stunned. Mostly what she felt was the strong and certain need to protect herself. She was in serious danger of losing her heart to this man—if she hadn't lost it already. And he was seeing someone else.

That, she remembered now, was one of the reasons she should have moved while she had the chance.

"What?" he asked, touching her hair.

The tenderness in the brush of his fingers was as compelling as the aura of quiet power that always surrounded him. Combined, that gentleness and his strength were decidedly hazardous to her emotional health.

With a small shake of her head, she stepped back. "I was just wondering what that was all about."

"What do you mean?"

She told herself to let it go. It was a kiss. He'd been happy for her, so he kissed her. Just because he'd altered her heart rate and his breathing in the process didn't mean anything at all.

She'd never been very good at lying to herself.

"Never mind."

"Don't do that, Amy." Over the guarded gray of his eyes, the dark slashes of his eyebrows merged. "What is it?"

She couldn't believe he had to ask.

"You're interested in my stepsister. Remember?"

J.T.'s breath escaped in a rush. A twinge of something that felt like guilt vied with the need for self-preservation. He was on totally unfamiliar ground here. There was no way he had imagined her response to him. Just as there was no mistaking the way she'd withdrawn from him now.

He'd thought he'd been interested in her stepsister, too. Seeing the beautiful blonde ad exec that afternoon had also jolted him into remembering that he needed to get back to the Bride Hunt before she lost whatever interest in him she'd had. Candace seemed to be exactly the sort of woman he'd told himself he wanted: sophisticated and just cynical enough to ultimately appreciate an advantageous marriage. Yet when he'd seen her—even wearing the red satin dress that had hugged her every curve—he'd felt nothing. Certainly none of the pull he felt just thinking about the woman so warily watching him now.

The irony of that physical chemistry wasn't lost on him. He'd known all along that Amy was off-limits. Even if she and Candace hadn't been loosely related, he knew that Amy needed and deserved far more than he could ever offer. She needed a man who believed in love and commitment and sharing. A man who could give her more than the shell of a marriage he would attempt for the sake of saving what mattered to him and his brothers.

He didn't even know what real love was.

The one thing he did know as he stepped back was that he didn't want to cause a problem between her and her stepsister. Especially now that it seemed she might have made headway with her stepmom. He knew family was important to her, even if they did take shameless advantage of her at times. With her grandmother's memory failing more by the day, what family she had might soon matter even more.

"That was your fault."

Her shoulders straightened. "My fault? You're the one who…"

"Kissed you?" he asked, when she hesitated. "True. But

you kissed me back. Look," he said, glancing at his watch. He didn't care about the time. All he cared about just then was that she was back to looking more confused than accusing. "You don't want to be late meeting your friends. I'd better take a rain check on the champagne."

He had no idea what she'd been about to say. Even as she opened her mouth, her cell phone rang.

"Go ahead and get that," he told her, motioning to where she'd left the instrument on the coffee table. He couldn't believe how he'd just complicated the situation with her. For himself, anyway. "I'll let myself out."

J.T. rarely had reason to concern himself with complications where women were concerned. Mostly because he'd never put himself in a position where difficulties might exist. He never made promises. He always used protection. And he never allowed a woman to get close enough to think their relationship had anywhere permanent to go. He'd encountered a couple of women over the years who put more meaning in a long weekend together than he'd ever intended, but for the most part, to his knowledge, he'd never done anything to complicate a relationship.

Until last night.

All he'd done was kiss Amy. Yet, he had the feeling the consequences of that bit of spontaneous combustion weren't going to simply disappear.

The thought only added to the agitation that had plagued him since Gray had phoned a few hours ago. The call had been about work, but his oldest stepbrother had mentioned that Justin was marrying the mother of his child. The wedding was the first week in December, three weeks away. It seemed Alex had someone in his sights, too. Gray wasn't even looking yet, but the pressure had just increased on them both.

Amy was standing behind him. He could feel her. Her presence added an entirely different edge to the restiveness that had returned in spades.

"Kay said you want to see me."

J.T. turned from where he stood by the repaired laundry room wall in the basement of Elmwood House. Setting his paint roller in the tray, he picked up the cloth draped over the ladder and wiped white enamel from his hands.

He had sensed Amy there, watching him. But even before he turned, what he'd sensed most was the caution he could now see etched firmly in her unadorned face.

He decided he liked her better with the more sophisticated makeup she'd worn yesterday. She looked too vulnerable without it.

"I wanted to know how you think Edna is today."

With her hands in the pockets of her open coat, Amy remained in the doorway. Jared had a streak of paint on his chambray shirtsleeve. It was his eyes she noticed most, though. Those guarded depths still betrayed fatigue. But then, he always looked tired when he returned from one of his trips. She knew, too, that he was pushing now to get his work finished here.

That was probably a good thing. The sooner he finished, the sooner he would leave.

"She seems the same as last week." She didn't want him being concerned about her grandmother. She didn't want him doing anything to jerk around with her heart, or her heart rate for that matter. The concern he always seemed to feel for Edna made it even harder for her to keep the distance she knew she needed to keep with him. "She's forgotten about her flowers, but she still thinks Mom is alive.

"So," she continued, before he could do something endearing and tell her he was sorry, "Kay said she invited you and Mike for Thanksgiving dinner next week." The director, who seemed ten years younger having all that stress removed, had told her she couldn't think of a more fitting way to thank the men than to share that holiday with them.

"She said Mike already accepted, but you told her you couldn't make it. I imagine you have family commitments."

Tossing the rag aside, J.T. walked over to where she stood. She wanted distance. That was evident by the way she hadn't even entered the room.

At the moment he wasn't sure what he wanted himself— other than for Harry to take a flying leap with his ultimatum. He wanted it all to be over. One way or the other. More than anything he wanted to go back to being simply who he was. No hedging. No evasions.

He jammed back the useless thoughts. He wasn't about to blow things for his brothers. One set of consequences at a time was enough to deal with.

"Actually, I avoid family gatherings whenever possible," he admitted, letting her know that much about who he really was. "I've never been much on holidays."

Something like sympathy swept through the caution. "I don't suppose you were," she said, considering. "It had to be hard without your mother there."

The cynic in him edged closer to the surface. Her assumption had hardly been the case. A man couldn't miss what a man had never known. Or so he wanted to believe. "That wasn't it. It had more to do with the stepmothers who did show up."

"Stepmothers?" The soft wings of her eyebrows rose. "How many times did your father marry?"

"Four. I only had two stepmothers, but his first wife showed up once in a while. There was always a battle about whether or not their respective sons would spend the holiday with them, or they would spend the holiday with us. I remember a lot of theatrics and tears."

He also remembered sitting alone in his room when he was young playing video games because there was no one wanting to be with him for the holiday. Not that Alex or Gray eventually wanted anything to do with their respective mothers' manipulations, or that J.T. ultimately bothered to care about being left out. Not having a mother had become an odd sort of blessing in those bizarre, dysfunctional scenarios. Still, for J.T. a holiday meal had come to hold all the appeal of a root canal.

"You have stepbrothers?"

Having revealed—and recalled—a little more than he'd intended, he let her query go with a flat, "I do."

Amy didn't know which to ask first; how many stepsiblings he had, where they were, if they were close. She settled for what bothered her most at the moment. "If you don't get together with your family, how do you spend Thanksgiving and Christmas?"

"Most of the time I work. That's what I'm doing this year," he told her, jamming his hands on his hips. "I'm leaving right after the ad presentation this week."

There was so much she didn't know about him, she realized. So much she wished she did know. Her second attempt to obtain a credit report and business information on him had yielded nothing. Candace felt certain that was because he'd worked out of the country for so long, and that the bulk of his assets were foreign. Candace had also said she'd look into it herself. As busy as Amy had been, it had been easy to let the matter go. All that had really mattered to her, anyway, was that Jared seemed to be an inherently decent and caring man who for whatever reasons seemed to bear his personal burdens alone.

She didn't want the empathy that came with that thought. She understood that kind of emotional solitude all too well. Yet he could have confided in her had he trusted her enough. Considering what little she truly did know of his background, it was entirely possible that he did have a confidant somewhere. For all she knew, he could have confided all she didn't know about him in her equally unrevealing stepsister.

Hating the twinge of envy she felt at the thought, she focused on what Kay had asked her to do. Since Jared had declined dinner, she wanted Amy to try to get him to stop by for dessert. She'd insisted that their celebration wouldn't be complete without him.

"You'll work Thanksgiving Day?" she asked.

"I'll be traveling that Thursday. I'm coming back to work the long weekend so I can finish up here. But I won't get in until late afternoon."

"Dinner is scheduled for three. Dessert will be around four."

The tension she'd noticed in him before seemed almost palpable as he slowly scanned her face. His handsome features seemed inscrutable, his thoughts too guarded for her to imagine. It was only when his eyes moved to her mouth and her heart bumped her breastbone that she realized where his mind had wandered.

"Where will you be?"

"Here. I always spend the day with Grandma."

His eyes lifted back to hers. She knew by the deep breath he drew what he was remembering. She was remembering it, too. Those sanity-robbing moments of heat she'd felt in his arms threatened to sabotage her common sense even now. It had only been a kiss. But that kiss had rocked her to her core.

She could only imagine what an incredible lover he would be.

"Then, I'll think about it," he said, and reached to tuck back the hair brushing her cheek.

"Jared, don't." She swallowed, stepping back from his touch and the awful longing she felt to be back in his arms again. "I can't do this. I don't know what you want from me. I don't know what you want from Candace."

He hadn't thought. He hadn't intended to touch her at all. "Amy…"

"Don't," she begged, her voice hushed as she stepped farther from his reach. "I care about you. And about her. But mostly right now I care about not having you jerk around with—" my heart, she almost admitted "—with me," she said, "while you figure out who or what you want."

The sound of the door opening met the thud of heavy boots on the stairs.

"I have to go," she told him, backing even farther from the tension that had his jaw locked tight. "Have a safe trip."

"Hey, Amy."

"Hi, Mike," she replied, making herself smile at the burly, good-natured plumber descending toward her. "Why are you working on a Sunday?"

"Chicken and dumplings."

She'd forgotten about that. J.T. heard her say as much just before she disappeared up the steps—leaving him to wonder what in the hell he thought he was doing.

By the time he'd left Kelton & Associates three days later, he'd finally figured it out.

Part of it, anyway.

Chapter Ten

J.T. had been in his hotel room less than half an hour when Candace reached him on his cell phone. She'd dropped hints about getting together after the presentation, which had been totally first class and everything he wanted, but she'd dropped the subject as soon as he told her he was leaving for Seattle that evening.

From the unfamiliar hesitation in her voice, he had the feeling the subject was about to come back up.

"…won't keep you but a minute," she was saying, only to give a faintly exasperated sigh.

He could hear Amy's voice in the background. He just had no idea what she said in the moments before Candace returned to the line.

"I'm so sorry, Jared. Could you hold for just a second, please?"

Amy had been out of the office when he'd arrived for his

presentation that afternoon. Heather, the agency's new auburn-haired receptionist had greeted him with the enthusiastic sort of professionalism that clung like a caffeine high to many of the KA associates. He liked that energy. It got work done. She hadn't been able to tell him when Amy was expected back, though. Neither had Candace when he casually asked if her stepsister was around.

To her credit, Candace had been profuse with her praise for how skillfully Amy had handled the fund-raiser. She even told him she'd suggest to her mother that they put Amy in charge of all their clients' publicity events.

"Only if you give her a staff of her own," he'd said, then watched her blink her baby blues at him as if she hadn't a clue why that would be necessary.

"I'm sorry," he heard her repeat. "A client needs to change her ad before it goes out it the morning." That conclusion was accompanied by another sigh.

"Anyway," she continued, brightening, "I was just thinking. You said you'd be back Thanksgiving afternoon. We always go to my grandparents' house for dinner... my mom's mom and dad," she explained, "so why don't you join us? They always have a crowd. My grandfather is into the art scene," she told him, "so you'd meet lots of interesting people. You might even make some profitable business connections," she added, sweetening the deal. "We don't sit down until six. You'd be back by then, wouldn't you?"

J.T. walked past the muted talking head on CNN and added his shaving kit to his leather duffel bag. Connections or not, he would decline.

"I don't know for sure what time I'll be in," he replied, telling her what he'd finally told Kay. He just hoped she'd accept the response and not press. He had no desire to get into how he avoided holidays and the baggage that came with them. Not again. And not with her. "But thanks for the offer. I appreciate it."

"No problem," she murmured. "Just thought I'd ask. Except for today, I haven't seen you in a while."

He hedged. "We've both been busy."

"I know." She all but sighed the words. "You should have some free time soon, though, shouldn't you? You bought drinks the last time. It's my turn."

J.T. came to a halt halfway between the closet and the foot of the bed. Closing his eyes, he pushed his fingers through his hair, expelled a long, low breath.

He didn't want to do this. He didn't want to meet for a drink. He didn't want to pretend to care about her so she'd care about him enough to marry him. She was pleasant, educated, undeniably attractive and her career would keep her busy enough—unless, as his wife, she decided she had no need to work. But that point was moot.

He felt nothing at the thought of seeing her. To be fair to her, he could no longer let her think he was interested in her as anything other than a business associate.

"It's going to be a while before I have any free time," he told her, skipping over mention of the drink, hoping she'd take the hint. "After I get things wrapped up at the home, I'll be leaving the country again. I've been away from that project way more than I should have been."

"Of course." Professional to the core, Candace's tone dropped only a couple of degrees. "I understand completely. I'll see you then for final approval on the ads sometime in April or May. We need at least a three-month lead for the magazines."

"Sounds good. And, Candace," he said, too relieved that she'd made it easy to quibble about timing. His name would have to be changed in those ads, but he couldn't do that until

July. He didn't want the press discovering Plan B unless he actually had to use it. "Thanks again for the campaign. You and your team nailed it."

She told him she was glad he liked it. Moments after that, she'd said goodbye and he was off the phone.

The reprieve he felt lasted mere seconds. It leaked out along with the breath that puffed his cheeks and lowered his knotted shoulders. The pressure was off to work something out with Candace, and he wasn't going to even think about the Bride Hunt until after the first of the year, but he had no idea what he'd do after that. The whole premise felt wrong. Even more so now that he'd attempted to implement it. He could hedge and evade with the best of them. But he wasn't comfortable with outright deception at all.

He wasn't going to worry about that little dilemma right now, though. He needed to finish packing and get himself up to Seattle. He had meetings with his design team and with the city planning department lined up for the next couple of days. His first appointment was at nine in the morning. Next week, he had meetings with Gray on the potential Singapore project. He'd then head back to Portland to finish up at the home.

He figured it wouldn't take more than a few days to complete the small expansion he'd made to the sunroom by knocking out an interior wall to an unused storage area. The larger expansion, the one that required a building permit to extend into the yard, would have to wait for better weather next summer. Kay thought the money for that would come out of the profits from the fund-raiser. Like Edna's care, when the time came, he'd cover the cost of it himself.

He swept one last glance around the nondescript but functional room. Not seeing anything he'd forgotten, he grabbed bags, blueprints and briefcase.

Then he thought of Amy.

She had deliberately avoided him that afternoon. There was no doubt in his mind about that as he headed out into the rain. If she didn't want to see him now, that was fine. But he would see her when he returned. Before he walked away from her, he needed her to know that he wasn't the kind of guy who played two women against each other. That had never been his intention. He couldn't tell her what his intentions toward Candace had been without having her think him an even bigger louse than she probably already did. But it was imperative that she know he had never intended to cause her any trouble.

He'd never talked to her about going back to school, either. She might think it none of his business, but someone had to tell her she needed to do something for herself for a change.

Jared was right.

Amy conceded the thought as she followed the beams of her headlights along the dark, rain-slicked street. The slap of her windshield wipers competed with the rushing air from her little Honda's heater.

In the five minutes since she'd left her grandmother watching *Home for the Holidays* after Thanksgiving dinner, she'd come to two conclusions. She truly missed the woman her grandma had been. She missed her wit, their long conversations and just being with someone who really knew and cared about her. And Jared was right about her having put her future on hold.

She had opened the envelope he'd left on her entry table—the one he said they could discuss later—the evening he'd left it there. The moment she'd seen the university catalogs with their respective oceanography departments marked with paper clips, she'd known what he'd wanted to talk to her about.

Her first reaction had been that she didn't have time to go back to school. Not with the obligations she had. But even as she started to close the door on the thought, the part of her that wanted more, needed more, had kept it open by a crack.

Now, fighting the effects of a bittersweet day and thinking of what Kay had said at grace about the home having its future back, she had to acknowledge that there might not be anything in her own future but more of the same if she didn't lay the groundwork for changing it now. If she went to night school or took classes online, she could at least complete everything but the classes requiring on-site labs. She would just have to talk to Jill about not scheduling whatever it was she needed done for her on a class night.

There was something else she needed to do, too. She needed to thank Jared. She wouldn't even be considering the idea had he not totally ignored her rationale and brought her the catalogs. She just wished she hadn't fallen in love with him. There wasn't a doubt in her mind that she had, either. She'd just had no more business doing that than she did feeling as if he'd let her down.

She'd known all along how urbane and worldly as he was. For all she actually knew about him, he could have women in Seattle and Singapore and she and Candace were just diversions while he was here. Candace herself had been known to see several guys at the same time with varying levels of interest. Considering that, it was entirely possible that they had some sort of understanding. Amy just hadn't had the impression that her far more sophisticated and experienced stepsister had been interested in anyone but Jared since he'd shown up at their office door.

Still, despite the fact that she'd done a miserable job of protecting her heart, she needed to thank him. Yet again. Or so she was thinking when a loud bang accompanied the jerk of her steering wheel. Every nerve in her body had jumped when her car started thudding along the dimly lit street.

She knew to ignore her first instinct and not slam on the brakes. She'd figured that out when she'd had a flat last year and just missed having the truck behind her skid into the back of her car. According to the nice officer who'd helped her change her tire, the second thing a person needed to keep in mind was to maintain a firm hold of the steering wheel. Since she already had it in a death grip, she had that covered, too. With no cars behind her, her initial startle calming, she let the car slow on its own and eased to a stop under a streetlamp.

To her right was the dark, open space of a golf course. To her left rose a hill of shrubs and trees that formed a barrier between the street and the business park beyond it. At five o'clock on Thanksgiving those businesses would be closed.

Up ahead, she saw nothing but the dark that had fallen half an hour ago, and little circles of illumination from the streetlamps disappearing in the distance. The view behind her appeared equally deserted.

The bad news was that the early-evening traffic on a holiday seemed to be a tad light. The good news was that her discouragement over her grandmother had been startled into submission.

"The end to a perfect day," she muttered, and pulled her cell phone and wallet from her purse. Finding her auto club card, she punched out its phone number and sat on hold for five minutes listening to the rain on her roof before a dispatcher came on the other end of the line. When he did, he told her it would be three to four hours before anyone could get to her.

She thanked him and told him she'd change it herself. She knew how to change a tire. She just didn't want to get out in the rain and do it. What she wanted and what she got were rarely the same, though.

Figuring it futile to sit there hoping some Good Samaritan

would happen by and rescue her, she killed the engine, un-fastened her seat belt and pulled the lever that opened her trunk. It wasn't raining hard. At least, not as hard as it could have been. She couldn't sit there and wait for it to stop, anyway. This was the Northwest. It might not let up until June.

Wrapping her hoodless trench coat around her, she headed for the back of her car and lugged the spare tire from its well under the mat. She had it leaning by her decidedly flat right rear tire when she realized why the tire hadn't seemed very heavy.

It was the tire that had picked up a nail and gone flat last year. She'd intended to get it fixed, but that had been the week she'd manned a hospitality suite after work at a local convention for Jill. With the other tire serving her purposes just fine, the repair had totally skipped her mind.

Annoyed with herself for forgetting, at the tire on the car for blowing out and the timing in general, she'd started to haul the other tire back to the trunk. Just as she did the rain turned to drizzle, that heavy kind of wet that didn't lean to one side or the other, but came straight down and totally soaked everything it touched.

Cold rain seeped through her hair to her scalp as she hoisted the tire back in. She could feel it on her neck as she wiped her hands on the utility towel wrapped around the jack and slammed the lid of the trunk. By the time she jumped back inside her car, water was running in rivulets down the side of her face.

Now chilled and wet, and with at least a three-hour wait ahead of her if she called the car club again, all she wanted was a ride home.

Hoping they wouldn't mind her interrupting their holiday, she called her next-door neighbors. She got their answering machine.

Her neighbor on the other side was away for the long weekend. So was the couple across the street. Jill and Candace would be at Jill's parents' house an hour across town. She wouldn't bother them, anyway. They'd be sitting down to dinner soon.

Even with the heater blasting, she shivered. Her flats were soaked, her feet wet. Her hair and the collar of her turtleneck were drenched. She knew Jared should be back about now, but as torn as she was about him, she regarded him as her last resort.

The drum of rain on the roof grew louder.

It was now officially pouring.

Droplets shed from the sleeve of her coat as she picked up her cell phone from where she'd left it on the console. Just because she'd made the mistake of falling in love with the man didn't mean he couldn't come give her a ride. It wasn't as if he ever had to know how she felt about him, anyway.

J.T. had left Seattle later than he'd planned. When his cell phone rang and he noticed "Kelton, AE" on its little blue screen, he was just north of Portland.

"How did the dinner go?" he asked.

"You were missed," he heard her reply. "But that's not why I'm calling." A quick hint of indecision entered her soft voice. "Are you back in Portland yet?"

"I'm about twenty minutes out. What's wrong?"

"I have a flat tire." Resignation slipped into her tone. "If you don't mind, I could use a ride home. The auto club can't get here before eight or nine o'clock. "

He could feel himself frown. Beyond his windshield wipers, the luminous stripes on the freeway flashed by. "Where are you?"

She told him she was by the golf course a couple of miles from her grandma's. He knew where that was. The area was considered safe, but he also knew there were no houses or businesses along that particular stretch of roadway.

"Are your doors locked?"

"They are."

"Is there much traffic?"

"Not really. But I'm okay," she insisted, sounding as if she wouldn't admit being otherwise anyway. "Or will be when I can dry off."

He didn't like her sitting in her car in the dark alone, even if was early in the evening yet. Wanting to keep her on the line until he reached her, he asked why she was wet and learned about her flat spare tire and how she'd forgotten to get it repaired. That reminded him of her front bumper.

"Since you never took care of your spare, what about the dent in your car? Did you ever get that fixed?"

She hesitated. "I've been busy," she reminded him.

"I'll take that as a no."

Her comment this time was silence.

He'd already sensed the same guardedness that had been there the last time he'd seen her. Because of that, J.T. honestly hadn't much cared what they talked about. He'd just wanted to keep her talking to him. But now seemed as good an opportunity as any to bring up one of the two subjects he'd intended to discuss with her before he left again. She'd just reminded him of her tendency to put everyone else's needs ahead of her own.

He hoped she'd be more receptive to this particular conversation now than she'd been the night of the fund-raiser. Then she'd said that it would ruin her good mood. Since her present mood probably wasn't all that great, he figured she didn't have that much to lose.

"You know, Amy," he began over the beat of his windshield wipers, "forgetting to fix a flat because you were busy taking care of something for Jill isn't anything by itself. Neither is not fixing a dent because you've been tied up with that fund-raiser for the home. But it's always going to be something.

You're always going to be too busy taking care of someone else to take care of what you need to do for yourself."

He fully expected her to protest his assessment. At the very least, he thought she might try to change the subject.

"I know," she admitted, her voice hushed.

It was his turn to hesitate. "And?"

"I'm going to night school."

He'd never met anyone else who could catch him so off guard. At the moment, though, he was more interested in the relief he felt at her decision. He just wasn't sure which pleased him more. That she would give herself a shot at her dream, or the way some of her reserve seemed to fade as she thanked him for the catalogs. She knew he had a lot going on, she told him, so she especially appreciated his taking time to get them for her.

He didn't want her thanks or gratitude. After admitting that his assistant had tracked them down, all he wanted was to know when she planned to start.

They were still talking about the logistics of taking the classes that required her to be on or near the ocean when he finally saw her little black sedan sitting alone in the rain under a streetlight.

Making a U-turn because he'd come from the opposite direction, he pulled up behind her and leaned across the seat to open the passenger door. She was already out of her car, stuffing her cell phone into her coat pocket as she hurried through the rain to his SUV. Seconds later she was inside, slamming out the downpour.

"You're not wet," he said the moment the door closed. "You're soaked."

"Only a little."

She had a true gift for understatement. In the brief moments the interior light had been on, he'd noticed dark patches of damp across the shoulders and down the sleeves of her coat. The fabric looked to be water-repellent, but not waterproof. What he'd noticed most was her hair.

In the green glow of the dashboard lights, he watched her comb back that wet, dark silk with her fingers. "Are you warm enough?"

Her glance made it as far as his chin. "I'm okay," she assured him, "Thanks for getting me."

"Not a problem."

The reserve was back. She'd barely made eye contact with him before her focus landed on her knees.

"So," he said, refusing to let her lapse into silence as he pulled away from the curb. "We were talking about you asking Jill for the summer off next year to take one of the diving labs."

"Right," she murmured, and picked up where they'd left off by telling him she had no idea how Jill might respond to that request. She then worried aloud about whether coming home on weekends to see her grandmother would be enough to keep her somehow in her grandma's memory.

The conversation seemed normal for them. It was just the ease they'd once had that was missing. There was no mistaking the faint tension J.T. sensed in her. It was in the way she held herself as they continued to talk. And in the way she sought the darkness outside the passenger window when silence finally fell between them. He didn't doubt that the stress of Edna's continuing decline caused part of that disquiet. She seemed especially disheartened by it tonight. Yet, by the time he pulled up to her house and he'd hustled her up her front steps, there was no doubt that the bulk of that unease was because of him.

"I said you didn't need to get out," she told him, unlocking locks while he held the storm door open for her. The porch overhang sheltered them from the rain. The worst of it anyway. It beat down hard, bouncing up from the walkway and steps behind them. Her breath drifted off in a fog. "I can see myself in."

J.T. had heard what she'd said when he stopped the SUV and climbed out. He'd just chosen to ignore it. "I want to talk to you."

"We've been talking."

"Not about this."

In the pool of light on her front porch, he watched her push open her Bristol-blue door. The moment she stepped inside and flipped on the entry light, she turned to face him. The lamps she'd left on by the sofa spilled brightness into the comfortable room behind her.

"About what?" she asked, as he walked in and closed out the chill.

Her guarded features seemed even more delicate without the thick, dark bangs that usually covered her forehead. A lock of still-damp hair curved by her ear. The rest looked as if she'd shoved it back with both hands to keep it from sticking to her skin when she'd first escaped the rain.

The shoulders and sleeves of her long coat remained stained with moisture. The wet she'd added to it on her way in, now dripped onto the small patch of parquet flooring where they stood. He added his own little puddle to the floor from his brown leather bomber jacket.

"Dry off first," he suggested, wiping off his boots on the sisal entryway rug. "You're cold."

Amy was about to tell him she wasn't all that cold when the warmth of the room made her shiver. Standing there in her wet shoes, goose bumps forming everywhere, she looked from the disquieting determination in Jared's expression.

Since he hadn't taken the hint in the car, she'd try a different approach.

"I really appreciate the ride," she told him, toeing off first one ruined brown dress flat, then the other. "But you're just getting back into town, so I shouldn't keep you. You're probably tired," she pointed out, unfastening her coat. "And I know there's a lot of work to do at the home tomorrow. I imagine you want to start early."

She didn't want to sound ungracious. She truly did feel hugely grateful to him. The man had just saved her a semi-miserable wait in her car. Still, all she wanted now was a hot shower—and for him to not be so close. After the dispiriting day she'd had with her grandma, the latter more than anything. She was badly in need of a pair of arms.

Since he wasn't moving, she created distance herself by heading for the coat tree by the staircase. She'd just started to take off her coat when she felt its weight being drawn from her shoulders.

"I'm not tired." Taking the wet garment, Jared hung it on the brass tree himself. "And I'm not going anywhere until we talk. You can start by telling me why you want to rush me out of here. You might want to get out of those first, though."

Water droplets sparkled in his dark hair as he nodded to her feet. Following his glance, she looked down at the choco-late-brown tights she wore with her tweed jumper and turtle-neck. Rainwater had soaked both feet through.

She skimmed a glance as far as the placket of his thermal knit shirt. "I'm not trying to rush you."

He didn't respond to her feeble denial as she turned. She could, however, feel him frowning at her back while she headed across the carpet in her living room.

In the reflection of her dining room windows, she could see him shrug out of his own wet jacket. Shivering again as she entered the hallway and flipped on the overhead light, she reached into the bathroom and snagged a towel from the rack. Catching her own reflection in the mirror over the sink, she groaned.

He must have heard her.

"Are you okay?"

No, she thought, *I'm not. I'm cold. I look like something the cat wouldn't even bother to drag in, I feel like crying and I wish you'd go away.*

"Amy?" he asked, his voice closer.

Taking the towel, she walked out, running it over the back of her hair. She'd get out of whatever was wet after he left.

"You know, Jared, now really isn't a good time."

"Fine," he said, giving in a little too easily. "Just tell me why you want to get rid of me and I'll go."

"I never said I wanted to get rid of you."

"You haven't had to."

"Jared…"

"Talk to me, Amy."

"There's nothing to talk about."

"Not true." His eyes held hers, unwavering. "There's a problem. I want you to tell me what it is."

Chapter Eleven

J.T. suspected he already knew what Amy's problem was. As she stood in the space between her living and dining rooms looking none too comfortable with him, he just wanted to make sure nothing else had cropped up that he'd need to deal with.

When no response was forthcoming, he decided to help her out.

"Is it because you think I'm playing you?"

Amy blinked at Jared's bluntness. The unnerving man filling the space a few feet away was nothing if not direct.

Telling herself she might as well be direct, too, she held her towel against the belt of her jumper and crossed her arms over the thick blue terry cloth.

"I'd say that's pretty much it."

"That's all?"

"Don't you think it's enough?

"Maybe you don't," she admitted, thinking how incredibly

naive she must sound to him. She sounded naive even to herself. "I am so not in your league, Jared. I'm not even close." She'd known that from the moment she'd met him. The knowledge hadn't stopped her from wanting the impossible, but she'd at least never fooled herself into believing she had any sort of a future with him. "It's obvious why you're attracted to Candace," she conceded. "What I still don't understand is what you want with me."

His eyebrows merged. His voice went utterly flat. "You're serious."

"Why do you say it like that?"

"Because you really don't have a clue, do you?"

"About what?"

The moisture in her hair teased out the scent of her shampoo. Or maybe it was the scent of her skin that drew him closer. If her confusion was any indication, the pretty woman who looked a bit like a street urchin at the moment honestly had no idea what she did to him. What she was doing right now, simply being so close.

Wanting to ignore the way his body tightened, he said, "About you. About me and your stepsister." That was the issue that needed clarification most. His inability to be with the younger woman without wanting to touch her was his problem. "There isn't anything between us. There never has been."

"Jared, please," she muttered.

"We had a drink together. That's all. I never took her out after that. I never even called her unless we had business to discuss."

Pure skepticism lurked in her weary eyes.

He hated that the doubt was there. He had no idea what Candace might have said about him, or what impressions she might have given anyone about their relationship. He did, however, get the sense that the woman watching him so warily assumed there was far more than had actually existed.

His eyes narrowed. "Just how involved do you think we were?"

"I honestly don't know." Her glance shied away. "I just know you both seemed really...interested."

"I was interested. At least, I thought I was." He just couldn't confide the nature of that interest. Not without creating huge problems for himself and complicating the hell out of the immediate situation. "But I never even kissed her. Never," he repeated when she looked up in confusion.

"I'm far from being lily white, Amy. But I don't cheat on a woman when I'm seeing her." That was what he'd needed to tell her before he left next week. He hadn't bothered to wonder why it seemed so important that she know that about him. He'd left women with less than favorable impressions before. Sometimes the circumstances were his own fault. Sometimes not. There was just something about this particular woman that wouldn't let him leave with her thinking he'd tried to take advantage of her.

"Just in case you think I have someone else stashed somewhere," he added, an edge of self-defense in his tone. "I don't."

The only woman he was interested in was her. No one else.

The silent admission caught him unprepared. So did the absolute truth in it as he watched her struggle to reconcile what she'd thought with what she now knew. She looked entirely too vulnerable standing there hugging her towel, too exposed by the confusion she didn't have time to mask.

Mostly, she looked entirely too tempting.

A muscle in his jaw jerked. He should go. He'd said everything he'd needed to say. Almost.

"This wasn't something I thought we should talk about at the home," he said, explaining why he'd been so insistent just now. "Since I'll be out of here in a few days, I didn't want to leave with you thinking I was jerking you around."

For a moment Amy felt too disconcerted to speak. She didn't doubt a word of what he'd said. As he'd systematically shattered her assumptions, he'd looked and sounded as adamant as he had when she'd suggested he'd make more points with Candace working on a project more visible than the home. He'd made it clear then that he wasn't trying to make points with anyone. All he'd been thinking about was his own need for escape.

She'd often wondered since then if he'd actually found it.

She wondered now if she could find a convenient hole to crawl into.

"I don't know what to say," she confessed. "'I'm sorry I thought you were being a jerk' seems a little inadequate."

A faint smile tugged one corner of his mouth. "As long as you believe me, I'll take it."

"I do. And I am sorry. I just didn't know what else to think."

"Don't worry about it." He nodded to the towel. "Go get yourself dried off. I can let myself out."

"Wait," she said, before he could take much more than a step.

Awkwardness gave way to a whole new sort of disquiet. Two minutes ago, she'd desperately wanted him to leave. Her home. Portland. Now the part of herself she'd been trying to protect needed far more time.

"When do you have to leave?"

"I don't have to go anywhere until the first of the week."

She lifted her chin, tried for a smile. With one more loss piling onto her day, she had a feeling the smile didn't work. "I think I'm really going to miss you."

Her guileless admission tugged J.T. back. He didn't want to leave, either. Not her, anyway. With her looking so susceptible to him, he just couldn't remember why he'd told himself it was best for her if he did.

Certain it would come back to him, he lifted his hand, tucked back a drying tendril of her hair. Her weary words only made leaving now that much harder. "Don't say that," he murmured.

The way her head moved almost imperceptibly toward his touch didn't help, either. Neither did the effort he'd seen behind her smile.

That struggle had hit him like a fist.

"What's wrong?" he asked.

The high, snug collar of her sweater was still fairly wet. As she shook her head, so was the feel of the hair behind her ear when it brushed against his hand.

"It's nothing." Nothing she wouldn't get past, she might as well have said.

He brushed the underside of her jaw with his thumb. "Try again."

At his quiet command, she gave a tired little shrug. "It won't sound logical," she warned him softly. "It's just that right now feels a little like it does when I'm with Grandma. You're standing right here. And we're talking to each other. Yet, I miss you as if you're already gone."

Two months ago what she'd just said wouldn't have made a bit of sense to J.T. Now, he understood completely.

The thought that she might miss him that badly tugged hard at something deep in his chest. With that unfamiliar yearning furrowing his brow, he cupped his hand to her shoulder.

"How was she today?"

That was one of the things she would miss most about him, Amy thought. He was one of the few people who asked about Edna as if he really cared about what he heard.

She only hoped he wouldn't stop touching her. That made little sense considering how that small contact tightened the knot behind her breastbone. But she couldn't deny how badly she needed the concern he'd always seemed to have for her. "She enjoyed getting dressed up."

"But...?" he prodded.

The simple weight of his hand on her shoulder made her want his arms even more. Her grandma wanting to wear a dress and jewelry had been about the only positive she'd been able to find. "Even with the turkey and everything on the tables, I don't think she ever got that it was Thanksgiving. She spent most of the time in the community room waiting for my mom." The strength disappeared from her voice. "She thought Mom was coming to pick her up for lunch."

Her hushed admission deepened J.T.'s frown. But it was the look in her eyes that made him forget to recall why he'd meant to leave her alone. He'd seen that same expression whenever she was faced with something about Edna over which she had no control. She always sought to make the best of the situation despite that lack. Only this time, she couldn't seem to hide the sadness she usually tried to mask along with all the other disquiets she handled on her own. That inability could have been because the day had been a long one for her, though he knew she'd had much longer. It could have been because she was standing there damp and bedraggled.

It could have been any number of reasons, he supposed. But all he knew for certain was that he couldn't let her stand there trying to be strong all by herself.

With a tug of his hand, he drew her closer.

"Then after that," he said, continuing from where she'd left off as he slipped his arms around her back, "you got a flat on the way home." She offered no resistance. She simply moved into his embrace while he spoke and fisted his shirt in her hands. "This sounds like one of those days you mentioned that builds character."

With her forehead resting against his chest, Amy nearly sighed in relief. Finally folded in his arms, she sank into the delicious warmth of his strong, hard body. As she did, she closed her eyes. If she imagined hard enough, she might be able to recapture the too-brief sense of security she'd experienced in his arms in the elevator. She'd give anything for even a glimpse of that feeling right now.

"Those are weeks," she reminded him.

"Right," he said against the top of her head. "Bad days. All you get out of them is that they get better."

Hers definitely had. Surrounded by his strength, she could practically feel the tension drain from her body, easing away the more awful parts of the day. "I can't believe you remember that."

J.T. brushed the crown of her head with his lips, felt the slight weight of her body relax a little more against his. "I remember everything about you." That was part of his problem. "I can't seem to get you out of my mind."

"You make that sound like a bad thing."

He'd never admitted anything like that to a woman before. "Just a confusing thing," he corrected. "I told myself I should leave you alone, but I don't want to."

With her cheek resting against his chest, she tucked her head toward her chin. "I don't want you to leave me alone, either."

The admission was little more than a weary whisper.

"Then, I guess I'm not going anywhere right now."

At his quiet assurance, he felt her back rise with a deep breath of relief, then fall as she slowly released it. She felt so small to him, almost delicate as he stroked the length of her narrow back. Reaching the base of her spine, he slowly followed that same path up between her shoulder blades.

He'd never just held a woman before. Just held her and let her lean on him while he slowly caressed the tension from her body. He wasn't even sure he knew what he should do. Sex was one thing. His instincts were just fine there. But this wasn't about getting each other naked, though she really did need to get out of her wet clothes. He was simply out of his element with her. All he had to go on was his gut.

From her muffled response long moments ago and the way she curled against him now, she didn't seem to notice he was in unfamiliar territory. It was as if she needed to be exactly where she was.

It occurred to him as he carried his touch up to stroke her head, that he needed to be right where he was, too.

"You know, Amy, you said you don't know what I want from you." His voice was low, his tone as quiet as the beat of the rain on the dining room windows. "I didn't know, either," he admitted. "But I do now." He slipped his hand from her hair, continued caressing her back. "This. This is what I want."

He wanted her to let him hold her, to comfort her. Somewhere beneath that alien feeling existed the need he'd felt all along to protect her. Even from himself. But mostly what he felt just then was the desire to take care of her when she'd had a bad day. Or a bad week.

A bad month, for that matter.

He'd never known those needs before. The strength of them might have unnerved him, too. Or at least given him more pause. But the longer he held her, the more impossible it became to ignore the effects of her scent as it moved from his lungs into his blood, and the feel of her slender little body shifting against his.

With her hands between them, he couldn't feel the firmness of her breasts against his chest. But a layer of denim and her skirt and tights were all that separated their thighs. As he continued to stroke her back, every time his hand reached the base of her spine, he had to fight the urge to either pull away or press her closer.

He wanted more than just to hold her. Far more. He knew the sweetness of her mouth. What he wanted now was to know the taste of her skin, the feel of it bare beneath his hands. He wanted to know her textures, her shapes. He wanted to know the little sounds she made when she was mindless with need, and the feel of her soft hands on his body.

What he didn't want was to move from her.

He eased his arms from her, anyway. Reaching between them, he circled her wrists with his forefingers and thumbs.

As he did, he felt the tension he'd eased from her muscles slip through her again.

Ducking his head, he brushed his lips to her temple. "Do you have any coffee?"

Amy blinked at the middle of his shirt. Confusion masked the banked yearning in her tone. "Sure." Her brow furrowed as she looked up at him. "You want coffee?"

"No," he admitted, his breath warm on her face as he brushed his lips over hers. The contact was brief, the merest stroke of skin over skin. "It's just that we need to do something before I kiss you."

Her heart jerked in her chest. "You just did."

"That wasn't a kiss," he insisted.

The longing she'd veiled threatened to surface as his smoky-gray gaze moved over her face, lingered on her mouth.

"It wasn't?"

He slowly shook his dark head. "Not even close."

"Oh," she breathed.

"Yeah," he murmured back. "Maybe you should show me how it's done."

His last words were a brush of breath against her lips.

Amy sighed at the contact, felt a little ache open under her breastbone.

The feel of his lips against hers held the same incredible gentleness she'd felt in him before. She wanted that gentleness. She wanted whatever he was willing to share with her.

But he was waiting, wanting her to take the lead when she had no idea where she was going.

It wasn't as if she'd never been kissed before. She'd just never been kissed well. Not the way he'd kissed her when he'd melted her bones and taunted desires she hadn't known existed.

Lifting her hands from where he'd held them in his, she curved her fingers at the sides of his face. His lips felt smooth beneath hers, the night-time stubble of his beard, deliciously rough. Remembering the first touch of his tongue to hers, she tipped his head, seeking that more-intimate contact.

Warmth pooled low in her stomach when he opened to her. Still holding his face, she kissed him more deeply, mating their mouths the way he had done. Wanting nothing more than for him to feel what she felt, she leaned closer, trying not to sink against him as their tongues tangled.

His breathing seemed a little more shallow to her when she withdrew to kiss the corner of his mouth and finally drew back.

He brushed his thumb over the hollow of her throat. "Do that again and I won't be going anywhere tonight."

Long moments ago it had occurred to Amy that, if he wanted to hold her, that meant he might need holding, too. And that maybe, just maybe, he needed her right now as badly as she needed him.

She swallowed. Hard. "Promise?"

Her eyes barely met his before they fell to his chest. Even then, J.T. knew without a doubt what he'd seen in her expression. Wanting her to look at him, he cupped her face with one hand and lifted it back to his.

Heat curled low in his gut. Need was there, stark in the depths of her dark eyes. So was the longing for respite he suspected she hadn't wanted him to see, but didn't have the strength to hide.

She seemed to realize he saw it now. Her lips parted on a

shuddering breath. Caught by her yearning, the profoundness of it, he caved in to the needs clawing at him and covered her mouth with his.

Amy felt his gentleness shift. In the space of seconds, a foreign sort of hunger replaced it. As if encouraging her need with his own, he drew her against him, pressing her stomach to the hard length behind his zipper.

Her breath hitched at that contact. Or maybe that painful sound had been his. All she knew for certain was that her knees felt ready to buckle as he kissed her more deeply, creating utter havoc with her senses and taking away the loneliness deep inside her. He made her ache, made her want.

She'd wanted him even before he'd touched her.

His voice was a deep rasp in her ear. "I want you in bed, Amy." Tension coiled through him. Ruthlessly controlled, but definitely there. "If that's not what you want, we'll go make coffee."

He was giving her a chance to back away, to ease the heat curling like smoke between them.

It was a chance she didn't want.

"I don't want coffee."

"Good," he growled, and started backing her down the hall.

She felt his hands at her waist, working the buckle of her belt. She didn't remember when she'd dropped her towel, but she must have because an erratic heartbeat later, her arms were around his neck while his hands worked down the back zipper of her jumper.

The tweed fell in a pool at her feet. With his mouth clinging to hers, she stepped over the puddle of fabric and felt him tug up the hem of her sweater. He had it as far as the bottom of her bra as they passed the bathroom. By the time they reached the laundry room, he was coaxing her arms through the sleeves while his mouth worked over hers. They'd just turned the corner to her bedroom when he broke that debilitating contact long enough to pull the damp knit over her head.

It didn't occur to her to make them slow down. With his broad hands warm and seeking on her bare skin, the aching sense of urgency he created within her rose right along with her goose bumps.

"My shirt." Little paths of fire darted through her as his lips caressed the side of her neck. "Your turn."

He seemed to think she knew what she was doing as she tugged the heavy cotton from his jeans and he backed her toward her bed. Heaven help her, the only thing she knew for certain as they tugged the shirt over his head and he tossed it in the direction of her sweater was that she loved him.

Anxiety swept through her as the rest of their clothing landed in a heap, but that apprehension had more do with insecurity than fear. She understood the mechanics of making love. It was actual experience she lacked. Yet, the thought that he would finally know just how inexperienced she really was faded with the feel of his mouth claiming hers once more.

She'd felt his tension before. With the corrugated muscles of his chest pressed to her bared breasts, what she felt now was his hunger as it radiated through her, sensitizing her nerves, obliterating all the anxieties she simply didn't want to deal with.

Wanting more, needing more, she curved her hand to the back of his head as they fell in the shaft of hallway light onto her unmade bed.

The shiver running through her as he pulled her comforter over them no longer had anything to do with being cold. The heat of his body had long since warmed her. The feel of his hand wandering up and down her back as he'd held her had soothed even as it had aroused. Now, even as he sensitized nerves she didn't know she had, it was the knowledge that he had wanted to hold her that squeezed so hard in her chest.

No man had ever cared enough to know how badly she needed that. But then, no man had bothered to know her, to care about her, the way this man had done.

Instead of disappearing as other men had when they'd learned of her responsibility to her grandmother, he'd helped her find a way to keep the older woman where she needed to be. Instead of standing by while she'd sold her home, he'd helped her find a way to keep it. Instead of letting her put off the possibility of the career she'd once dreamed of, he'd encouraged her to pursue it.

He knew what was important to her. As she sought the feel of his harder, rougher body, she just wished she knew what truly mattered to him.

Knowing she mattered to him somehow was all she needed to know for now. Never in her life had she felt so desired, so cherished, as she did as he trailed his lips down her throat, to her breasts, over her belly. But it was her need for him that drove the erotic game of follow the leader that ultimately had him pushing his hands through her hair and rasping her name in her ear.

J.T. was ready to die from want. The woman in his arms was beautiful in her desire for him, artless in her need as her small soft hands stroked and explored. She was such a sensual woman, trembling at his touch, sighing at the feel of his hands roaming her body. Her skin tasted impossibly sweet. The texture of her flesh felt like warm satin. But it was the feel of her responding to him, taunting his considerable control that finally had him fumbling beside the bed for his pants and his wallet.

He knew he wouldn't last long as he rolled the protection over himself and eased his weight over her. Not this time. Not with her kiss-swollen mouth seeking his as she reached to draw him closer.

He had never known the need to claim a woman before. But that was the need that drove him now as he curved her legs around his and pushed himself forward. With his control hanging by a thread, the tightness he met was almost more stimulation than he could bear.

He hissed in a breath, made himself go still. "Amy, you're so…"

"Don't stop. Please," she begged, urging him closer. "They say it doesn't hurt much at all."

The raw need coursing through his body demanded completion. Yet, somewhere through that swirling mist of burning nerves, he realized what she'd just told him. Incredulity vied with conviction. Certainty with disbelief. It had never occurred to him that she might be a virgin. But even as he realized that no other man had been with her, the heat took over.

She whispered his name, the sound of it a breathless plea.

He whispered hers back, possessiveness sweeping through him as he eased forward, catching her little moan with his mouth. He made himself remain still, gritting his teeth against the mind-numbing feel of her, waiting for her body to become accustomed to his. She allowed only a few thudding heartbeats before she moved beneath him, and made it impossible for him to hold back any longer.

On some barely functioning level of consciousness, it occurred to him that he'd once thought of her as a breath of fresh air. In the moments before he gave in to the red haze of heat surrounding them, he realized that for years he'd been starving for oxygen.

The rain had stopped. In the silence, J.T. lay with Amy's legs tangled with his, her head on his chest, her hand over his heart. With his arm around her, he could feel her deep, even breathing.

Gray daylight peeked around the edges of her curtains. The digital clock on her nightstand read 8:02 in neon green. He kept waiting for the restiveness to start creeping through him, that edgy sensation that told him it was time to slip from the bed and be on his way before complications set in. Yet he'd been awake for nearly an hour and all he'd felt was the need to stay right where he was.

It had never occurred to him before that there was actually a difference between having sex and making love. Yet, making love was what they'd done. Especially when they'd taken it more slowly after awakening around midnight, and slower still when she'd turned in his arms a few hours later and he kissed away all the new little aches he caused.

He couldn't believe how completely she'd given herself to him.

The furnace kicked on, the rush of air through the vent beneath the window ruffling the bottom of the curtains. There was no doubt in his mind that she cared deeply about him. Or, at least, the man she thought him to be.

The thought effectively destroyed the compelling sense of peace.

Guilt replaced it. So did the equally guilty and profound realization that he needed this woman in his life. With her, he didn't feel the slow-simmering agitation that threatened to consume him, or the need to be anywhere other than wherever he found himself. He wanted her. He wanted to be with her.

Old habits demanded that he deny those needs—even as Harry's demands surfaced to insist he grab what he had.

Ruthlessly, he shoved aside his last thought. He couldn't subject her to the pretense. He wanted her to know him, to know who he was. With the realizations hitting hard and fast—and with her now stirring in his arms—what he recognized most was the need for more time.

The sudden tension in Jared's hard, honed body had wakened Amy from her dozing. Enticing sensations of security, of sanctuary vanished as memories of last night flooded back. Thoughts of repercussions and potential regrets flowed right over them.

"How do you feel about spending the day in the snow?"

Jared's voice was a sleepy rasp against her forehead as he pulled her closer. His question wasn't the most romantic, but it went a long way to dispell the insecurities that had awakened with her, and the awful fear that all he'd want to do now was leave.

"I'd love it. But don't you have to work at the home?"

"I'm taking the day off." Skimming his fingers lightly over her arm, he caused her to shiver. "If you'll take it off with me."

Beneath her palm, she felt the strong, steady beat of his heart. Her own gave a shamefully joyous and hugely relieved leap. "Won't that put you behind schedule?"

"Not if I work twice as hard tomorrow."

"I'll work twice as hard with you."

She felt the weight of his leg hook around hers. Slipping his hands down her side, he caught her by the waist and tugged her over him.

She'd barely felt his hard body beneath hers when he pulled her up. Lifting his mouth to the pulse hammering in her throat, he murmured, "You have yourself a deal."

"My car." With her body instantly responding to his, she could barely think. "I can't leave it where it is. I need to get it towed to a garage and have the tires fixed."

His hands had tightened at her waist. He nuzzled the side of her neck, flicked her earlobe with his tongue. "After we get up, you can give me your keys and I'll take care of it. When I get back," he promised a moment before he started to make her mindless, "we'll go play."

Chapter Twelve

Jared had been gone long enough for Amy to dry her hair and put on makeup when she heard her cell phone ring. Thinking it might be him, she abandoned the search of her closet for just the right sweater and jeans and dug the phone from her purse before it could go to voice mail.

The name on the caller ID simply said "Private Caller."

Wondering if it might not be him anyway, she answered with a curious, "Hello?"

"Amy, where are you? It's Candace."

Anticipation flattened. Candace only called when she wanted something. "I'm home. But I'm leaving in about an hour…"

"Stay there. I'm on my way. There's something you need to see."

Amy opened her mouth to ask what that something was. The click on the line told her Candace had already cut the connection. Unable to imagine what was so urgent, she headed back to her closet nursing a vague sense of unease—and the hope that whatever Candace wanted could be dealt with in a hurry. It would be awkward for her still to be there when Jared returned. Amy wasn't entirely sure what was happening between herself and Jared. She knew what she hoped it would be, what she wanted it to be. But whatever it was, it was too new to share, especially with someone who'd given every indication of wanting him to be interested in her herself.

She had decided on her good jeans and, after ten minutes of vacillating, a black-and-white Alpine knit sweater when her doorbell rang.

Candace's hand was already on the handle of the storm door when Amy flipped the latch. She didn't wait to be invited in. Looking fabulous in her quilted Burberry jacket, designer jeans and high-heeled boots, she stepped into the entry radiating a sort of agitation that wasn't familiar at all.

Concerned, Amy motioned her into her living room.

"Candace, what's wrong?"

She had a magazine in one hand. Her shoulder bag dangled from the other. The bag was dropped to the overstuffed chair she'd stopped behind. The magazine, she kept.

"I found out why we weren't able to get any information on our client," she said, sounding calm, not looking it. "It's because he's not Jared Taylor."

She held out the copy of *Forbes*. "I'd borrowed this from my grandfather last night. I thought an article on the cover looked interesting, so I took it home to read. What I found on page twenty-seven was even more enlightening."

Amy flipped to the dog-eared page.

"HuntCom Leads Industry in Global Expansion" read the title of the piece. Beneath that title, the large-type lead-in to the article mentioned the computer giant's expansion in India.

That was as far as she got before her glance shifted. It promptly froze on the photos on the opposite page.

Two of the photos were of work sites, huge projects obviously under construction. One, according to the caption, was of J.T. Hunt who was overseeing the New Delhi campus's construction.

The color image of the dark-haired, incredibly handsome heir to at least part of HuntCom's fortune was unquestionably of the man who had just shared her bed.

Amy blinked at Candace. "J.T. Hunt?"

"The second son of Harrison Hunt."

"The billionaire?" Amy asked, though why she had no idea. Everyone knew Harrison Hunt was as rich as Rockefeller. She even knew he had sons. Three or four, if she remembered right. Though, at the moment, she was drawing a blank on what she'd heard about any one of them.

"That's him," Candace confirmed. "Owner and founder of HuntCom, based out of Seattle. J.T. is in charge of property acquisition and development. He's the architect who designs all of their facilities."

For a moment Amy said nothing. She just stared at the picture while disbelief vied with a sickening certainty and a few other feelings she couldn't quite define.

"He's had plenty of opportunities to tell me who he is. He could have told me at our initial meeting," Candace pointed out, starting to pace. "He told me then that confidentiality was important to him. But he either didn't trust me or the agency enough to confide the information.

"He said his partners didn't know he was leaving so he couldn't risk them learning of his new venture," she continued. "I assured him as I do all our clients that everything about him and his ad campaign would remain under wraps until he wanted information released." She reached the tall, cylindrical fish tank. Seeming more concerned by the man's lack of confidence than anything else at the moment, she frowned at the ferns waving gently in the crystal-clear water. "I'd just like to know who he didn't trust. Me…or the agency."

Apparently expecting no response, she turned on her heel. "He's obviously leaving HuntCom to set up his own architectural firm." She offered the conclusion as she paced back toward the chair. "What I don't understand is why he let us think he was doing it on a shoestring. He even made a point of telling me he had to keep his costs down. And why didn't he just give you the money for that home instead of going on about how he could save money by working on it himself? I went onto the computer last night and pulled up all kinds of information about him. The man is filthy rich on his own."

Annoyance had joined the agitation in her voice. As she recapped her dealings with him, that irritation seemed directed mostly at herself for not having picked up cues.

"Once I realized who he was," she said on her way past the coffee table, "I remembered reading about him being into yacht races and mountain climbing and just about anything that could be labeled 'extreme.' It's been a couple of years since I'd come across anything about him. And it's not like I followed the Hunts except for how my stock did with their company," she qualified, turning at the dining room, "but it had been so long since I'd seen a photo of him that I hadn't remembered what he looked like. When he showed up at our office, I thought he was just some great-looking guy who wanted an ad campaign."

Amy had sunk into the chair opposite the one occupied by the expensive alligator shoulder bag. Since Candace had gone silent, she looked up from the magazine to see her standing with her hands on her hips and a frown marring her exquisite face.

"I'm glad he and I never really got together," she said,

sounding as if the frown and the admission were for herself. "I'd hate to fall for some guy who knew he wasn't being honest with me."

Her words put a knot in Amy's stomach.

"Anyway," she muttered, seeming to dismiss her near miss as nothing of consequence on her way back to the fish tank, "I figured you'd be seeing him sometime in the next couple of days. I know you two talk," she reminded her, sounding more like the self-assured woman Amy knew her to be. "And, like you said, maybe all you talk about is whatever it is he's doing at that home. But I got the distinct impression when he was in the office last week that he might have a bit of a thing for you. That's why I thought you needed to know about that," she said, nodding to the magazine. "Just in case you think he's serious."

Candace was actually being protective of her. The unexpected kindness registered even as Amy closed the incriminating pages.

Tossing the magazine onto the coffee table as if it might bite, Amy pushed her fingers through her hair. She hadn't said a word while Candace talked herself through her professional and personal conclusions about the man obviously neither of them knew. Growing more uneasy by the second, she found she didn't have a lot to say now, either.

"I'll definitely keep it in mind."

There was no refuting his identity. Even if the photo could be dismissed as simply bearing a truly remarkable resemblance, there were too many other coincidences. J.T. Hunt was an architect. He was overseeing a project halfway around the world. HuntCom was based in Seattle.

Still, even with what Candace seemed to consider irrefutable evidence, Amy felt a desperate need to hear Jared's side of the story before she condemned him. He was a good man.

A generous, caring man who'd simply longed for escape from something sucking the spirit from his soul. She sensed that in the deepest part of her being. There *had* to be a logical explanation for why he hadn't told her who he was.

It seemed Candace had expected more from her than what she'd received. As Amy rose, battling all that disquiet, her stepsister's knowing blue eyes narrowed on hers.

"Oh, Amy." Her voice went flat with conclusion. "You're involved with him already."

In the absence of an immediate denial, comprehension moved through her expression. As if she was beginning to understand why he had never really pursued her, she looked at Amy with a quiet sort of sympathy.

"End it before he does," she said with the certainty that tended to accompany any advice she offered when it came to men. "The Hunt brothers never get serious about any relationship," she warned. "That article even refers to them all as confirmed bachelors. Jared…I mean, J.T.," she corrected, looking truly concerned, "is especially known for playing the field. On the Internet last night I found articles about him and some model he was dating in Monaco. And an actress in France. I forget her name, but she's huge over there. The articles were older, but if those are the circles he ran in then, he's probably still running in them now."

And what sort of chance do I have against competition like that? Amy thought. "I would imagine he is," she agreed, surprised by her stepsister. Not by her advice. All things considered, it was totally sound. What caught her off guard was that Candace wasn't acting as if she found it hard to believe that someone like J.T. Hunt, or Jared Taylor, would be interested in Amy to begin with.

"You know, Amy," she said, her tone suddenly confiding. "I don't know how involved you are with him. I'm not asking, either," she assured her. "You know who he is now, so you can make your decisions from there. Just do yourself a favor and don't get in over your head with him. That guy is even out of my league."

Hearing her stepsister echo what she had thought—and told—Jared about herself, Amy managed a faint smile. It seemed she and Candace had something in common after all.

"I know who he is," she assured her. It was a little late to avoid getting in over her head. But she'd always been a strong swimmer. It seemed she was about to learn how she handled being in the deep end of the pool. "He's J.T. Hunt and he's a client. I can take it from there."

Something like surprise—or maybe it was respect—moved into Candace's expression. "You know, Amy," she said, tipping her head as she considered her. "I really think you can." With that admission, her voice softened. "Are you going to be okay?"

"I'm fine."

"That's what we all say," her stepsister muttered and moved in to give her a designer-scented hug. "Call me if you need to talk."

For the first time since they'd met at their parents' wedding years ago, Amy thought she might actually do that. "Thanks," she said, then motioned to the coffee table. "Do you mind if I borrow that magazine?"

Moments later Candace was out the door and Amy was back at the coffee table, reading the six-page article that mentioned J.T.'s degrees from MIT and Harvard, his design awards, his passion for challenge. Then she sat back and waited for him to return.

J.T. knew something wasn't right the moment he walked into the warmth of Amy's home and hung up his coat. Earlier, she'd given him her car and house keys so he could let himself back in. Now she stood facing him in her living room, her arms crossed over a magazine and her pretty features as guarded as he'd ever seen them. Though she'd dressed for snow, she didn't look anywhere near ready to leave.

"Your car will be ready this afternoon," he said, because that's what he'd been thinking about when he'd opened the door. That and the reservation he'd made for them for dinner tomorrow night. "I told the guy at the tire shop that we might not be able to pick it up until tomorrow."

Her response was the lift of her chin, and a quiet "Thank you" as he stopped in front of her.

She didn't make him ask what was wrong. She simply held out the magazine for him to take.

He'd barely noticed his own image looking back at him when she spoke with utter calm.

"Why didn't you tell me who you are?"

J.T.'s first thought as he stared at the page was that he was nowhere near ready for this conversation. His second was that he was screwed.

He met the clear disquiet in her eyes. There was accusation there, too. And hurt.

He'd never meant for this to happen. "I was going to."

"When?"

He hadn't figured that out yet.

The magazine landed on the table with a soft plop.

"I told you before that there were things I couldn't talk about…"

"Like your identity? It's not as if the world doesn't know you."

"It's not that simple."

"Then, please," she asked. Begged, actually. "Simplify it for me."

The plea in her eyes tore at him. So did his obligation to keep Harry's rules for his brothers.

He reached for her, wanting to reassure her that nothing had really changed between them. That nothing needed to change.

She stepped back before his fingers could brush her arm.

"I wish I could," he muttered, and jammed his fingers through his hair instead. He just couldn't explain anything without breaking those rules. Ever since he'd left her bed, he'd been trying to figure out a way around them. The irony was that he felt as close as he ever would be to fulfilling his end of the agreement they'd all signed.

Except the damage was already done. She knew who he was.

"It can't be that difficult," Amy insisted, more than willing to help him out. "Is it because of your new business? Because you didn't trust the agency to keep your plans confidential?"

"It's nothing like that."

"Then what was it? And when were you going to tell me? I need the truth," she insisted, sounding as deceived as she was trying not to feel. "I need to know there's a good reason you let me make love with you when you knew I had no idea who you really are." Her voice caught at the enormity of his omission. "The truth is the very least you owe me."

The calm she struggled to maintain seemed in serious danger of slipping. She felt it in the sting of unshed tears in her eyes, heard it in the betraying tremor in her voice.

"I know I owe you that, Amy. I do," he insisted, needing that hurt to go away. He just didn't know how to tell her that she had literally stumbled into his plans when he'd least expected find the woman he would actually want to marry. Except by doing just that—telling her.

"Come here." Taking her hand when he would have rather drawn her into his arms, he tugged her toward the dining room table. The first time he'd been there its surface had been covered with old photos and albums. The shiny mahogany now held the faint scent of lemon wax, a trio of fat sea-green candles and the course catalogs, dog-eared and scribbled on, that he'd left for her.

"This is going to sound bizarre," he warned.

"I don't care how it sounds as long as you're honest with me."

"I will be. I promise." Pulling out a side chair, he nudged her onto it. "I just need you to promise me that what I tell you stays between us. I don't want to mess things up for my brothers. I have no idea what would happen if word got out about what my father is doing, but I don't have time to figure it out right now."

Desperately needing to hear whatever he would say, Amy nodded. "I won't say anything," she promised as he sat down in a chair facing her.

With his size elevens planted a yard apart, he rested his forearms on his denim-covered thighs and clasped his hands between his knees.

"I never set out to deceive you, Amy. You have to believe that." Last night had snuck up on them both, but the deception he'd been operating under had felt wrong for weeks. Faced with its effect on her, and the way she no longer welcomed his touch, he was more than willing to be rid of it.

"When I first went to Kelton & Associates, it was to see if it was the kind of agency I wanted for an ad campaign. I didn't make an appointment under my name because I didn't know how many agencies I'd have to interview before I found the right one. Everything else I told you and your stepsister at the time about needing to keep things quiet for a while was the truth.

"The reason I'm working on starting my own firm," he continued, "is because I need a fall-back plan. Harry…my father," he explained, "wants me and my brothers to marry and give him grandkids. If we don't find wives by next July, he's going to sell off HuntCom and take away everything that each of us values most. The threat is collective. If one doesn't comply, we all lose out. I figured his idea had no chance of succeeding, so having my own business in place when he pulled the plug seemed like the only logical thing to do."

Disbelief vied with incredulity. "You're being forced to marry?"

"That's one way of putting it. But I've just…"

"No, wait," she asked, searching the tension in his features while she tried to understand what she was hearing. "Your new business," she prefaced, "you're going into it because you'll lose your position in the company if you don't marry by his deadline."

"More than likely."

It was no wonder he'd been so unenthused about what he was doing, she thought. All that manipulation was undoubtedly part of what he'd been trying to escape. That need to escape made definite sense to her, though little else did just then.

"You still could have told us who you are once you'd decided on us. You could have told me," she insisted, because his failure to do that was what mattered to her most.

"I couldn't," he countered. "One of the stipulations is that we can't let the women know we're his sons. His wives were all gold diggers and he doesn't want any more in the family.

"I didn't want to get married. I had no intention of ever marrying," he told her, being as honest with her as he could. "Then I met Candace and thought the idea might work after all. That's why I didn't let her or anyone else know who I am."

The knot living in her stomach tightened. "Because you thought you wanted to marry her."

"Because I thought I 'might' want to," he clarified.

"And she had no idea she was being auditioned."

The flat conclusion in her voice worried J.T. So did her phrasing, though he could hardly refute it.

Until now she'd seemed blessedly willing to listen, to accept. As she rose to stand behind the chair, he had the uneasy feeling she might not be so receptive to anything else she would hear.

The tension stealing through his muscles had him rising, too. "You wanted the truth," he reminded her. "I'm just giving it to you. I told you there was never anything…"

"I believe you about that," she told him. "I really do." This wasn't about her stepsister. It wasn't about anyone but the two of them. "I believe everything you've said. Every word," she assured him, because no man would admit to something so convoluted and calculating unless it really was the truth. "There's just one thing I need to know." She had dozens of questions, actually. But only one mattered to her just then.

"Am I a prospective candidate, too?"

The feeling that she might no longer be open to what he said solidified. "It's not like that with you."

"How do I know that…J.T?" His name seemed so foreign to her. She had fallen in love with a man she really didn't even know. She didn't even know what J.T. stood for. "How do I know that you're not just getting desperate and you saw me as more malleable than my stepsister? How do I know that I wasn't just a convenient possibility?"

He could hardly fault her the distrust robbing the light from her eyes. He just didn't know what to say that wouldn't sound as if he was playing her exactly as she'd just implied.

He could tell her how much he cared about her. How he wanted to take care of her and Edna, if she'd let him, or simply help her if that was what she wanted. But the admission would sound too opportune right now. He could tell her he needed her in his arms, his bed and his life. But she could easily think he was grasping for whatever he thought she needed to hear.

He'd spent most of his life telling himself he needed no one, that he was fine on his own. Feeling something precious slip through his grasp, his basic sense of self-protection wanted to fall back on that defensive position. The part of him that had felt such incredible peace with her didn't want any part of it.

"I don't know how you can know that," he admitted. "Nothing I can say right now will matter, will it?"

"I doubt it," she agreed, wrapped in her own self-protectiveness. "Right now," she echoed, " I think you should just go."

"Amy…"

"Jared…J.T.," she corrected, her agitation rising as she crossed her arms more tightly. "The last thing I ever want to be to someone is a means to an end. Please. Just…go."

In the absence of any argument that wouldn't just sink him further, J.T. reached to touch her cheek. The way she ducked from the contact ripped at him, but all he did was drop his hand. "I'll see you later," he promised, and turned to grab his coat.

This wasn't over, but he knew she wouldn't be receptive to hearing that just then. Without another word, he headed out the door, shoving aside regret and frustration as his considerable resourcefulness, or maybe it was his survival instincts, formed Plan C.

Amy was beginning to understand why J.T. Hunt avoided holidays. All the celebrations, the expectations and the trappings simply made a person feel…trapped.

Her disillusioned thoughts had been with her even before she'd left Elmwood House. Christmas Eve was fairly quiet at the home, but the tree and mantel decorations had been pretty, and a few of the residents' family members had been there. What had drained the spirit from the gathering for her had been all the questions about the man she'd spent the past month trying hard to not think about.

Everyone at the home still knew him as Jared. And nearly everyone who had the ability to remember him had asked if she'd heard from him. They'd wanted to know how he was, where he was and if he'd be in town for Christmas.

The only thing she could offer with any certainty was that he would not be there for the holiday.

That had disappointed Kay and the staff. They'd wanted him to come for Christmas dinner. So had Mike, who'd said they'd talked about gearing up for a climb next summer. Now that Mike and Kay were dating, he spent even more time at the home.

Amy was truly happy for the two of them. But aware of their disappointment that Jared wouldn't be there, and hearing his name over and over, had only reminded her that he'd disappointed her, too.

She'd avoided him before he'd returned to Seattle. He'd made no attempt to call or see her before he'd left, either. When he'd called a week later, she'd let voice mail pick up. The third time she'd done that, he'd left a message telling her he knew she was avoiding him and that he was in India. He'd be back the end of the month. He'd call her then.

Today he'd sent roses.

Not to her. To her grandmother. Her grandma hadn't known who the "Jared" on the enclosure card was, but she'd loved the flowers. She'd been stroking one of the lovely red buds when Amy had left.

It wasn't quite raining, but the fine mist leaking from the night sky necessitated the use of her windshield wipers. In the dark, Christmas lights glowed from the houses she passed on her way to her own.

She had no other plans for the evening, but the senses of disenchantment and loneliness she felt had nothing to do with going home to a house with only fish for company. It didn't even have to do with missing the woman who once would have been able to tell her how long it took for a badly bruised heart to heal. She had friends she could visit. She just didn't feel like celebrating when the person she wanted to be with had an agenda that had ruined her ability to trust his motives. Without trust, there was no security. Without security, she was better off on her own.

With a sigh, she turned off the Christmas music on the radio and turned the corner to her house. She'd had enough of Rudolph. She would pour herself a glass of wine and call Jared tonight. She'd heard that mixing wine with a phone call to an ex-lover was a really bad thing to do, but he was the only ex-lover she had and there were a couple of things she wanted him to know. First, she couldn't accept the tuition voucher he'd had his secretary send her. She didn't want his money. She also wanted him to know that when he returned to the States, she'd appreciate it if he'd not show up at her door. As much as she missed him, seeing him again would only confuse her already totally torn feelings about him even more.

She was wondering what time it was in India when she noticed a sleek black Jaguar parked in front of her house. She'd just turned in front of it to pull into her narrow driveway when Jared—J.T.—got out.

Wondering if her mind hadn't simply conjured him up, she hit the brakes and glanced back in confusion. He was truly there. And he was heading for her car.

She didn't bother pulling all the way back to her single garage. Leaving her little sedan in the light spilling from her dining room windows, she grabbed her purse, took a breath to calm her heart and met him by her frostbitten azalea bushes.

She didn't intended to sound so accusing. "You said you wouldn't be back until the end of the month."

"It's good to see you, too."

The searching way his glance slid over her took a bit of the starch from her stance. "I was going to call you."

"When?"

"Tonight."

"Good that I'm here then." One dark eyebrow arched. "Can we go inside, or would you rather stand out here and get wet again?"

The mist was fine, more of a fog that put halos around the streetlamps and porch lights. But it wouldn't take long for it to dampen their hair or start to bead on their coats.

Not caring to think about what had happened the last time she'd been truly wet from the rain, she turned to her porch and hurried across her tiny patch of front lawn to the steps.

He held open her storm door. Her pine wreath with its bright red ribbon swayed slightly as she unlocked the main door and pushed it open.

The scent of pine from the unlit tree in the far corner of the room greeted them as he shut out the cold. In the light from the lamps she always left on, she dealt with her coat and turned to face him. She wouldn't allow herself to consider why he was there. The possibilities were too disconcerting.

Totally unprepared to see him, she grabbed for something conversational. "Is that your car?"

"One of them. I had to drive down from Seattle. All the flights were booked and the crews for the jet have the next two days off."

The sense of being hugely disadvantaged increased. Plunging her hands into the low pockets of her red tunic sweater, she took in the unrevealing, too-handsome lines of his face. One of his cars, he'd said.

"You have a jet?"

"It belongs to the corporation."

Of course it does, she thought.

Her glance slipped over his tall, broad-shouldered frame. He wore black slacks and a gray cashmere sweater that turned his eyes the color of old pewter. His black leather jacket and shoes looked suspiciously Italian. When he lifted his hand to push back his neatly cut, faintly graying dark hair, a gold Rolex flashed in the entryway light.

Jared Taylor had been impressive enough. J.T. Hunt was downright imposing.

She reminded herself that she'd seen him naked.

The thought did nothing to ease the tension coiling in her stomach. Half of that tension came from him, she was sure. She could feel it radiating from his long, lean body as she turned into her dining room to close the drapes and flip on its overhead light.

"How long have you been here?" She reached for a pull cord. In the night-blackened window, she could see his reflection moving behind her.

"About half an hour. You were still with Edna when I called over at the home to see if you were there. Kay said she didn't know if you had any other plans tonight, but she let me know when you left." His reflection disappeared as fabric swayed. "I thought you might go on to Jill's if things were still working out with you two, so I figured if you weren't here in half an hour, I'd come back in the morning."

"I don't do anything over the holidays with her or Candace," she said, closing the drapes on the other window. "They always spend the week with Jill's parents at their cabin." She didn't bother to mention that while they were gone she tended their houseplants. "They're in Aspen."

He'd stopped in front of her little tree, all six, skinny decorated feet of it. She would have loved tall, lush and full, but the corner by her dining room table was the only place to put a tree and narrow was all that would fit.

"Kay knew you were here?" she asked.

He made a humming sound as he frowned at her tree. "I had the feeling you'd just avoid me if you knew I was here, so I asked her not to tell you. I needed to talk to Mike, anyway," he said, sounding as if asking about her were almost an afterthought. "We've been talking about a climb next summer, I was just checking dates." He frowned at the tree's base. "How do you turn the lights on?"

Walking over to the modest Noble fir, she crouched and stuck the plug into the socket behind it. Ornaments that had gleamed dully in the overhead lights, now sparkled in a cacophony of primary and pastel colors as a few hundred tiny white lights reflected their shiny surfaces. The quantity of lights was overkill. But it was her tree, and she liked it.

"Wow," he muttered. "That could bring in planes at LaGuardia."

"Is there a reason you're here? Other than to insult my tree?"

"I want to talk to you," he said simply. "And it's a great tree. Skinny. But great."

"Jared... J.T...."

"It's Jared." He'd liked the sound of that name coming from her. "Jared Tyler Taylor Hunt. Taylor was my mother's maiden name. She was going for the alliteration." He shrugged. "Or so I've been told."

He touched one of the ornaments, a pink one with "Amy's First Christmas" embellished on it in mostly flaked-off glitter. "You've had these a long time."

Many of them were from her childhood. Memories she saved from Christmases she could no longer remember in any real detail. Some she couldn't remember at all.

"A few of them," she replied, certain he must think her horribly sentimental.

"A decorator always did our tree. Or maybe it was a florist.

All I know is that it always had a theme and everything matched. I've never had one of my own."

With the tip of his index finger he bypassed a globe of cobalt blue and nudged a three-inch-long shape of crystal.

"What's this?" he asked as she wondered at what he was revealing about himself, his past. Mostly, she wondered why he was revealing it at all.

"A glass slipper," she replied quietly.

Turning it to its side, he read the gold script running from heel to toe. "Happily ever after…"

"It came from Disneyland," she said, thinking she really should get rid of that one. She'd actually once been naive enough to believe happily-ever-after was a possibility. With her heart warring with her head over the man frowning at her ornament, happy-enough-for-now even seemed like a stretch.

"You never did say why you're here."

At her quiet reminder, J.T. let the piece of crystal fall back into its place. He wanted nothing more than to reach for the woman watching him so warily, but he had no reason to believe she wouldn't just pull away. He'd rather lose what assets he now had left than have that happen again.

She wanted to know why he was there. He could have told her he'd come to arrange an endowment for Elmwood House that would carry it for another twenty years. Kay had seemed a little speechless when he'd mentioned his intention. He'd also asked her to send Edna's bill to him for as long as the older woman remained there. Kay hadn't become any more articulate after she'd discovered who he was when, for billing purposes, he'd given her his real name and address.

He also could have told Amy that he'd just needed to see her for himself and make sure she was all right.

Instead of delaying though, he threaded his fingers through

his hair and got to the point. "I'm tired of going though the motions, Amy."

Wariness remained, but concern entered her lovely brown eyes. "I'm not sure I know what you mean."

"I mean I'm tired of just checking things off on my list of things to do. I've spent my whole life pursuing and acquiring." And demanding more of myself with each success, he thought. "But somewhere along the line I stopped finding any pleasure in what I've accomplished or done."

The admission made him want to pace. Needing to see her eyes, he stayed right where he was.

"I've gone my whole life running from one project to the next, one venture to the next, because I was afraid of what I might find if I ever slowed down. When I finally did slow down," he admitted, "it was because of you."

He took a step toward her, relieved when she didn't reclaim that small distance. "When I was with you I didn't feel what I can usually only escape sailing, or climbing or buried in work. That was why I stayed to work on the home. I didn't just need the escape. I needed what I felt with you."

Her glance faltered.

The instant it did, he stepped closer. "I know you doubt me," he said, wanting to address fears before they could fully surface. "I don't blame you. I'd bolt from any woman who'd deceived me the way I did you. But when this all began I was only thinking of my job and my brothers," he defended. "I didn't know I was going to find you.

"I fell in love with you, Amy." He spoke the quiet words with utter calm. Inside, his heart raced as it did when a climbing rope slipped. "I didn't plan for it to happen. I didn't ever expect it to happen. It just did. If there's any chance you care about me, I don't want to let you go."

Never in her life had Amy felt as torn as she did at that

moment. The man she loved had just said the words she'd longed to hear, had ached to hear. Yet what she felt more than the joy his admission should have brought was the awful uncertainty that kept hope at bay.

Struggling, she searched the compelling, masculine lines of his face. The lines around his eyes seemed deeper to her. Though his voice sounded strong and certain, he looked weary. The soul-deep fatigue she'd sensed in him from the beginning tugged hard. Even before he'd really known her, that fatigue had been there.

"You know I care about you, Jared. I love you, actually." He had to know that. She wouldn't have given herself to him so completely had she not. "But I know you need a wife to keep your position."

Looking strangely relieved, one eyebrow arched. "You love me?"

Crossing her arms against his quiet charm, she narrowed her eyes. "That's not the point."

"Right," he muttered. "The point is that there's this need for me to get married hanging out there."

"That would be it."

She loved him. Feeling as if he'd just been handed the biggest reprieve of his life, J.T. reached his hand toward her cheek.

"I don't need to get married," he assured her, watching her try to resist his touch, grateful that she couldn't seem to. "I don't have my position anymore. At least I won't after the first of the year. I gave it up. And my inheritance. And the island." That had really hurt. "You said you didn't know how you'd ever believe I cared about you," he reminded her. "Getting rid of the obstacles seemed the best way.

"That doesn't mean I'm poor," he qualified, encouraged by the way she gaped at him. "I have money of my own." Millions, actually. "But I want to go ahead with the firm here.

You need to be close to your grandma. And I think I can really get into being my own boss.

"I just need another chance with you," he told her. "On our terms. No one else's."

Amy said nothing. For long moments, she simply stared at him while hope burst past uncertainty. Doubt and distrust landed in a heap at her feet. "You gave up everything? For me?"

He gave a shrug. "I didn't know what else to do."

Amy's heart was beating hard in her throat when he motioned to the slipper sparkling on the tree. "I don't need to get married," he stressed. "But I want to. I have nothing to gain by marrying you but a shot at that fairy tale. But first I need you to come back to Seattle with me."

She was still stuck on him having given up his inheritance and an island for her. That island had to be the one he said he loved to sail to. The one he'd taken pictures of whales from for her.

"Why?" she asked, the word sounding a little choked.

"Because I need you to help me talk my dad into letting the agreement stand for my brothers. I should be able to get out of it since I don't have anything to gain by meeting his demands. I'm sure we can make the argument that disqualifies me."

"By the way," he said, easing her into his arms. "What do you want for a wedding present?"

With her hand flat against the soft leather covering his chest, she tipped back her head. Being held by him was the best gift she could have right now. "I don't need a wedding present."

"Sure you do. Why don't I buy the ad agency? Then, Jill and Candace can work for you."

A hint of devilment danced in his eyes.

His protectiveness of her was showing. As much as she loved that it was there, she didn't want or need that sort of payback. "I appreciate the thought," she assured him, curving her hand to his face, "but I don't want that agency. You know working there is mostly a means to an end for me."

"You have different means now." He lowered his head, brushed his lips over hers.

Amy sighed at the contact.

"I'll give you anything you want." He carried that soft touch to the corner of her mouth. "You can do anything you want." On his way to the other corner, he brushed her lower lip. "We'll get a staff to take care of everything if you still want to go to school." He felt her breath tremble against his cheek. "And when you're ready, we can make babies."

Amy lifted her head, searched the smile in his eyes. "You want babies?"

"Yeah. I do." He'd never thought about family before she'd come along. Except how to avoid being part of one. He'd known since the day he'd met her, though, how important family was to her. Somehow it had come to matter to him, too. Especially the idea of having their own. "Do you want to go practice?"

Amy's heart felt as if it might burst from her chest when she caught the gleam in his eyes. She said nothing, though. She simply smiled as she curved her arms around his neck and rose on tiptoe to give him the kiss he'd been teasing her with. He'd told her once before she should show him how it's done. Apparently, that was what he wanted now.

She kissed him long and hard. He kissed her back, a little more fiercely, leaving no doubt in her mind that he had missed her as much as she had missed him.

Long moments later, with her body sagging against the hard beat of his heart, he swept her up in his arms. Moving past the glittering tree holding bits of her past, he carried her down the hall toward their future.

On the way, he whispered against her forehead, "I'll take that as a 'yes.'"

Epilogue

The protective feel of Jared's arm at her waist drew Amy's glance to his strong profile. He wore a tuxedo as easily as he had worn denim. Her own gown, black and strapless, was simplicity itself. It was the wide diamond choker and cuff bracelet he'd bought for her to wear with it—and the two-carat-diamond and platinum engagement ring on her finger—that added to the feeling of having stepped into a fantasy.

Soft music drifted around them.

Jared had received the usual corporate invitation to the black-tie party his father always held between Christmas and New Year's, but he hadn't planned to attend. With three hundred guests milling about, he'd said his presence would hardly be missed. His father had requested he attend, though. Specifically, that he attend with his fiancée. *Requested.* Not insisted or summoned. Apparently, the difference was huge.

That difference, and her suggestion that they use the opportunity to get their talk with him about his brothers over with, was why they were now in the circular gallery above the festivities, watching Harrison Hunt—all six-feet-six, tuxedo-clad inches of him—approach them with a white business envelope in his hand.

With a frown, J.T. recognized the letter as the one he'd sent two weeks ago, disinheriting himself from everything except his family. His relationships with his father and brothers, such as they were, he wanted to keep.

Behind Harry's black horn-rimmed glasses, his still-shrewd blue eyes narrowed. "This is really what you want? To give everything up?"

J.T. felt Amy tense. With his arm still around her waist, he gave her a reassuring squeeze. She was doing him proud with her usual, commendable job of masking her disquiet.

"I told you when you called a few days ago that it's not what I want," J.T. said evenly. "But it's what I have to do." Because you've left me little choice, he thought. "All I want now is Amy. And to make sure Gray and Alex keep what's important to them if they comply with your terms."

Harry didn't acknowledge this last statement. As if intending to ignore it, his focus shifted to the woman he'd barely met.

Surprisingly, his voice lost a hint of its steel. "Amy."

"Sir?"

"What J.T. did, and what he's said about you, tells me you're the very sort of woman I'd hoped he'd find. We don't have time to talk right now. Guests," he explained, motioning to the crowd below. "I just wanted to put an end to this business of him disinheriting himself. I still want grandkids," he explained, "and I'm not having my grandchildren lose what's rightfully theirs.

"Take this." Harry handed the letter to her. "Do what you want with it. Tear it up. Burn it. Frame it. As far as I'm concerned, I never saw it."

From the inside pocket of his tuxedo jacket, he withdrew another envelope. "And this is yours," he continued to J.T. "Since I'm not accepting your letter, your position with the company and your inheritance remain as they are. As far as Hurricane Island goes, it's now yours. That," he said as J.T. took the envelope he offered, "is the title. I've transferred it to you."

J.T.'s brow furrowed. "You're giving me the island?"

"You don't want it?"

"Of course I do. But what about Gray and Alex? The only way I don't jeopardize their interests is to give up everything."

"You did give it up. I'm giving it back. Consider it an engagement present. And don't worry about your brothers. The agreement is still binding for Alex and Gray. If I know them, they'll find a way to keep what they want just as you and Justin did."

An unfamiliar sort of gratitude nudged at J.T. Not for the size of the gift, but for what it represented. In his own odd, emotionally detached way, his father was telling J.T. that he mattered to him. He was trying to be decent. Having come to appreciate Amy's refusal to harbor resentments, and suspecting that was why she and Jill had finally made peace, he decided it was time to start letting go of a few resentments of his own.

He slipped the envelope into his inside jacket pocket. "In that case, thank you. For all of it," he added, and held out his hand to shake his father's.

Harry had never been into paternal hugs, back slaps or handshakes. At least, not with him. As it was, J.T. couldn't remember ever having shaken his father's hand—until Harry clasped his now.

His mouth pinching, his father gave a hard nod. "Good, then." He pulled back. "We're done."

"Just one thing," J.T. said, stopping the big man before he could walk away. "I told Gray that I'll finish up in India, but then I'm staying stateside." Thanks to the woman beside him, he'd finally found the excitement that had been missing from nearly every aspect of his life. He truly wanted the architectural firm that had once merely been Plan B. He would keep it small, though, so he could still consult for HuntCom if Gray needed him. And so he could take Amy to all the places he knew were on her wish list. "I want to be closer to the family we're going to start."

Harry's glance darted to Amy. "I thought you were putting off kids until you finished school."

"We want you to know your grandchildren. So we'll get help," Amy said, still not sure how she and Jared would coordinate their lives. She needed to remain close to her grandmother. And Jared wanted her to travel with him when she could. They'd work it out somehow, though. Everyone was having to make adjustments. Even Jill.

Maybe Jill most of all.

Amy had already been with Jared in his condo last night when her stepmother had called her on her cell phone. Jill had wanted her to coordinate a last-minute New Year's Eve party. New Year's Eve was tomorrow. When Amy had told her she wouldn't be able to help because she was out of town with her fiancé, Jill had chuckled at what she'd assumed was a joke. She'd then alternated between disbelief and delight when she'd realized Amy was quite serious—and that her fiancé was the client Candace had already told her was actually J.T. Hunt. Jill had then moved into stress mode because she would now have to hire an office manager, a personal assistant and a part-time accountant to replace her stepdaughter.

Candace's only comment when she'd come on the line, since Jill had called on their way back from Aspen, had been a quiet, "Way to go, girl."

Amy now watched Harrison Hunt look from her to the tall,

handsome man at her side. He said nothing, though. He just gave them both a tight nod that was as close to genuine satisfaction as he was likely to get, and disappeared in the direction of the elevator.

Jared's hand settled on her bare shoulder as he turned her to face him. "That wasn't so bad."

"Not bad?" Stunned by Harry's generosity, incredulity vied with relief. "You have your inheritance back, Jared. You protected your brothers' interests. You have your island."

Arms that had become blessedly familiar curved around her. "You're forgetting something."

She couldn't imagine what that something could be.

"I got the girl."

Her relief moved into a smile as she looped her arms around his neck. She loved the way he looked at her. The way he touched her. She loved the heady knowledge that they were now there for each other. Mostly, she just loved him.

Rising on tiptoe, she lifted her lips to within a breath of his. "You definitely have the girl."

He smiled, too. She felt it when he caught her last words with his mouth. Then the smile faded. With the music drifting from below, he gathered her closer, drawing her against him and into a kiss filled with possessiveness and protectiveness. Gentleness and promise.

There was gratitude in that kiss, too, along with a quiet sort of amazement that still had J.T. wondering at the odd workings of his fate.

He once never would have believed it possible, but he'd actually found what he hadn't believed existed—with the woman he hadn't realized he'd been looking for. He'd meant it when he'd told her he wanted a shot at the fairy tale. Until he'd met her, he'd just never realized how essential such a dream could be.

As for Amy, secure in the arms of the man who would have given up his claim to a fortune for her, she felt just like Cinderella at the ball.

* * * * *

The search for the perfect bride
continues next month with
THE BILLIONAIRE AND HIS BOSS
by Pat Kay
The third book in the new Special Edition miniseries
THE HUNT FOR CINDERELLA
On sale January 2008,
wherever Silhouette Books are sold.

When Kimberley Blackstone's father is
presumed dead, Kimberley is required to take
over the helm of Blackstone Diamonds. She
has to work closely with her ex, Ric Perrini, to
battle not only the press, but also the fierce
attraction still sizzling between them. Does Ric
feel the same...or is it the power her share of
Blackstone Diamonds will provide him as he
battles for boardroom supremacy.

Look for

VOWS &
A VENGEFUL GROOM

by

BRONWYN
JAMESON

Available January wherever you buy books

To fulfill his father's dying wish,
Greek tycoon Christos Niarchos must
marry Ava Monroe, a woman who
betrayed him years ago. But his soon-to-
be-wife has a secret that could rock
more than his passion for her.

Look for

THE GREEK
TYCOON'S
SECRET HEIR

by

KATHERINE
GARBERA

Available January wherever you buy books

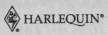

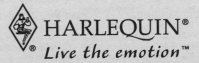

REQUEST YOUR FREE BOOKS!
2 FREE NOVELS PLUS 2 FREE GIFTS!

SPECIAL EDITION®
Life, Love and Family!

YES! Please send me 2 FREE Silhouette Special Edition® novels and my 2 FREE gifts. After receiving them, if I don't wish to receive any more books, I can return the shipping statement marked "cancel." If I don't cancel, I will receive 6 brand-new novels every month and be billed just $4.24 per book in the U.S., or $4.99 per book in Canada, plus 25¢ shipping and handling per book and applicable taxes, if any*. That's a savings of at least 15% off the cover price! I understand that accepting the 2 free books and gifts places me under no obligation to buy anything. I can always return a shipment and cancel at any time. Even if I never buy another book from Silhouette, the two free books and gifts are mine to keep forever.

235 SDN EEYU 335 SDN EEY6

Name	(PLEASE PRINT)

Address	Apt.

City	State/Prov.	Zip/Postal Code

Signature (if under 18, a parent or guardian must sign)

Mail to the **Silhouette Reader Service™**:
IN U.S.A.: P.O. Box 1867, Buffalo, NY 14240-1867
IN CANADA: P.O. Box 609, Fort Erie, Ontario L2A 5X3

Not valid to current Silhouette Special Edition subscribers.

Want to try two free books from another line?
Call 1-800-873-8635 or visit www.morefreebooks.com.

* Terms and prices subject to change without notice. NY residents add applicable sales tax. Canadian residents will be charged applicable provincial taxes and GST. This offer is limited to one order per household. All orders subject to approval. Credit or debit balances in a customer's account(s) may be offset by any other outstanding balance owed by or to the customer. Please allow 4 to 6 weeks for delivery.

Your Privacy: Silhouette is committed to protecting your privacy. Our Privacy Policy is available online at www.eHarlequin.com or upon request from the Reader Service. From time to time we make our lists of customers available to reputable firms who may have a product or service of interest to you. If you would prefer we not share your name and address, please check here. ☐

Inside ROMANCE

Stay up-to-date on all your
romance reading news!

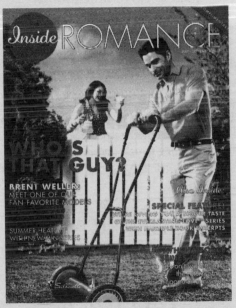

Inside Romance is a FREE quarterly newsletter
highlighting our upcoming series releases
and promotions.

Visit
www.eHarlequin.com/InsideRomance
to sign up to receive our complimentary newsletter today!

IRNI107

nocturne™

Jachin Black always knew he was an outcast.
Not only was he a vampire, he was a vampire
banished from the Sanguinas society. Jachin, forced
to survive among mortals, is determined to buy
his way back into the clan one day.

Ariel Swanson, debut author of a vampire novel, could
be the ticket he needs to get revenge and take his
rightful place among the Sanguinas again. However,
the unsuspecting mortal woman has no idea of the
dark and sensual path she will be forced to travel.

Look for

RESURRECTION: THE BEGINNING

by

PATRICE MICHELLE

Available January 2008 wherever you buy books.

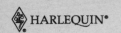

Silhouette®

COMING NEXT MONTH

#1873 FALLING FOR THE M.D.—Marie Ferrarella
The Wilder Family

When Walnut River General Hospital received a takeover offer from a large corporation, Dr. Peter Wilder butted heads with board member Bethany Holloway, a staunch supporter of the merger. But soon Peter realized he had a takeover target of his own: Bethany's heart.

#1874 HIS SECOND-CHANCE FAMILY—RaeAnne Thayne
The Women of Brambleberry House

Returning to her seaside hometown was hard on widowed fifth-grade teacher Julia Blair. But then she saw the For Rent sign on the rambling Victorian and knew she and her twins had found home. Of course, it helped when she realized the workman in the backyard was Will Garrett, her childhood sweetheart all grown up....

#1875 THE BILLIONAIRE AND HIS BOSS—Patricia Kay
The Hunt for Cinderella

Philanthropist Alex Hunt needed to find a bride within a year or his wealthy father would disinherit him and jeopardize his charity work. So, to avoid the gold diggers, Alex took a fake name and a blue-collar job…and formed an instant attraction to his new boss P. J. Kincaid. But was P.J. also pretending to be someone she wasn't?

#1876 YOURS, MINE…OR OURS?—Karen Templeton
Guys and Daughters

For ex-cop Rudy Vaccaro, buying a 150-year-old New Hampshire inn was a dream come true. But his preteen daughter felt very differently about the matter—as did Violet Kildare, the former owner's maid, who'd been promised the property. Sympathetic, Rudy let Violet keep her job…not knowing he was getting a new lease on life and love in return.

#1877 YOU, AND NO OTHER—Lynda Sandoval
Return to Troublesome Gulch

Police officer Cagney Bishop had always lived in the shadow of her bullying police chief father—especially when he ran her first love Jonas Eberhardt out of town. Now Jonas was back, a wealthy man, funding the local teen center to show that Troublesome Gulch hadn't defeated him. But would Jonas's true gift be to offer Cagney a second chance?

#1878 FOR JESSIE'S SAKE—Kate Welsh

Abby Hopewell felt betrayed by men—especially her only true love, Colin McCarthy. When they were young, he'd callously left her in the lurch and split town. Or so Abby thought. Now Colin was back, his daughter, Jessie, in tow, and Abby's bed-and-breakfast was the only place to stay. It was time to revisit the past....